Get Your Coventry Romances Home Subscription NOW

And Get These 4 Best-Selling Novels *FREE*:

LACEY
by Claudette Williams

THE ROMANTIC WIDOW
by Mollie Chappell

HELENE
by Leonora Blythe

THE HEARTBREAK TRIANGLE
by Nora Hampton

A Home Subscription! It's the easiest and most convenient way to get every one of the exciting Coventry Romance Novels! ...And you get 4 of them FREE!

You pay nothing extra for this convenience: there are no additional charges...you don't even pay for postage! Fill out and send us the handy coupon now, and we'll send you 4 exciting Coventry Romance novels absolutely FREE!

SEND NO MONEY, GET THESE
FOUR BOOKS FREE!

C1280

**MAIL THIS COUPON TODAY TO:
COVENTRY HOME
SUBSCRIPTION SERVICE
6 COMMERCIAL STREET
HICKSVILLE, NEW YORK 11801**

YES, please start a Coventry Romance Home Subscription in my name and send me FREE and without obligation to buy, my 4 Coventry Romances. If you do not hear from me after I have examined my 4 FREE books, please send me the 6 new Coventry Romances each month as soon as they come off the presses. I understand that I will be billed only $10.50 for all 6 books. There are no shipping and handling nor any other hidden charges. There is no minimum number of monthly purchases that I have to make. In fact, I can cancel my subscription at any time. The first 4 FREE books are mine to keep as a gift, even if I do not buy any additional books.

For added convenience, your monthly subscription may be charged automatically to your credit card.

☐ Master Charge ☐ Visa

Credit Card # _____

Expiration Date _____

Name _____
(Please Print)

Address _____

City _____ State _____ Zip _____

Signature _____

☐ Bill Me Direct Each Month

This offer expires March 31, 1981. Prices subject to change without notice. Publisher reserves the right to substitute alternate FREE books. Sales tax collected where required by law. Offer valid for new members only.

KISSING COUSINS

Anna James

FAWCETT COVENTRY • NEW YORK

KISSING COUSINS

Published by Fawcett Coventry Books, a unit of CBS Publications, the Consumer Publishing Division of CBS Inc.

Copyright © 1980 by Anna James

All Rights Reserved

ISBN: 0-449-50122-1

Printed in the United States of America

First Fawcett Coventry printing: December 1980

10 9 8 7 6 5 4 3 2 1

The author wishes to acknowledge the invaluable assistance she has received in research from the archives of the Thomas Cook Group Ltd., and from the staff at the London headquarters of the Group's Public Relations Office.

CHAPTER ONE

THE NANNIES of Frinton-on-Sea, that exclusive and somewhat windswept holiday resort on the east coast of Her Majesty Queen Victoria's Brittanic isle, have never quite forgotten the bright summer's day of a certain season in the mid-1850's when Henrietta de Vere Smith, an attractive but self-willed child of the aristocracy, pulled the golden curls on each side of the handsome head belonging to her cousin Roddy until he squealed, and then—as further punishment for stepping on the sandcastle she had just built with her own fair hands—pushed him off a fairly low breakwater and into two feet of gray ocean and swirling seaweed.

The fact that Roddy, who was three years old at the time and therefore the same age as his antagonist, was wearing the long petticoats sported by Victorian children of both genders (the word *sex* was forbidden even to those Earth-Mothers the Nannies themselves) made the experience all the more hurtful to his already well-developed sense of masculine pride, and it was with a sense of relief that he was whisked out of his sodden skirts forever by his own nurse, and into a dashing if miniature facsimile of the naval uniform worn by every member of the Queen's own senior service. In fact the incident seems to have given him a taste for uniform that was to stay with him into his adult life, carrying him through not only to leadership of the army cadets at the great and noble English public school where his education was completed after Frinton-on-Sea—but also over the threshold of the Royal Military College at Sandhurst itself, in preparation for what was to be a dedicated career as a soldier.

In the meantime Henrietta had never quite forgotten the moment when she had peered over the breakwater to make sure she had not injured her cousin too seriously, and had experienced a strangely hurtful and yet warming sensation in the pit of her stomach at the sight of the small, brave boy who was struggling manfully to his feet, his golden curls entwined with the gleaming fronds of seaweed which gave the resort its bracing and briny reputation. She was not to know it for more than a decade, but the sensation was akin to love, and to hide it she had blazed at him with her blue eyes and high young voice, telling him to get up at once and not act like a baby.

She continued to reprimand her cousin in this vein, in fact, for some years, and the playful feud maintained on each side had developed into a thoroughgoing, comfortable state of war by the time Roddy had decided on his career. It was about this time that Henrietta, now an elegant creature with a seventeen-inch waist, a gift for languages, and a mane of chestnut hair that was the envy of every London debutante, realized the true nature of her feelings for her cousin. And in her self-willed fashion, she imagined that the feelings were doubtless reciprocated, and Roddy would be proposing on the eve of his enrollment at the college as a military cadet.

On the day in question, Roddy did present himself, an arrogant and handsome figure, at the door of Henrietta's great family house in fashionable Belgravia. He had come to say goodbye to her mama (his own mother's sister) and to collect a handsome tip into the bargain. He also hoped to impress Henrietta with the dashing cut of his new uniform, which had been tailored in Saville Row, and had cost his father the better part of a month's income. But as Henrietta (who had beaten the parlormaid to the door by a good five seconds) ushered him in he was aware of nothing more stimulating than the usual friendly glare from the blue eyes that shone under the soft dark curls arranged carelessly over the smooth high forehead.

"You look far too handsome to go for a soldier, Roddy," was the nearest his cousin got to a compliment as she held the door wide for him. "And I daresay Mama will shed tears at the sight of your uniform."

"No need to talk such stuff and nonsense, Henrietta." He strode past her as he spoke, and her eyes followed him, a shade less scornfully perhaps, but he was not to know this. "I'm not off to war, you know. The college is only an hour away, or an hour and a half at the most. And the chaps get London-leave, or get to the races, at least once a week."

"I am quite aware that you cannot be off to war, Cousin," she answered blithely as she led him up the wide staircase to the first floor. She paused, her slim hand on the golden balustrade, and glanced back at him with a look intended to set his heart beating rather faster than it already was. "For at this moment in time there aren't all those many wars about. A few skirmishes on the wild northwest frontier of India, it is true. But it is entirely characteristic of you, is it not, Roddy, that you decide to go into the army when there is no war about?" She bounded up the last few stairs, and—accustomed to her teasing—he bounded after her, smiling. But waltzing a turn or two on the landing, she stopped, and looked rather seriously into his eyes. "But I am glad. For I would not have harm come to you, Cousin."

There was a brief moment of silence between them, and Henrietta found herself disappointed that Roddy did not take advantage of their temporary isolation and proximity, in the passage outside her mother's drawing room, to broach the matter that was closest to her own heart. But as he made no move, she soon broke the silence with a little laugh, and assuming a demure countenance, ushered him into the presence of her mama.

"Aunt Constance, how good to see you!" Roddy spoke with well-feigned pleasure, advancing stalwartly across the deep red pile of the drawing room carpet as if into the lion's den. Henrietta's mama awaited her nephew with small lace kerchief clutched in one hand at the ready for what tears might come, and a picture of her sister, Roddy's mother (painted by a second-rate artist whom she had never admired) on the small table that flanked the blue velvet chaise longue where she was in the habit of passing her afternoons. She herself presented a picture of robust but dignified middle-age, and a commanding presence.

It was the sight of the portrait that had made Roddy falter, imperceptibly, and then regain his nerve before his manly advance into the ornate room. He knew that there was no love lost between Constance de Vere Smith and her sister—who had so badly let down the de Vere de Veres, Constance maintained, by marrying beneath her. As this was almost impossible to avoid, considering the elevated social status of the de Vere de Veres, Roddy chose to ignore the matter as much as was possible, and saw it as merely an expression of the impossibly bigoted temperament displayed on all and sundry occasions by Henrietta's mama. Though he would not admit it, he was ready to ignore a great deal that might otherwise annoy him—if it meant that he was able to enjoy Henrietta's own company without complications. For very good company she was, he allowed—and that was as far as he went along the path of thinking what he felt about his spirited and exquisitely attractive cousin.

What was really wrong with Roddy in the view of Henrietta's mama was that he had to work for a living. Her own son, Henrietta's brother Charles, had been to school at Eton where he had acquired a certain skill in translating Latin verse, and had long since found life as a country gentleman a perfectly satisfactory way to exist. It was true that Roddy's father was a very successful solicitor, but that was only one step removed from *Being in Trade*. And the resultant income, apparently, did not run to allowing Roddy to idle the Season away and marry a girl of good family.

What was equally certain in the mind of Henrietta's mama was that Roddy was not going to marry Henrietta, who was destined for higher things. She now began to weep gently in fact, explaining that she sorrowed not only because the poor boy was obliged to go in for a profession, but also because he had to depart for the alien and distant climate of Surrey, so far out of town, in order to start in it at all.

Taking the free, dry hand his aunt now offered him, whilst Henrietta herself looked on without a smile, Roddy kissed her warmly on the brow. "Steady on, Auntie. It's not time for tears, y'know. If truth were told, I'm off to enjoy myself. And don't forget your own brother made a fine career in the cavalry. We make good soldiers, the de Veres."

He did not turn his head when Henrietta greeted this remark with a loud and scornful sniff. It was a well-known family secret that the deVere de Vere in question had died not in battle, nor even quite in the saddle, but he happened to have been on leave, and hunting in Ireland at the time. And it was rumored that his stirrup cup had been so heavily laced with Irish whisky against the chill of the dawn before he cried after the hounds that he had promptly fallen at the first jump. The thought of which seemed to give Henrietta's mama the excuse for an even swifter flow of tears, during which Roddy and Henrietta eyed each other warily across the room.

When she had dried her eyes, replacing her handkerchief firmly in her reticule, Constance gestured to the portrait beside her.

"I have always wanted you to have this," she said, truthfully. "And now it seems the perfect moment has come. Take it, Roddy. Keep it on the wall of your little room at Sandhurst. Keep it forever."

Apparently too moved to speak, Roddy took the picture of his mother (they had a replica, slightly more of a likeness, at home) held it to his chest, and bent once more to embrace his aunt. A stifled choking sound then came from the high windows at the far end of the drawing room, where Henrietta seemed to be deeply engrossed in the cry of a knife-grinder and the whirr of his machine in the London square below, at the same time burying her face in the heavy crimson silk curtains. The fact that she was not weeping had been clear to Roddy from the moment she had stifled the first impulse to laugh, and crossing the room to the windows, he gave his cousin a sharp, comradely, and quite unromantic nudge.

The gesture was meant as a conspiratorial, even affectionate little token. But to Henrietta's way of thinking it was yet another in a sequence of stupidly annoying events. She had spent all morning preparing her dress and her hair for Roddy's call. She had swept ahead of him when he arrived with all the allure at her command. Reading the most promising significance into the fact that he had even arranged to call on her mother, now that his career—such as it was—lay ahead of him in no uncertain terms, Henrietta had fully expected the afternoon to lead to a declaration. All the other girls who had been debutantes with her that Season had begun to announce their engagements, and she had been looking forward to joining their ranks. And all that Roddy could manage, it seemed, was a friendly nudge in the softest region of her lithe, uncorseted young frame.

On the verge of departing for the Royal Military College, Roddy looked dangerously as if he were not going to propose.

But the truth of the matter was that Roddy, unnerved as always by his Aunt Constance's patronizing manner, had even forgotten his plan to ask permission to take Henrietta out to tea. He had enjoyed the walk round to the house in Belgravia. It was a fine afternoon, and he could have strolled with Henrietta in the Park before calling in at one of the great Knightsbridge hotels for tea. Whether or not he would have actually got as far as proposing marriage was unlikely, as he was also looking forward to savoring a few months with his fellow officers as a young bachelor. He wished to be uncommitted, to see his way more, before he let Henrietta know that he returned her affection. If ever that seemed the right thing to do. For he had often lately mulled over the fact that in a wife he would want rather more respect than Henrietta seemed prepared to offer, and could only hope that she would grow out of her pertness towards him. Until she showed some signs of maturing, however, he still thoroughly enjoyed her companionship. And it was therefore with a quite genuine expression of astonished innocence on the handsome young face beneath the short-cropped golden curls that he now watched Henrietta turn on her heel without a word and glide imperiously out of the room.

When Henrietta's mama followed the exit of her daughter with yet another display of grief, Roddy felt, justifiably, that he had almost had a surfeit of their temperamental household for the day. Muttering his farewell, he hurriedly left the drawing room and closed the door carefully behind him. But once on the landing he paused, reluctant to leave the house without a more friendly word with his cousin. And slowly descending the wide stairs, he began softly (for fear of unnecessarily arousing the servants) to call Henrietta's name.

Before he had reached the front door, he was rewarded by a discreet cough, coming from the direction of the morning room. He noticed that the door to this room had been left partly open, and without pausing to think twice he walked straight in. He found his cousin standing drawn to her full height, though still an inch or two lower than his own square shoulders he was glad to note, before the great marble fireplace. It was clear from the way in which she held her chin high, aggressively so, and from the bright tears that glistened unshed in her great blue eyes, that she was in an emotional state of mind.

"I say, old girl!" Roddy cried when he saw her. "Don't take on so. I don't know what I've done to deserve it, I'm sure. And if you're upset that I can't get to next week's party at the Muggeridge place, well don't forget we've three more dances lined up before Christmas. I'll not let you down."

"It's not what you've done, Roddy." Henrietta's tone was icy. "It's more what you have not done. And what you let *others* do. I watched you with Mama. I thought she'd walk all over you. You know how she loves scenes. And I—I did expect you to ask her, to ask her..." her voice trailed away, and she realized, not for the first time, that she was not so emancipated a young woman that she could ever speak of marriage to a man before he had broached the subject to her.

"I did want to ask her, dammit," Roddy cried, irritated by the continued complaining tone in which Henrietta spoke. "It's a delightful afternoon, and I had no desire to take tea indoors here when we could be out in the Park. If you hadn't swept out like that, I'd have popped the question...."

"Oh, Roddy!" Henrietta's face lit up, and she moved swiftly from where she stood, and curled happily into a great bronze leather chair, smiling up at her handsome cousin.

"Yes," Roddy continued. "I know she'd not have liked it. But I'd have insisted. I fully intended to ask to take you out to tea." With a manly shrug at the thought of his temerity and the way in which it had come to nothing, Roddy sat in the chair facing Henrietta. And to his bewilderment she leapt to her feet, once more in a blaze, and once more flounced out of the room. There was nothing for it, he told himself, but to follow her. In the hall, he found her again, standing with the front door held wide open to facilitate, no doubt, his immediate flight.

"We can't go on like this, old girl," he told her quietly, looking vaguely about him for the hat he had left in the hall on his arrival. Her show of emotion had by now thrown his poise to the winds, and had he known what she wanted he would have been quite unable to oblige. Instead, he gave her a brotherly tap on her nearest shoulder, retrieved his hat at last, and with "Don't forget to keep me a waltz or two at those three dances," stepped out onto the streets of Belgravia and took two or three deep and restoring gulps of uncomplicated fresh air. Upon which Henrietta slammed the door in his wake, and rushing back into the morning room and the refuge of her favorite chair, burst into angry tears.

"Will he never have the courage to *do* anything?" she wailed to herself, and when she had run out of tears and bad humor she tidied her hair in the mirror above the fireplace, and began to plan what she would wear for the next dance at which she would meet Roddy again. By then, she thought happily as she went to her bedroom to look through the gowns mama had bought for the Season, he would have settled down at his horrid old military college, and might be quite glad to see her. If she were in luck, she might even get to know which adventurous region of the great British empire he intended to honor with his labors as an officer and a gentleman once he had got through his training.

But Henrietta was not to be so easily gratified. In

the months that followed, she saw Roddy at the three dances, danced all their favorite waltzes with him uneventfully, and watched him increase in good manners and matching poise in his dealings with the other young women of their acquaintance. She met several of his young officer colleagues, and heard that he was "a crack shot, a good sport, and a first-class horseman." But all this she already knew. What she still did not know by the end of his first winter away was where he went on his periodic leaves of absence that were evidently not spent in town—and where he hoped to serve his Queen on his graduation at the end of the year.

The following Season was well under way, and Henrietta, still unbetrothed, was passing each evening dismally with her parents in the usual round of dining out with relatives and friends, when a visit by way of a change to the opera house again brought Henrietta to the realization that something quite new and unexpected had happened to her cousin.

The orchestra was tuning up in preparation for an overture, when a rustle of interest spread through the stalls and then through the circle, as two shadowy figures entered the royal box and stepped forward into the light. At once the audience came to its feet, and a flutter of applause followed.

The Prince of Wales, a dashing figure in evening dress and white tie, smoking a large cigar, was accompanied by his wife, the Princess Alexandra. In her low-necked crinoline of the palest pink, a choker of pearls gleaming softly at her long, graceful throat, Alexandra looked as beautiful as the legends about her claimed. Bowing slightly to the audience, she took her seat. The prince also seated, the audience resettled, and the overture began its jaunty, Italian melodies. It was not until at least fifteen bars from the beginning that Henrietta registered with a low gasp and a quick turn of her head again to the royal box that she knew the young equerry who had stepped forward to hold the golden cane chair for the princess as she took her seat. It was Roddy. In uniform, golden curls well-brushed, gloves impeccably white, he now stood to attention in the deeper recesses of the box. He was clearly on duty.

As the heavy, silken opera house curtains swished dramatically apart, and a duet between two sopranos began its attack on the story that was about to unfold, Henrietta found herself drawn back to the stage by a sharp rap on the knuckles from Constance de Vere Smith's fan. As soon as she found an opportunity to explain what had distracted her to her mama, she did so, in a soft whisper that nonetheless prompted loud hissing and shushing from the members of the audience close by. This did not deter Constance from at once examining the occupants of the royal box through her exquisite mother-of-pearl and tortoise shell opera glasses, to Henrietta's acute embarrassment.

While Henrietta's father pretended to follow what was happening on stage, now that a tenor had joined the sopranos and a team of peasants were dancing round the trio while they explained their life stories to each other, his wife continued to scrutinize her prey, and finally lowered the glasses and firmly shook her head. Then to her companions' immense relief, she turned her attention to the music.

It was in the interval that she told Henrietta she had been mistaken. How could such an undistinguished young man as her sister's son ever hope to find himself in attendance on royalty? There had been a superficial likeness, it was true. But there were so many young men in uniform this Season. (She implied that Henrietta's cousin was one of the many fish in the sea her daughter had so far failed to net with each word that she uttered.) The very idea of Roddy as equerry, even for an evening, was absurd. And yet, as they walked back to their seats, Constance was preoccupied, and did not quite manage to disguise the fact that she was itching to turn her gaze once more on the royal box.

But they were all to be disappointed, for the time

being. Clearly impatient of the tenor and his brace of sopranos (whom Henrietta herself had to endure for two more hours), the royal party had taken advantage of the interval to leave discreetly.

Still convinced that it was indeed her cousin whom she had seen that night, Henrietta wasted no time at their next meeting—at a summer supper dance held at an elegant whitestone house in Regent's Park. She asked him lightly if he had seen the opera in question. They were dancing a waltz, as usual, and before he answered Roddy neatly reversed.

"Oh yes," he told her, airily as the dance itself. "I was there with H.R.H. He didn't take to it, and we slipped out before the first interval. Doesn't do to be seen to leave, you know, m'dear. It offends the artistes dreadfully."

Astonished by his display of total honesty, there was nothing Henrietta felt she could reply, and for the rest of the evening she was extremely thoughtful. As it happened, Roddy was staying in town for the night with one of his fellow officers at their club, and when her carriage was called she accepted his offer to drive back to Belgravia with her with alacrity. As they bowled round the Park and turned south for Marble Arch, she gazed out at the stars, and hummed happily to herself at the memory of the music. Roddy joined in, only too pleased that the evening seemed to be coming to a close uneventfully. But he was wrong.

"Roddy?" Henrietta spoke his name softly.

"Henrietta?" It was an old game they had played as children. The idea was that the first to start a real sentence was the loser. But Henrietta seemed to have forgotten the rules.

"If you are in the habit of meeting with His Royal Highness, I suppose the matter of where you will be serving when you get your commission must come into the conversation. They say the prince is very interested in foreign politics. And in the empire. Even if it's his mother who is the Empress."

"Oh, he'd make a splendid ruler. H.R.H. is as keen as mustard, I'm sure of that. And well-informed. But she'll never let him have his head, of that I'm equally sure. You know what mothers are, Henrietta."

Henrietta sighed. "Yes, indeed I do, Roddy. And I sometimes think I'm as surrounded by a maternal empire as *he* is... His Highness, I mean."

Roddy made then as if to take her hand, sympathetically, but she withdrew slightly into her corner of the carriage. "I suppose he'd like to see someone like you, someone he knows and trusts, looking out for things in India—or somewhere like that. They say there's a great deal to be done out there." She gazed wistfully up at the stars, as if to convey that they too watched down over Pathan tribesmen and wild Hindu hordes.

Roddy coughed nervously. He was thankful they were now approaching Hyde Park and would soon be at Henrietta's door. "I wouldn't say that exactly, old girl. For one thing, as I told you, H.R.H. doesn't have that sort of pull. And—well, he seems to have other things in mind for me. I must say, I like the fellow enormously. You know where you are with him. And we have some splendid times, we aides-de-camp."

"Aides-de-camp?" Henrietta turned fully to face him, her blue eyes wide with undisguised horror. "You mean helping out, at his—his events?"

"Yes," Roddy told her staunchly. "Events. Soirées. That sort of thing. All has to be organized, you know. I met H.R.H. on college maneuvers, you see, and I was in charge of the mess for the night, and—well, to be blunt about it, he liked the way I did things."

"Did things?" Henrietta's eyes were now cold as steel in the dark of the carriage. "What things?"

"Look here, Henrietta," Roddy came back icily himself. "It's my job. I do what I'm told. He asked for me, and for the time being that's what I have to do. If he sent me to India, I'd have to go there, too. But it just doesn't come to that sort of thing. He's in London; he

has a very full life. He needs all the help he can get."
Something in her cousin's tone warned Henrietta then that perhaps this time she would be well advised not to provoke him further. She was so upset at the thought of her handsome Roddy as what she could describe to herself as nothing more than lackey to a prince that she wished in any case to be alone with her thoughts and her disappointment. And she had to admit reluctantly that she liked the loyalty and enthusiasm with which Roddy himself talked of the prince in question.

Fortunately, the carriage drew up almost immediately at the de Vere Smiths' door, and Roddy leapt out, making for the pavement so that he could be there to help Henrietta alight in place of the coachman. His obvious fondness for her, in the way in which he held her arm, and guided her to the great door, softened her heart for a moment, and Henrietta was about to ask him would he not like to come in for a nightcap—brandy perhaps—with her father, when her cousin gave her arm a brotherly squeeze, and turned and walked back smartly down the steps. Dismissing the carriage on Henrietta's behalf, he then turned back to where she stood watching him in the lamplight, raised his hat, bowed, and marched away. In that moment, Henrietta knew what it must feel like to watch a beloved soldier march off to his fate at The Front.

"Only he's not fighting at any front," she told herself bitterly, and as she waited for the butler to open the door to her summons, she stamped fretfully up and down on the wide top step with her small feet. For a summer's night, it had turned exceedingly chilly.

CHAPTER TWO

IN THE WEEK or two that followed, with no date fixed in her diary for any social occasion at which she might next chance to meet her cousin, Henrietta tried constantly to come to terms with what seemd to be his new way of life. She rode frequently in the Park with her best friend, The Honorable Alice Manners, her burnished head under its gleaming top hat held high as she averted her gaze from the admiring eyes of the gallants who watched her progress from the railings of Rotten Row. She shopped assiduously, for gloves and shoes and shawls, only to fling them haphazardly into the recesses of her wardrobes when they were delivered to the house. She began a journal, in a large book bound in red leather, only to abandon it one rainswept evening on the third page, across which she scrawled impetuously:

Nothing ever happens!

No sooner was the ink dry than she ran from her room and took the unprecedented step of knocking at her mother's boudoir door, in the hope of finding some grain of comfort in the strong-minded platitudes which she knew Mama would proffer should she admit to her ennui. But her hand fell to her side as she remembered that her parents were dining away that evening, at the house of old friends who were on leave from service with Her Majesty's diplomatic service in the far east. She regretted now that she had refused earlier that day to go with them. She had feared that any account of distant places and adventures in foreign parts would only serve to aggravate her need to flee her far too comfortable nest and her parents' rule.

She told herself that if she fled it would only be to seek some reality—whether in a neat house north of the Park as Roddy's wife, or as an adventurous Victorian lady at her adventurous soldier husband's side. But that was just the problem. Roddy showed not the slightest intention of seeking either the neat domestic hearth, or the untidy skirmish of the battlefield. And lately, he showed no sign either of risking the untroubled streets and squares of Belgravia itself.

As she made her way restlessly downstairs and crossed the hall to the green baize door that led to the kitchen quarters, she tried once more to tell herself that there was much for which to be thankful. It was not exactly her cousin's fault, she reasoned, that he had not been sent to India. When he was fully trained, and the days at the Royal Military College over, it might in fact turn out that there was no real war for him to go to. And if she were honest with herself, to see him go off into battle might mean nothing but the substitution of months of dread for his safety in the place of the present weeks of stupefying uncertainty.

If only, she sighed, he had proposed to her on that day he had come to make his farewell to Mama. At least she would have known where she stood.

"Are you there, Mrs. Pillet?" she called miserably, standing at the top of the stairs that led into the sanctuary of the cook's domain. She waited for an invitation to descend which she knew, since her childhood days, would be forthcoming.

"Why, Miss Henrietta!" The cook's white hat and starched apron glimmered beneath her. "You're a rare enough visitor these days. Feeling peckish, I suppose?"

"Oh, I couldn't eat a thing, Mrs. Pillet," Henrietta's voice lightened as she ran down into the warmth of the kitchen. There was a delicious smell of fresh-baked bread in the air, and on the black stove a heavy enamel saucepan simmered with quiet promise.

"Not even a taste of my blanky de veau?" Mrs. Pillet asked.

Henrietta half slumped at the scrubbed white table in the center of the room, and eyed the stove. "Well," she sighed, "I would not like to hurt your feelings by a refusal, Mrs. Pillet. Just the merest taste, perhaps?" Mrs. Pillet's blanquette de veau was famed for its creamy subtlety, and now she came to think of it she was perhaps a little hungry, and after all she would be saving all the fuss of dining alone upstairs if she gave in now to the temptation.

Moments later, she cut delicately into a morsel of veal, and smiled across into Mrs. Pillet's wordly-wise old eyes.

For a second, she was reminded of the discerning blue-gray eyes of the gentlewoman who had been her Nanny. She was transported to the scene of her childhood summers, and could almost hear the rattle of stones and splash of seawater as she and Roddy ran together along the beach at Frinton.

It was then that she remembered a louder splash, and gleaming gold curls, and eyes gazing into hers in bewildered but heroic suffering. She had hoped such things of Roddy. And now, caught up as he was in the whirl of life round Prince Edward, she knew she would never have the opportunity to plan a future with and for him. He would grow away from her, of that she was certain. He would dance attendance on the prince, and the royal inertia would rub off onto him, and he would sink lost forever into the quicksands of boredom and high living.

It was no good, she told herself as she dug less elegantly now into Mrs. Pillet's blanky de veau. Her cousin was lost to her, and she might as well give in to it. She would put his indifference out of her heart, and his career out of her mind. She had no power to run his life for him. And perhaps no right? She smiled across at the cook, accepted the offer of a second helping, and as the plump white figure rustled to and fro in the warm room, resolved that as soon as she had tried a dish of Mrs. Pillet's trifle she would go straight to her room, reopen her journal, and on the next untarnished page set down her newfound wisdom.

She was in the same hard-won, equable frame of mind a whole week later, and looking her most delightful in amber silk trimmed with ecru lace, on the night Mama and her father took her, for her birthday, to the opera once more. They were a little late in arriving, and by the time they found their seats, in the front row center of the circle, Henrietta was breathless with happy anticipation. She gazed briefly at her program, and as the overture began her eyes wandered with rapt interest round the rest of the darkening, now silent theater. It was then that she saw Roddy again. This time he sat only slightly in the shadows of the royal box. In the foreground were the prince, and his elegant companion—whom Henrietta took at first to be his wife. But as she continued to watch, unaware as Roddy was of her gaze, she became puzzled at the attentive way in which he leaned over the shoulder of the woman beside the prince. Surely this was not etiquette? Surely the Princess Alix would not have invited such proximity?

And as her eyes became accustomed to the darkness, Henrietta saw that the woman was not Alexandra. She was a stranger, of strangely dark beauty. She flirted equally with the man at her shoulder, and the man at her side. Bronzed ringlets shone in the lights from the stage as she turned a graceful neck. As the music receded to a far distance, and became a ringing in her burning ears, Henrietta avidly studied the sensuous, sophisticated movements of the woman who seemed to take so much of Roddy's attention. From that moment, she loathed her, without knowing who or what she was. It was as if she personified the uselessness and sloth that she feared would set in for Roddy if he did not see active service, and really start to live, once his time at the college was over. And when the woman in the royal box laughed silently at a remark from Henrietta's cousin, at a solemn moment on the stage, Henrietta's fury blazed, silently, within her.

This time, however, it seemed that the performance pleased the royal party, and by the first interval they were still in their curtained box. Try as she might to pretend she was not watching them, as by now was almost the entire audience, Henrietta had at last to lift her head openly, her attention drawn to her cousin's presence by her father and mama. Mama was speaking loudly, anxious that those nearest to them—and those further afield—should be aware that her own nephew was now a companion to royalty. But Henrietta's father spoke softly to his daughter. "Why, words almost fail me, Henrietta. Do you see her as I see her? Such a beautiful woman. And Roddy thinks so too, by gad. Haven't you noticed?"

"Noticed what, Papa?" Henrietta spoke as civilly as she could in view of the circumstances. She was fond of her father, and never spoke harshly to him if she could avoid it. He had quite enough to suffer in that line of country from her mother's tongue.

"Why the likeness! It's amazing, Henny. She's the split image of *you*, my girl. Your twin sister!"

And in an appalled silence that lasted the rest of the evening, Henrietta sat going over and over in her mind the nightmare fact that if Roddy was attracted to this woman then it must be because he might once have also been attracted to her. For her father was right. She and the woman who knew how to flirt simultaneously with royalty and with Henrietta's own handsome young cousin were as alike as two opposite profiles on a golden, polished coin. The same shape of head, the same rich coloring, and—the same proud look.

Not knowing how she reached the end of the evening, Henrietta thanked her parents on their return to the house for her birthday outing, and pleading a sudden fatigue after so much excitement, she almost ran to the sanctuary of her room. There she flung herself down on her bed, still fully clothed, and cried her heart out until she slept. It was thus that her mother found her, an hour later, having been prompted by her husband to look in and see if the girl was all right. It was so unlike her to go to bed without being reminded how late it was.

The presence of her mother in the room made Henrietta turn uneasily in her sleep, and for a moment she awoke. The obvious distress on her swollen face, the tangled copper of her hair on the pillow, prompted Constance de Veré Smith to cross the room to her daughter. There was rarely a show of tenderness between them, but in this instance Henrietta almost welcomed the rather heavy maternal embrace.

"It's no good, Mama," she began to sob again. "He'll never amount to anything. And now...that woman..." she threw her head back on her pillow, gulping down angry tears. "Papa says she's like me!"

"What nonsense men talk, my dear. There's nothing remotely like you in that dreadful creature. It was a trick of the light. Maybe only the color of your hair. If her's was natural, that is, in the first place."

Strangely comforted by her mother's astringent reply, Henrietta resolved to cry no more that night. She sat up, gulped back a sob, and began to disrobe while her mother fussed about the room. "I have quite made up my mind, Henrietta," her mother continued, pretending to restore order on a quite orderly dressing table as she spoke. "There is nothing for it but the best cure of all. Not time. Not a whirl of parties. But— travel! We are going to take advantage, you and I, Henrietta, of those splendid new tours planned for the adventurous traveler by Mr. Thomas Cook and his son. We are going to forget Master Roddy and his unforgivable behavior for once and for all. We are going to see the world!"

With this proclamation, which seemed to her to solve at one blow her daughter's worthless heartache and her own desires to do something fashionable of which she could boast to her friends on her return, Henrietta's mama blew out the lamp which she had borne into the room before her on her arrival, and marched off to her slumbers.

Henrietta, left in darkness, limp with sorrow, but not totally distraught, stared into the shadows. Then, as she nestled into her soft feather pillows and stretched her long limbs between the cool white sheets of her high bed, she reflected that to make anything of her life she was, indeed, going to have to put her cousin— and that dreadful woman—out of her mind. One had one's pride, after all. It would be for the best.

And she had to admit, as she slid at last into a delicious sleep, that she was truly attracted to the idea of seeing something of the world. If only it need not have been with her indomitable mama....

CHAPTER THREE

IN KEEPING with the tradition by which the female members of the de Vere de Vere family were accustomed to act promptly once their minds were made up; (before any of their long-suffering menfolk could summon the strength, no doubt, to stand in their way) Henrietta's mama called her into her morning room early the next day and placed in her hand the address of Mr. Thomas Cook's booking office in Fleet Street, and a banker's draft drawn on her own account in a Bond Street banking house. It was for a handsome sum, and would more than cover the cost of the holiday she had in mind.

"I have in mind, my dear Henrietta," she told her subdued daughter, "a few weeks in Paris now that the French have settled down briefly to living in peace. And possibly something a little unusual to follow. I am told that the castles—the châteaux—of the Loire valley are not to be missed. You will enquire for the routes and the hotels—only the best, of course—suggested by Mr. Cook? And no doubt I can leave it to you to book tickets, on the first available day of the new year. I am tired of it all, and if it were not for the supper dance at Wellington House on the last Saturday this month, I declare I would shake the dust of London off my feet this very afternoon."

A little pale after her experience of the previous evening, Henrietta nevertheless did her utmost to listen to her mother through the clouds of her own thoughts. When she thought of the proposed journey to Paris she imagined herself and Roddy strolling together down the Champs Elysées, only to come down to earth with the realization that it was on her mother's plump arm that she would be leaning. The mention of the châteaux of the Loire brought on an even fiercer attack of melancholia: castles made one think of Windsor, and at Windsor was lodged the royal family, and within the bosom of that family these days could be found her cousin—and no doubt that woman who had graced the royal box the night before. Henrietta sighed wearily.

She was looking particularly attractive, though she did not know it, in a walking outfit of pale lemon velvet trimmed with black. She had intended to take the family carriage to the home of her best friend, The Honorable Alice Manners, who lived only two squares away from the de Vere Smith residence. Then she proposed to walk in the Park with Alice, for it was a fine day, and tell her all that had passed on the evening of her birthday... except, perhaps, for a true description of the beauty of the woman who had accompanied H.R.H.—and Roddy.

"Henrietta!" Her mother brought her sharply back to the task in hand. The banker's draft was tucked in her reticule, and a list of errands that would take all morning if Henrietta did not hurry was added to it.

Suddenly there was no time for sighs, and with a spark of her old spirit in her eyes as she settled back in the carriage, Henrietta decided that if Mama insisted on travel then she would travel with goodwill. In fact if she could only shake off her disappointment in her cousin, she could almost persuade herself to travel even further afield than the Continent. She leaned her head against the velvet rest, and gazed out onto the bustling London streets. Did the streets teem with people like that in the northwest frontier towns, she wondered? Frowning, she told herself that if they did it was nothing to her. Everyone knew that Paris was *the* city to visit. She must count her blessings—and forget her visions, now thwarted forever it seemed, of riding with Roddy into the slopes of the hills of Kashmir, a silken Indian shawl slung casually across her shoulders, the remorseless sun of far lands beating down, glinting on the gold band on her left hand. . . .

Fortunately at this moment the carriage came to a halt with a jerk, outside the house where Alice Manners lived during the Season. Dismissing the driver, with the explanation that she and her companion for the morning would take a hansom later, Henrietta crossed the pavement and mounted the elegant marble steps that led to the entrance. Almost at once the door swung open, to reveal Lord Manners' (Alice's father's) butler standing with The Honorable Alice herself jumping up and down in a state of considerable excitement at his side.

Ceasing her athletics briefly in order to embrace Henrietta, Alice led her friend, still skipping rather than walking, into the small morning room on the far side of the spacious hall. She explained that she had heard the carriage draw up, and hoping above hope that it was the de Vere Smiths', she had time only to make sure that her mother was engaged on the day's menus with Cook in the study, and had raced downstairs to be sure of greeting Henrietta in private.

"For you see, my darling Henrietta," she cried, her

golden curls dancing as she pushed the visitor onto a chaise longue and snatched her reticule from her, throwing it on a distant chair, "there is something that only *you* are to be told! *No* one, but *no* one—except Maria Newcastle, whom I am to meet at The Chocolate House in Bond Street in less than an hour—is to know except my darling Henrietta."

"Bond Street? Good, that is where I also have to be, in less than an hour." Henrietta, who knew Alice's confidences of old and was aware that if she allowed her to speak at all they would be closeted for the rest of the morning, started to her feet. But her friend promptly pushed her back down onto the seat.

"Can't you guess? Don't you think I look—different? Oh, Henrietta, I'm so happy!" Alice whirled away for an instance, hugging her rather homely frame with strong young arms, then turned back to gaze into Henrietta's eyes with her own nearsighted, slightly squinting orbs. With a shock of intuition laced with immediate, cold jealousy, Henrietta knew before Alice spoke again what it was that she had to say. Her ears sang and her eyes clouded with unshed tears at her own lone plight as she heard the flow of the well-worn phrases—always so fresh and significant when each girl came to the moment when she could announce, with pride and shining eyes, that—she was engaged!

Sure enough. "I'm engaged! Secretly engaged! It happened last night, and he had to go straight to India, so there's not even a ring to prove it. But he says I'll have his dear dead mama's engagement ring when he's told the family. And his name is Gerald. Gerald Morton." Henrietta looked blank. "The Mortons of Buckingham. Shire, not Palace." Alice shrieked her young girl's laughter at her own joke, and whirled about the room again. And at that moment Henrietta actively hated her own best friend.

"Now, Henny," said the innocent object of her jealousy, retrieving her friend's bag and raising her from where she sat only to embrace her again. "Now, let's

31

send for a hansom and get down to Bond Street. I can't tell my parents until Gerald has formally asked Papa, and I'm bursting to tell Maria. Then there'll be just the three of us, and you can both help me decide about the wedding."

The Chocolate House in London's smartest quarter was perhaps not the best place in which to discuss such a well-kept secret as Alice's betrothal to Gerald, but Henrietta was in no mood to advise discretion to anyone. In a state of stunned amazement that plain, excitable Alice, whom she had known all her life, had managed to become engaged when she herself had flunked it, Henrietta allowed herself to be drawn into the street, into a hansom, and into The Chocolate House, which buzzed with activity at this time of the morning.

Sure enough, Maria Newcastle, a young married woman who had been Debutante of the Year some three Seasons previously, had taken a table in the center of the room, and waved to the two friends as they arrived. Aware that all eyes were upon her, probably because the whole of London must know of her cousin's behavior at the opera the night before, Henrietta advanced to the table, her head high. She was extremely glad that she was wearing the yellow outfit. She knew that it became her coloring perfectly, and on occasions such as this one needed to look one's best.

There was no pity, however, in the exuberant greeting Henrietta received from Maria Newcastle. The older woman examined her admiringly, and told her how well she looked. Alice impatiently drew her friend's attention to herself, and asked her did she not find that she too was blooming? And within seconds, at the top of her voice, had told her news to the whole of London.

Exhausted at the very thought of the chatter that would follow, Henrietta asked if she might have her chocolate at once, as she had many errands to complete for her mama. There were some broken spectacles to be taken for repair to Mr. Dixey's establishment three doors away, and then the much further errand in Fleet Street to the offices of Mr. Thomas Cook. It was so difficult to obtain a hansom in Bond Street at this time of day that she wanted to bring the chocolate party, and incidentally the painful talk of betrothals, to an end as quickly as possible.

But at the mention of Thomas Cook, Maria Newcastle gave a glance of interest. Finding some solace in the thought of her imminent departure abroad, Henrietta explained. And the news of the de Vere Smiths' plans to travel certainly seemed to detract from Alice's own announcement. Until, that is, Henrietta mentioned Paris and the châteaux of the Loire... which had the effect of making Maria Newcastle raise her elegant, plucked brows in mock horror.

"But Henrietta, you must be mad! If your mama insists on travel, then, my dear, *travel* it must be—go as far as you can while she's in the mind to buy your ticket. It will make a new woman of you."

Henrietta was not sure that she liked the implication that she needed to be made over like a discarded dress, but her reaction went unnoticed as Maria continued. "It did of me. And you can go to Paris any day. In fact if you take a further tour you will no doubt have to pass through the city, anyway. Even the Loire is then but a stone's throw. No—I insist. I shall go to Fleet Street with you myself, this very instant."

She rose, and Henrietta hastily gathered her primrose skirts and made to depart. But again, Maria sat down. Henrietta and Alice followed suit, half hypnotized in spite of themselves by the beguiling fashion in which Maria laced a dimpled chin on a slender hand and frowned.

"Of course, it is still very novel. And there are grave risks attached to such an excursion. But if H.R.H. can do it, then why not you and your mama?"

"H.R.H.? Is the prince going to France again?" Henrietta's heart beat faster. She knew that the Prince had a great weakness for all things French, and her imagination bounded ahead to visions of what the innocent Roddy would make of such a trip at the side of a veteran of French fleshpots. She tried to appear only slightly interested.

"Not France, foolish girl. Although of course his entourage will take the Newhaven-Paris-Italy route, no doubt. And the French adore him. But—I have said too much. I was sworn to secrecy." Her voice dropped to a discreet whisper. "Not even the... the dear lady at Windsor herself is to know. H.R.H. enjoyed himself too much for the Queen's liking on his official visit. She is to remain in blissful ignorance of the fact that he plans to return—incognito."

"Return? But where?" Alice helped out, shifting athletically on her small chair.

"A private party. Just a few friends." Maria went on dreamily. "By private steamer. Only the aides-de-camp involved are in on the affair, and it so happens that one of the young men is a—a dear friend." Maria fluttered her lashes. She was a very liberated-mannered woman, indeed.

At the mention of the aides-de-camp Henrietta went white. Now she felt that her heart would stop, it raced so under her tight yellow bodice. To disguise her agitation, she opened her reticule, and drew out the banker's draft, studying it earnestly as if she had never seen it before. "Where is it that they are going, Maria?" she asked casually. "And where is it that you think I should go with mama?"

"Didn't I say? I thought I mentioned it? Oh Henrietta, you will never regret it! The great river, the desert, the moonlight, the pyramids!"

"Pyramids?!" Alice and Henrietta gasped in one voice.

"Why, of course there are pyramids. And it's the height of fashion to have seen them. That's why, if I know Constance de Vere Smith, your devoted mama, that is, she'll not make you alter the booking when you go home with your deposit paid this very afternoon. Come, Henrietta. You are going to Egypt!" And within moments of the announcement, Henrietta found herself outside in the street, on the first lap of her journey up the Nile.

Maria Newcastle had been entirely correct in her surmise that Henrietta's mama would not lightly turn down the plans for a trip that would put her in the avant garde of her own small social circle. To her knowledge, no one of that circle had yet braved the journey to Egypt except under military orders or in an excess of zeal in the matter of acquiring antiquities for the London museum. These reflections occurred to her while she listened gravely to her daughter's explanation that the banker's order had paid for a deposit only on a journey that would take them through, and then rather farther than, France. Secretly, she allowed herself a moment's fantasy; if she agreed to the plan her daughter had brought home from Fleet Street, who was to tell what marvels might come of it? She herself might come upon some small token of the ancient past in the sands of Egypt, and bring it home, to present it to the British Museum in a gracious little ceremony to which she would invite all her friends. Even her sister, Roddy's mother, would be impressed. At the thought of that young man, however, Henrietta's mama pulled herself sharply back to the present and the whole business of rehabilitation for her daughter and their hurt pride.

"It is a great pity, all the same, to miss the châteaux of the Loire, child," she told Henrietta. She had to be allowed some show of still being in command of the project, after all.

"But it's still a river, Mama. And such a great river! The Nile!" Her eyes were sparkling, for the first time for days, and her mother could not help noticing that the Egyptian vacation seemed to have fired her daughter's spirits at last. She looked quite her old self.

Henrietta, in fact, was making a bold attempt to conceal the vested interest she had in following Roddy and the Prince of Wales on their clandestine journey. And once she had made up her mind to risk everything—Roddy's friendship, as well as his trust, and certainly her own pride—she had found herself positively enjoying the idea. She had come home that morning full of repressed excitement, and quite determined to get her way. But it would never do for her mother to detect that.

"Well," Constance de Vere Smith reflected, "It is true that I am utterly weary of the present social round. The Season has been exhausting. Not a new face on the scene for a month. And we shall need completely new outfits, of course. Your father will have to be told that we face the hazards of sunshine, sand and drought. The matter of parasols is of the utmost importance. One to compliment each of our gowns... or should we wear topees?"

"Oh, Mama! Then you agree?" Henrietta flung herself at her mother in a rare moment of rapprochement. Although they were as close as mother and daughter can be, in the teeth of her mama's autocratic tendencies, a show of affection between them had not been encouraged on either side. The de Vere de Veres were made of sterner stuff, and the addition of a Smith to their ranks in the mild person of Henrietta's father had not exactly added to the family's capacity for rapture. It was Henrietta's lot so far in life to conceal the passionate nature that slept in her young breast.

But Constance even allowed herself a slight smile on her face as she returned her daughter's embrace and then swept across her boudoir to her secretaire. "Now what was the name of that complexion cream I heard of from the French ambassador's wife at dinner last week?" she murmured. "The poor creature had spent years in Africa before they were posted to London, and her condition had remained quite remarkably attractive despite the disgusting climate."

"There are worse things than sunshine, Mama." Henrietta sat in the chair beside the desk, and began mentally to make a list of her own needs.

"Dear child, there is *nothing* worse than sunshine to the English complexion. And when you return to Mr. Dixey's shop for your father's mended spectacles, pray ask his advice in the matter of smoke-colored glasses. Two pairs, I think, and a third in case. When we are traveling overland we shall watch our baggage like young eagles, and I shall make sure to keep everything of value in the very center of the tent, however inconvenient. They say that these Bedouins have very long arms, and it is nothing for a marauder to reach under the guy ropes, the very lifelines of the roof over one's head, and just *take* for the asking!"

With increasing admiration of her mama's obvious knowledge of how to survive on the adventure that now was the vista before them, Henrietta found herself making lists assiduously for the remainder of that day, and it was only as she copied at her mother's dictation the name of a Persian insect powder recommended by Keating's for use in the tropics, that it dawned on her that she was taking an appalling risk in proposing to travel so far afield with Mama. The plan had started with France only, and it was true they would have a night at least in Paris—but then! Three months of the new year would be spent in close proximity to a woman who waged war on thieves and fleas before they had even left home. She could not even begin to imagine the vigor with which her mother would go into action if and when she found herself face to face with her nephew under an Egyptian sky—and learned that she had been duped by her own daughter into breaching the tombs of kings only to satisfy a commonplace matter of affection, and to achieve an uneasy rendezvous far from home for two young and wayward cousins.

For in her heart Henrietta had no doubt at all that she herself had only such a rendezvous in mind.

CHAPTER FOUR

IT WAS a small but intrepid band of travelers that assembled on a bright January morning some weeks later at London Bridge Railway Station, under the watchful care of a personal representative of their tour organizer, Mr. Thomas Cook. The representative was a Mr. Bedales from Leicester, a solemn and bewhiskered gentleman with, Henrietta thought, reassuringly gentle brown eyes. She looked on with some apprehension from behind the warmth of her high fur muff that hung from a band round her neck, as her mother started the tour in the manner which she no doubt intended to maintain throughout by buttonholing Mr. Bedales with a query.

"My daughter's saddle is already in the guard's van, sir," she informed him. "But I ask myself, who is to see it safely stowed at Newhaven, and how will it fare in France?"

Mr. Bedales bowed slightly, and began to usher Constance de Vere Smith towards a carriage reserved for his group. "I can assure you, dear lady, that we have representatives at all points in our journey who will provide you—and your baggage—with every care. It is true that you are responsible ultimately for the separate mobility—and payment—of your effects. But that does not mean you stand alone."

Watching her mama clamber as gracefully as was possible into the carriage, with a guiding hand from Mr. Bedales at a discreet strategic point somewhere beneath the folds of the serge bustle sported by all ladies that season, Henrietta began to wish that she had not followed the instructions of Maria Newcastle and Alice Manners in her selection of luggage deemed necessary for the three months she would be away. It was Maria who had insisted she take her own saddle. "It will be an added expense, of course," she had explained, "but you will not regret it. When you take to the road that will lead you to the lands of the Bible, you will thank your stars that at least you are seated on familiar territory."

"The Bible?" Henrietta had replied, faintly. It was then that she had learned that the all-in-one tour on which she had innocently persuaded her mother to embark was not to end with the Nile. It was the custom, for those who still had the strength and the will, to continue by caravan overland to Jerusalem itself, before a return journey home the way they had come—through Italy. As Maria put it, what was the use of going so far, if you did not complete the pilgrimage? But Henrietta silently asked herself whether after whatever encounters awaited her beyond Cairo, if any, she would have the heart to forge on. It was a question no one as yet could answer.

She was following her mother along the station plat-

39

form in a similarly hesitant frame of mind, wondering if it was too late to turn back and cancel the whole affair, when a familiar manly voice hailed her, and she turned to see the burly, tweed-clad figure of her brother Charlie marching through the barrier.

"Charlie!" Henrietta's spirits rose as she ran back down the platform to greet him. Although they hardly ever saw each other since he had married and taken to country life, she had always been able to count on him to turn up trumps at awkward moments, and now here he was, doing exactly the right thing by coming to see them off.

He bent to kiss her, a brotherly peck on her straight nose, and brushed an imaginary stray fox hair from his chin as he encountered her collar.

"You smell delicious, Henny! And you'll need all the perfume you can stock up with where you're going, be warned!" He tucked her arm in his, and walked her smartly back again to where their mama now leaned from a carriage window, informing a cluster of fellow travelers that this was her son, Charles de Vere Smith, old-Etonian and gentleman farmer, come to see that all was well.

"Never fear, Mater," Charles told her cheerfully as she began a catalogue of things that could go wrong with the town house in Belgravia in her absence. "You know Pater is a sterling chap, and I've come up to town for a few days, so he'll not notice your absence at all."

Henrietta silently agreed with her brother, remembering that her father had not even expressed a wish to come to the station to see them off on the first stage of their epic journey. He had kissed his wife an absentminded goodbye at the breakfast table some hours before and gone to his club as usual, pausing only to skirt the mound of luggage that stood in the hall and regard it with a puzzled expression.

"You will make it clear to him that he is not to expect us back for quite some time, Charlie?" she asked.

"Never fear, Sister dear." Charles smiled. "But if it

comes to June or July and you're not back in the fold, I'll send out a search party. Don't forget I knew some of those Egyptian fellers at Eton. I'd soon get things sorted out if you went missing without leave!"

Constance regarded her son coldly. "You should not make a joke of such matters, Charles. You will make your sister nervous. And if we are not back by the month of May, let alone June or July, I for one shall be seeking an explanation from Mr. Thomas Cook in person. We are to join the Flemings at Henley. And Charles—I expect to see you there!"

Wondering how their parent could possibly be looking ahead to the monotonous social events of yet another English summer when the whole of the east was about to open to her, brother and sister smiled ruefully at each other, and Charles took Henrietta's hand and tucked it again securely into her muff.

"You'll look as jolly as a muffin under a topee, Sis dear," he laughed. "I've always said you're a winner, and I say it again. Let's hope you find the lucky man this time out, eh?"

His smiling expression turned to one of bewildered remorse as, at his last words, Henrietta's face crumpled, and she turned from him, bursting into tears. He turned to where his mother now glared furiously at him through her carriage window. Luckily, the other members of the party were beginning to attempt to take their places, and Constance de Vere Smith had to withdraw into the compartment to allow them to pass, before she was able to vent her spleen on her blundering son.

By the time the carriage was resettled, Henrietta had composed herself, and turned, sniffing a little, to smile up at her brother once more. "I'm sorry, Charlie," she said. "I know you meant no harm. But it is just because I seem to have missed the boat in that respect, at least for the past two Seasons, that Mama is going to all this trouble on my behalf. She is convinced that travel will solve everything—"

"And so it shall, Sis, so it shall." Charlie patted her

awkwardly on the shoulder, and opened the carriage door. "Now, no more tears. In with you, and may the best man win!"

Henrietta, torn between tears and laughter at her brother's incurable lack of tact, at last took her place in the carriage at her mother's side. Charlie stood well back from the train. Mr. Bedales opened the compartment door and took a corner seat on the far side from Mrs. de Vere Smith. There was a high-pitched whistle, a waving of flags and arms, a belch of steam.

Settling her skirts about her, Henrietta fluttered her hand again in farewell as Charles's figure slid imperceptibly away from view. Beneath them the thrilling surge of pistons settled to a heavy rhythm. A large fleck of grime appeared on the nose of a lady who sat opposite the de Vere Smiths. She lowered a thick veil over a pale spinsterish face. "How brave of such a young woman to travel alone," Henrietta thought, and then sat back in silent admiration as the young woman in question opened a dark blue vellum-bound writing book, and began to read what was obviously a first, handwritten entry in a journal. They were clearly in the company of an experienced traveler!

Henrietta's attention was soon diverted from the diarist when Mr. Bedales took it upon himself to make introductions all round between the other members of the party, and informed them that they were to take on an American gentleman in Paris, together with two or three distinguished fellow countrymen who would accompany them only as far as the Nile. And at Brindisi, when they boarded their vessel for Alexandria, further enthusiasts could be expected to swell their ranks.

The immediate company numbered eight, excluding Mr. Bedales, and apart from the spinster lady who was eventually introduced as Miss Summers from Finchley, they consisted of two married couples, a clergyman on leave, and a retired widower, Mr. Jonathan Fountain, who had made his fortune in coal and was about to spend it in the company of his elderly unmarried sister, a Miss Fountain from Harrogate.

To Henrietta's relief, her mother seemed to find no one in the assembly to whom she could take exception, and after a pleasant tea and an uneventful stroll round the harbor walls at Newhaven some hours later, they all boarded the night packet for France.

Twenty-four hours later, Henrietta sat opposite her mother at a small table in the dining room of the London and New York Hotel in, surprisingly, Paris, and worked her way with relish through a typically French table d'hôte, washed down by a rather rough red wine which greatly titillated the palate and went well with everything from the soup to the fruit and cheese. They had twenty-four hours in Paris, and there was much to see. A good meal was what was needed, and both mother and daughter ate heartily.

But Henrietta had only just cut into a splendid piece of Brie which the proprietor of the hotel, a Monsieur Chardon, had brought to the table for their admiring inspection in person, when she became aware that she was being watched from somewhere across the sparkling dining room. Her sense of discretion perhaps a little marred by the excellence of the wine, she looked up, and found herself looking into the eyes of a well-dressed, handsome man who sat alone at a distant table.

Within seconds, Henrietta lowered her gaze, remembering her lessons in decorum. But it was too late. The stranger, who was perhaps in his late thirties, dabbed at a fine ebony moustache, which was complemented by a neat imperial beard, with his large white napkin, and standing, bowed politely, not to Henrietta, but to her mama.

At that moment, Mr. Bedales happened to enter the dining room, and as the de Vere Smiths' table was the first on his right, naturally paused on his way to his own reserved table and bid them good evening. They were immediately joined by the handsome stranger, whom Henrietta now noticed was very elegantly dressed in an unmistakably English tailormade suit.

"Mr. Bedales, sir," the stranger began. Mr. Bedales turned. The stranger proffered a well-manicured, but strong, slightly bronzed hand. "Allow me to introduce myself, since I am to join your company. Monsieur Chardon, our host, had informed me of your description, and I was hoping to meet you after dinner."

The voice had a strange, soft twang to it, and the effect was pleasant. Henrietta realized that she was in the presence of that increasingly common phenomenon, an American in Paris.

"Dogharty, of Boston. At your service." The stranger bowed to Henrietta's mother, and then returned his admiring gaze at last to Henrietta herself. This time she felt that the proprieties allowed herself to incline her own head. Her newly-curled ringlets shone as she did so. She was thankful that she had changed into a particularly fetching but high-necked amethyst velvet gown for the evening.

When Mr. Bedales had concluded introductions all round, and proceeded to his own table, Brian Dogharty, who had clearly left his Irish ancestry behind him in a long distant past, asked the de Vere Smiths if they would not join him for a cognac in the hotel lounge, as he wished to acquaint himself more thoroughly with the itinerary, and could not think of more charming company in which to do so.

The man's almost English Boston accent obviously reassured Constance de Vere Smith, who agreed to meet him, with her daughter, in the lounge within half an hour. Pointedly, she looked at the unfinished slice of Brie on Henrietta's plate, and at the same time, showing herself to be the seasoned chaperone of many a London drawing room, added brightly that she hoped they would also be able to summon the other newcomers to their little group to join them there.

Thus it was that on the first evening of their journey through Europe to the great Nile, mother and daughter found themselves arranged on a high-backed red silk sofa in a Paris hotel lounge, the center of attraction in a small but growing circle that now included the distinguished fellow countrymen promised to them just out of London Bridge by Mr. Bedales.

Although she was still interestedly aware of the occasional admiring glance from the American, who characteristically had been the one to see that the party broke the ice at all, Henrietta found herself even more intrigued by the three men who had now been added to the group.

They were young, fair-faced men with a uniformly military bearing, and a rather limited vocabulary amply sprinkled with the "old girls" and "I say's" which Henrietta always tried to forgive in her conversations with Roddy. They were clearly not joining the tour for any kind of high jinks. They knew every step of the itinerary, but talked of it as if it were a campaign. And it was when one of them whispered discreetly to his companion that "they ought to make an early night of it, Paris being what it was, as they'd have enough late nights when they found themselves on duty with H.R.H.," that Henrietta, a rush of color in her young cheeks, and a palpitating heart caused not by the fine cognac in the glass in her hand, knew at once who these young men were.

She had, on her first night out from England, stumbled quite by chance into the company of her cousin's circle. The trio that now stood in a row, almost at attention, and made such innocent bows before they retired for the night, were the far from innocent young men who made up the duty roster as aides-de-camp to their truant prince. She thanked her stars that their obvious need for secrecy must have prevented them from bursting into friendly exchanges when they had heard the family name de Vere. They must know her cousin well. And their presence here no doubt meant that they were the back-up troops in a foray which Roddy himself must already have joined. As she returned their bows politely, her face still scarlet, she wondered just how far ahead of their party her cousin could be. Or was he already sporting at the heels of the royal party under an Egyptian sky? With an inward groan, she told herself that it would be days before she would know the truth of it all.

As if he sensed that she was undergoing some suppressed crisis, Mr. Dogharty leaned across to where she sat when the young men had left the salon, and offered her a second glass of cognac. Which she guardedly refused. She would need a clear head not to betray herself either to the company, or to her mother. With an effort, she tried to bring her thoughts back to the subject in hand, and smiling brightly told her benefactor that she would prefer to go through once more the arrangements for the trip on the River Nile itself.

"We go as far as the First Cataract, dear lady," Mr. Bedales, who had joined them by now, informed her.

Henrietta's mama placed her brandy-glass firmly on the table before her. It was empty. She regarded Mr. Bedales with a steely eye. "And pray, how many cataracts did you think we might tackle, sir?"

Her high, imperious tones soared to the decorative ceiling, and Henrietta, to the amusement of Brian Dogharty—whose eyes had not for one moment left her face—looked despairingly up at the clusters of naked cherubs who had witnessed the comings and goings of the Smiths of this world for several seasons and showed no signs of ever becoming used to their infinite variety.

In the exciting days that followed, Henrietta did not allow herself to be left alone at any time with the friendly American, though she was glad of his alert support at every turn, as her mother swung perilously from cable cars, slept deeply in airless trains, and stared triumphantly across the Italian Alps in their determined progress to Turin and at last to the shores of the Adriatic.

It was in Brindisi, where they had some time to

await the perfection of arrangements for boarding ship to Alexandria, that the further enthusiasts expected by Mr. Bedales to join their ranks for the Nile journey itself appeared.

Henrietta, who had now exchanged her warm clothing and deep colors for lighter travel wear, was repacking a valise she would not now need until their return journey when she became aware of voices she did not recognize in the courtyard beneath her hotel room. She crossed the bare, sanded floor and stood discreetly at the rounded window. Her curiosity was aroused by the French accent of one newcomer. Carefully, she leaned out a little, the vista of low white roofs from which the sunlight reflected strongly causing her to narrow her eyes. It was late afternoon, and the rest of their party was still in retreat after a lengthy luncheon and much Italian wine, consumed in spite of the teetotal-eye with which Mr. Bedales regarded them all from over the rim of his own glass of water at each repast.

With increasing interest, Henrietta listened to the conversation in the quiet of the courtyard. It was a discussion, bordering on argument, about the best arrangements to be made for the packing and despatch of certain antiquities. The smell of an excellent cigar wafted up to where Henrietta stood.

"I will not be diverted in this matter, monsieur," the Frenchman was saying, in rather good English. Henrietta could not catch the reply.

The Frenchman continued, somewhat excitedly, "You know the Egyptians do not take well to the systematic loss of their treasures in this way. Whether your . . . er . . . employer understands this or not. The British have been the worst offenders."

"My dear sir," his companion replied, "I understand these things, of course. But what is one to do? It is not as if tourism is exactly discouraged. And what pray have the Egyptians themselves done to preserve their treasures?"

"Ah! That will come. You will see. If, that is, there

is anything left for them to preserve by the time your countrymen have finished...."

"Would you say," the other answered dryly, "that your own countrymen are entirely innocent in this matter?"

There was an expressive silence. Then: "Shall I say that we at least have the future of such priceless treasures in mind, whereas a nation of individual colonial pirates are assembling them in London and elsewhere purely for their own gratification? They bring railways and religion in one hand, and—voilà! There is a puff of steam, a loud singing of hymns, and a very crowded cellar in your museum!"

As the voices were raised in further argument, the protagonists moved out of hearing, but Henrietta had heard enough to realize that if these were a sample of the rest of their party, then life was about to become much more interesting.

She was not to be disappointed. When at last their steamer carried them sturdily out into the Adriatic, she and her mother seated in cane chairs on deck under a canopy while a refreshing breeze whipped at their English complexions, Henrietta smelled on the same breeze the strangely seductive aroma of the cigar which she recognized from the time she had eavesdropped at her hotel window.

The man who turned the corner of the deck and strolled towards them was middle-aged, well-dressed in an unassuming light gray suit, and with sensitive lines to a cleanshaven face. In his hand was the remains of a cigar. He seemed to be preoccupied with the distant horizon as he took his exercise, but as he passed Constance de Vere Smith's chair and the Indian shawl over her knees slipped accidentally to the floor, he stopped with alacrity to retrieve it.

As he straightened and handed the shawl to her mother, Henrietta was aware of long, sensitive fingers handling the Kashmiri silk with some delicacy—and of deep gray eyes in a worn face.

"Pray, sir, am I not to know to whom I am indebted?" Constance de Vere Smith smiled graciously as the man relinquished her shawl into her own plump hands. She knew she was in the presence of a true gentleman, and he had an air of more sobriety and distinction than the other male members of their party.

"The name is Morton, ma'am. Lancelot Morton, at your service. Traveler—and archeologist."

It was as if he had chanced upon the magic formula which opened the cave of Mrs. de Vere Smith's sociability. The very word archeologist evoked to her somewhat limited thinking a conglomerate vista of towering monuments, buried treasure, and graceful if perhaps slightly damaged artifacts, placed at carefully chosen points of vantage in her Belgravia residence the moment she returned.

With some reluctance, Lancelot Morton took the chair at Henrietta's mother's side, and—genuinely reminded of some other recent matter of interest by the name he had given—Henrietta hastened to dam the flow of questions she knew would now beset the stranger if she allowed her mother to start the conversation. As restrainedly as she could, she leaned forward, and round the portly, beshawled figure of her mama, asked "Morton? It is a name I have heard very recently, and—I remember now, in very pleasing circumstances. Sir, are you by any chance related to the Gerald Morton who has just become affianced to my best friend, Alice Manners?"

The handsome man smiled. "Gerald Morton is my brother. My young brother. There is a wide gap in our ages, for my father married twice. My own mother died when I was a boy. But I'm fond of Gerald. He's a wild boy, but with a good heart. Off to India at the moment, so far as I know...."

"I have reason to know you are correct, sir," Henrietta smiled. This was perhaps the first man she had encountered since they left London in whose company she could relax. His credentials were established without question in their first, brief exchanges. His character was evident in those deep, tired eyes. "And he has left his heart behind him."

"It's a hard life on the frontier," Lancelot Morton went on, his eyes serious as he looked out to sea. The gray-green of the Adriatic reflected the sadness of Henrietta's mood as she thought of the life to which her friend would soon be called, a scene so close to her own heart. "He'll do well with a girl like Alice Manners at his side. She's an athletic little creature, if I remember."

Henrietta nodded in agreement. She resisted the temptation to add "and plain, and shortsighted!" After all, it was her best friend they were discussing.

Lancelot Morton gave a deep, sensual pull on the remaining stub of his cigar at that moment, and Henrietta thankfully let her ungracious thoughts of her friend waft away on the scented air that now surrounded her. She leaned back in her chair. On the portside, yards from where they sat, two dolphins played in the white spray that spread from the steamer's paddles. As she watched them twist and leap in blissful ignorance of the world's cares, the sheen of their backs and the blur of their bellies catching the light alternately at each turn, Henrietta wondered if perhaps she was going to be able to enjoy the voyage after all. She turned to express something of her sudden wave of happiness to her companions.

But as she did so a small, flamboyant figure came into view at the far end of the deck and strode fussily towards them. As he drew close to where they sat, he called Lancelot Morton's name. His accent was French. And without a word, their newfound acquaintance stood, bowed to the two women, and strode off to the saloon, his hand gripping the Frenchman's elbow so tightly that there was no question of the men taking separate paths.

CHAPTER FIVE

THE ARRIVAL in the sprawling, teeming Mediterranean port of Alexandria, from where they would take the long train journey through the Nile delta to the city of Cairo, marked for Henrietta a moment of truth. She was suddenly acutely aware of the great distance she had undertaken, not yet by any means completed, in pursuit of the man she loved. And it was not only a matter of miles, but of whole new worlds... worlds which began to hurl themselves at her senses as they came into port and a hundred smaller boats clustered about them, while thin high voices and thin brown bodies clamored for the travelers' attention. Every type of merchandise from pottery to lengths of cotton was held up for inspection, from the perilously narrow decks of orange-sailed boats. Would-be guides with rounded black faces under white turbans cried across the water in sing-song English that they knew of the best of hotels, and the holiest of mosques. Small boys, quite naked, dived and swam through the muddy waters towards them, brazenly touting for *baksheesh*.

At her daughter's side, Constance de Vere Smith loudly thanked her Maker for the comforting presence of Mr. Bedales, who shook his head and waved his arms discouragingly at all comers, and reminded his small band of tourists that they were provided with their coupons from his travel company for all they would need, and that Mr. Thomas Cook himself actively discouraged the indiscriminate paying of gratuities in these foreign parts. If they stood firm now, he exhorted them, they would find themselves under less attack when they gained dry land. And he was right. Once on the quayside, their baggage safely assembled in a great pile, the English travelers, with the American and Frenchman who now completed the number that would take the Nile steamer together, advanced without incident to the train.

Lancelot Morton and the French professor traveled in the second of the two compartments Mr. Bedales had managed to reserve for his party, and Henrietta had no inclination or time to dwell on the mysterious relationship between the two such contrasted men. Her attention was fixed, for most of the five hours they were on the train, on the landscape that stretched on either side of the railway ... a barren, almost treeless sea of gray-yellow mudflats, scattered with small villages of low, flat-roofed houses—and to the left of the train the twisting line of the river itself, broken only by roughmade bridges and strange, deserted islands from which great black-winged birds squawked into the sky like giant flies as they passed.

The real species of flies and midges and mosquitoes had already made their mark within the carriage, and although beneath a sensible veil Miss Summers of Finchley seemed able to remain calm before the onslaught, Miss Fountain of Harrogate fared rather worse, while her brother spent the entire journey waging war against the pests, with frequent reminders that In Yorkshire, where it seemed everything was always perfect, there were neither flies nor mosquitoes. Henrietta reflected silently that there was quite as formidable a list of natural hazards to be endured beneath the soil of that county by the miners who had made Mr. Jonathan the fortune that now enabled him to travel to the lands of cholera and sunshine.

Her attentions were also frequently drawn to the stoic behavior of the three young Englishmen who had joined them in Paris, and who now traveled opposite the de Vere Smiths, their backs to the engine. Although they continued to wear civilian suits, their bearing was so unmistakably military that Henrietta found herself thinking of Roddy every time she encountered a fierce blue eye or a fiercely-polished button-boot—both of which features applied to all three of the young men in question. She would have happily wagered six months of her allowance that these were Roddy's fellow officers, bound on the mission for which he had already been dragged from London.

But she dared not ask a single question of them for fear that her mother would not only correct her later for her forwardness, but would guess that it was her interest in Roddy that had brought both of them to Egypt in the first place. Fortunately, the trio's permanent silence, broken only by the occasional muttered expletive of admiration at the great speed their engine maintained, discouraged any such approach.

It was when the entire steamer party stood in the cool grandeur of the center hall at Shepheard's famous hotel at last, and the three young men left its ranks to join a frockcoated dignitary who awaited them with a sealed envelope held guardedly to his chest, that Henrietta knew for sure that they would eventually, inevitably, lead her to her cousin.

Now that she was certain that an encounter with Roddy lay somewhere ahead of her, on the winding river she had watched from the train, her emotions were in a turmoil. She climbed the wide hotel stairs to the room she was to share with her mother for one night hardly able to control the trembling in her limbs. She was sure that her shortness of breath would incur comment, and that the slow thud of her apprehensive heart rivaled the heavy, rhythmic flapping of the air coolers above them.

As she sat before the dressing table in their room and repaired her appearance in time for the late luncheon that awaited them in the dining room below, (they had left Alexandria about eight that morning) she looked into a flushed face, and eyes that brimmed with sudden tears. Supposing she did come face to face with Roddy? Suppose she did not?

That night she slept badly, unusual for her, and lay awake listening to her mother's heavy breathing. When Constance gave a little murmur in her sleep, Henrietta surprised herself with a little rush of sadness and compassion. How brave her mother was, how indomitable in the teeth of the unknown!

The next day, her spirits rose again. There was time for a tour of the city, and in particular of the markets and the most important mosques. Flanked by a retired clergyman who proved a useful mine of information in the religious field, and the admiring American, Brian Dogharty, who showed himself a man who could outbargain the slyest of merchants in the marketplace, Henrietta began once more to enjoy herself.

And in the white alabaster heart of the greatest of the mosques, her head bowed so that she could glimpse her own small feet in the soft slippers she and the others wore out of respect, Henrietta knew her first moment of peace for many weeks. The grand mosque of Mahomet Ali, whose tomb lay in its inner sanctum, was the most sacred of Cairo's ancient temples. The white alabaster walls, streaked with delicate lines of coral red, were a gleaming oasis in the heat of a desert land. There was no sense of time. Around the walls at some height ran exquisitely carved trellis screens, behind which the women of royal harems had for centuries watched the temple's ceremonies. Beneath them, acres of soft Persian carpet spoke of the artistry and wealth which served the prophet here. And yet the final note, Henrietta sensed, was of simplicity and dedication. In spite of its remoteness from her own religious experience, from the rigid solemnity of Victorian churchgoing as she knew it, she found it a very holy place.

In the dazzling light of the streets that clustered at the foot of the hill where the great mosque was built, Henrietta was thoughtful. She had noticed that Lancelot Morton, who accompanied their party, but at a distance, had been absorbed in a study of the white and coral alabaster. Unexpectedly so, for a man who must surely already be acquainted with the monuments around them. It was true that the alabaster was strange and rare, but the archeologist behaved as if he had never seen it before. And she knew for a fact from the conversation on which she had eavesdropped that he was no novice in the matter of antiquities.

Her attention was soon brought back to the present again, however, as they passed through a bazaar and Brian Dogharty, eyes gleaming above his splendid dark moustache and beard, gave a merchant at one of the stalls a hard time of it in reaching a price for a length of cotton Henrietta's mother had paused to admire. To Constance de Vere Smith's delight, they came away from the stall having acquired a splendid bargain. And the merchant, not in the slightest put out, bowed and smiled as they left.

"Sabah el-full!" he called to their departing figures, and Brian Dogharty turned, doffing his hat, and replied.

"Sabah en-nur!"

Impressed, Henrietta asked their escort what the words had meant.

"It's a common enough greeting out here," he told her. "The merchant simply told me it is a morning of fragrance, and I replied that it is a morning of light."

Enchanted by the romance of such an everyday exchange between total strangers, Henrietta walked on through the bazaar, her senses acutely aware of how close the words were to the truth: the air about her was heavy with strange, seductive perfumes, and with the spices used in the dark, cavernous restaurants which flourished every few yards; the light of Egypt was a clear, strong light, as if it were always morning.

It was at dawn next day, in the same clear light, that Mr. Bedales stood on the bank of the Nile and supervised the embarkation of the river steamer he had hired for the party in his care. Named—rather ineptly to Henrietta's mind—*The Sprite*, it was a long, stalwart craft, low in the water, giant paddles half concealed by its gray painted sides. At its prow stood the captain, a middle-aged Egyptian, excitedly directing what seemed to be his crew—a trio of white-robed, dark-skinned natives. At his side stood an Egyptian civilian, who Mr. Bedales explained with pride was Dr. Fayum, the ship's doctor, who was to travel with them for the whole of their voyage.

Apart from the doctor and the crew, they were now a party of sixteen in all, including Mr. Bedales himself, the number most comfortably accommodated by the Nile steamers. But when Constance de Vere Smith, who had already been persuaded to leave much of her luggage at the hotel in view of the limited size of the berths, stood in the doorway of the cabin she was to share with her daughter and complained in her loudest tones that she had expected at least double the amount of space to each passenger, Mr. Bedales overheard her and hastened along the deck to her side.

"I cannot promise exactly at what point in the journey I shall be able to offer you a cabin to yourself, dear lady," he comforted her. "But it is possible—even probable—that at least three of our party will be leaving us and, er, going their own way, in the course of the first few days aboard. When that happens, I shall of course see to it that the ladies of our party receive priority—and a single cabin shall be yours!"

Henrietta, who had already begun to unpack her valise and was choosing a gown for the gala dinner she believed would be served on their first night aboard, pricked up her ears. She had no trouble at all in guessing which three of the party Mr. Bedales mentioned. There *were* only three who traveled together: the young men of Roddy's stamp. Her guess at their identity had been right. They were on the very heels of the truant royal steamer. And Mr. Bedales knew it!

That evening, as she sat at dinner with her mama, her young face suffused with a glow that owed little to the excellent dry white wine that was served, Henrietta tried to put Roddy, now so near it seemed, out of her mind.

She wore a gown of palest lavender organdie, which she had chosen as it had the advantage of creasing rather less than other fabrics, and at her throat were the pearls her father had given her on the occasion of her coming-out more than a year ago. In her hair, which was dressed rather more formally than usual, gleamed a gardenia. She had placed it above one ear, while her mother remonstrated that not only was it most unsuitable, but they did not even know where the flower, which a smiling, white-robed steward had brought to their cabin that afternoon, had come from. To send a flower to an acquaintance of a few days was one thing, but to send it without a card was not the act of a gentleman.

Which of the numerous gentlemen at dinner that night it was who had so risked his entitlement to the name by the anonymous gift of the gardenia Henrietta was unable to guess. But she was pleasantly aware that across the red and gold of the dining room more than one pair of masculine eyes gleamed their approval at her appearance.

For the occasion, a small orchestra had been hired, and would leave *The Sprite* at dawn from some vantage point further upstream. With some ingenuity, Egyptian musicians had been found who knew how to play a series of waltzes which were already popular in England, and as the travelers finished their meal and left the dining room in small groups to walk the deck of the steamer under the stars, they were followed by the strains of a Strauss medley—while from the banks of the river there came in strange contrast the occasional bleating of a goat, or the rhythmic creaking of the *shaduf*, the water crane.

As she stood at the deckrail looking out across the water, the gentle chug of the steamer's paddles mingling with all these sounds of the night, Henrietta gave an exclamation of surprise when she saw on the distant bank the dim outline of figures of men and oxen still working at the irrigation of their fields.

"They say the river is the gift of life," a voice said at her elbow. "But all their lives are spent bringing its water to their land."

Henrietta turned, to find Lancelot Morton standing at her side. She would have known from the scent of his cigar who the speaker was, even if his fine features had not been outlined in the light of the flare that lit the deck behind them. Acutely aware that for the moment the same deck was deserted, and that her mother had gone to their cabin to recover from the effects of her first dinner afloat, Henrietta was at a loss to remind her companion that she was unchaperoned. His manner was so impeccable that she knew she was quite safe with him, but the training of long years, however much it went against the grain for a girl of Henrietta's spirit, was not to be denied.

"I—I was about to join my mother, sir," she began, wishing that she had a fan with her and could more easily disguise the conflict his presence aroused in her.

He smiled. "Of course. My apologies." Lancelot Morton bowed. He held out his arm. "Then let me escort you. It is at least a dozen yards to the steps, and then the stairway itself has to be negotiated. A challenge that your friend, my future sister-in-law, would find no problem at all, don't you think?"

Suddenly reassured by this reminder that her escort was soon to be so closely connected with her through the marriage of her best friend to his half brother Gerald, Henrietta relaxed. With a light laugh, and a last look across to the shadowy land, she took Lancelot Morton's arm.

But to her surprise, he led her not back towards the stern where they might most easily take the stairs to the middle deck and the ladies' cabins, but on towards the bows, so that as they walked they progressed in the direction taken by *The Sprite* itself, and Henrietta found herself caught up in the strange sensation of moving with the steamer, on into the night, to where the river waited for them. It was the most curious physical experience, almost like swimming, she thought, and before she could ask her companion to desist and take her to the stairs, she had floated the length of the deck and found herself standing at his side above the prow itself.

Beneath them, the dark waters bubbled and divided in the steamer's path. Behind them, the strains of the orchestra had faded, and the only sounds were the chug of the engine and the subdued voices of fellow passengers, who sat under the protection of the canopy on the lower deck. The air was heavy now with the rank smell of the river, and Henrietta was glad of her companion's penchant for good cigars. Raising her eyes, whilst she also contrived to hold her breath, from the swirl of the water at last, she exhaled, and after a pause decided that she should now ask Lancelot Morton to escort her to the cabins.

At that moment *The Sprite* had just maneuvered a bend in the river and was once more taking a course in midstream, coming out from the shelter of a small island to do so. For some yards the island had, combining with the bend in the river, concealed their view of what lay ahead. Now, as they gathered speed again, Henrietta's words caught in her throat.

From the prow where she stood she could see, quite clearly, a steamer somewhat the same as their own forging steadily away from them into the night. Its decks were brightly lit. Although it carried no flag that she could see, unlike the Egyptian and British flags that streamed from *The Sprite*, it was decked with bunting, as if it was *en fête*. To add to the impression of merrymaking, the sound of music echoed in its wake. But it was not the delightful elegance of Strauss that reached Henrietta's straining ears. It was the hypnotic drum and pipe of indigenous native music. The music of the bazaar... and, she thought faintly, of the harem.

As if sensing that she was more than normally surprised by the presence of the second steamer that sent a Vee of white foam towards them as it sped away from them in the darkness, Lancelot Morton took her arm.

"If I do not tell you now who they are, you will learn from all the gossips on board by tomorrow," he said dryly.

Henrietta froze. Surely Lancelot Morton did not know her secret? And if this was, as she now guessed, the Prince of Wales' own steamer ahead of them, why should this man rather than any other on board *The Sprite* have such information?

She listened with feigned indifference while he told her what she needed to know.

"I am perhaps not the only man on board who will make contact with them before the week is out. And, if I tell you why, it is for your ears alone. Can I trust you?"

He looked down at the alert eyes under the fall of dark hair. The gardenia shone in the half-light. "I know I can," he continued. "But discretion is important, not only because the very important personage in the boat ahead demands the utmost secrecy from me, having been tormented by tourists when last he took this route, on a more official excursion—but because I also require secrecy, in the execution of my own task. A task so heavy that I feel, now the moment is near at hand, the need to share something of the burden...."

He paused, as the solitary figure of a man approached the bows. It was Dr. Fayum. The doctor bowed to Henrietta. She returned his greeting, and looked anxiously at her companion to see whether he was to invite the Egyptian to join them. But to their shared relief, the white-clad figure moved on. The doctor was simply enjoying an after-dinner constitutional, it seemed. And yet it was strange that he should have appeared just as the royal steamer came into view.

"If you are referring to the official excursion I think must have been after the opening of the great Suez Canal, sir," Henrietta said levelly to Morton, "then it must be our own prince who sails before us. If you are unable to confide this in me, a mere nod of your head will be quite sufficient to confirm my suspicions."

Lancelot Morton surprised her then by giving a loud shout of laughter, his head thrown back to reveal strong white teeth and a brown throat. "I have chosen a willing conspirator, I see," he chuckled. "And my burden is, I declare, halved with the knowledge! But, to be more serious—when we link up with *The Centaur*—for that is the name of the boat the royal party has chartered—and link up we shall—then I, amongst others, shall be leaving *The Sprite*. But, unlike the others, I shall keep my actual berth on our own steamer, and shall return to it between my meetings with the prince."

Henrietta's mind reeled as she listened. If Lancelot Morton was telling the truth, then from the moment *The Sprite* caught up with *The Centaur* (the name had an ominous ring to it, classical reference or no), there would be much coming and going between the two steamers. And if Roddy was indeed in Egypt as aide-de-camp to H.R.H., then it could be only a matter of hours before he learned that his cousin was on his heels.

"Do I understand, sir," she asked, "that you yourself have business with the royal party of great import, but that you are prepared to confide it in me?"

"In some part, at least," he nodded. "I have the unpleasant task ahead of me of persuading our beloved prince to renounce an item of Egyptian antiquity which was presented to him, quite privately, during his last state visit. And I have reason to believe that he has it in his keeping on board the steamer, for there is no account of his returning with it to England last time."

"But why should he, His Royal Highness that is, be constrained to part with this antiquity? A gift is a gift," Henrietta defended the prince instinctively. She had always rather admired the handsome figure, and all Roddy had told her of his dilemma as heir to a throne that receded from him daily, had secretly aroused her understanding.

"Because it was not in the gift of he who gave it. Because it belongs to a fierce tribe of the eastern desert, from ancient times. And because if it is not returned to its rightful owners, then there are men who would use the whole situation to discredit the prince—even worse, his countrymen—at a point in time when their good influence is needed in this land."

Henrietta looked grave. She was enough of a patriot, and had enough fighting spirit, for the story to rouse conflicting emotion in her breast. She was informed sufficiently, by the numerous dinner parties she had recently endured in London, of the struggle for power and influence in Egypt between the English and the French—though little had she thought that she would ever find herself in close proximity to any facet of that struggle. The nearest, indeed, she had ever been to it had been her mother's repeated declaration that she would not buy a single share in the Suez Canal if Monsieur de Lesseps himself were to offer it to her, which so far he had not.

But on the other side of the coin was the dilemma which her companion faced. She did not envy him the painful task of seeking the return of a gift made to royalty, whoever the royal personage might be. And she found herself wondering how, if the gift were some ancient crumbling statue, or some weighty, gold-encrusted sarcophagus, Lancelot Morton might expect to transport the antiquity to its rightful owners if he achieved his goal in the first place.

"I would like to be of help to you, sir—"

He took her gloved hand briefly. "You must call me Lance," he said.

She looked up at him. In spite of the quite large gap in their ages, she found herself thinking that this man could be a true friend to her, and she to him.

"If perhaps in the more practical aspects of your almost impossible task? A helping hand?"

He took her elbow again, and this time walked with her towards the wide stairs that led to the lower deck. Before they descended, he paused again, and told her:

"It will not be necessary. The gift is priceless, but not large in size. Once I have persuaded the prince that it is in his best interests to relinquish it, I have only to return it secretly, and in person, to the tribe."

"The eastern desert must lie further than the First Cataract," Henrietta calculated. "So you would ride out to this tribe?"

Lancelot Morton nodded. "That is the least of my problems. You see, the antiquity is the most exquisite of jewels, a scarab of white and red marble made from the same stones that were hued for the ancient mosque of Mahomet Ali in Cairo, and set in fine gold filigree on a golden chain. It is therefore an object of religious devotion. And one which should not even be touched by the hands of an infidel."

"So there *is* real danger in your task?" Henrietta asked.

He nodded gravely. "There is no doubt in my mind," he told her, "that whoever engages in this matter will be dicing with death."

CHAPTER SIX

WHEN HENRIETTA AWOKE next morning she opened her eyes wide and found herself gazing at the mesh of a mosquito net beneath the curved ceiling of the small cabin she shared with her mother, unable to move far in the narrow berth without actually leaving the confines of her bed. To one side was the cabin window, firmly fastened. But beyond it she could hear the cry of a *fellah* as he urged his oxen into the day's work, and the chatter of the stewards who padded to and fro on the deck of *The Sprite* preparing for the passengers' appearance at breakfast. It was very early.

Her next sensation was one of apprehension, laced with acute interest in what the day might bring. A curious weight in the region of her heart told her that her cousin, now perhaps so close, was still the object of strong romantic affection and of unhappy doubt. But the other, more independent side of her nature, accounted for the light tread with which she soon moved about the cabin as she dressed for breakfast, and the little tune—somewhat eastern in style—which she hummed to herself, as she brushed her long hair and considered her situation.

Within two days of landing in Egypt she found herself the confidant of a distinguished if older man. Some second admirer, perhaps, had sent her the gardenia. The climate suited her, the other passengers were pleasant enough—and her mama lay unsuspecting of her daughter's rapid progress, sleeping the slumbers of a traveler well-pleased. The day's program included a visit to a town, the ancient capital of a Nile province, whose name eluded her. She knew only that they had traveled on during the night to reach it in good time for a daylight tour. The great pyramids of Giza and the strange step pyramid of Sakkara, now some way behind them, closer to Cairo, had been saved as the climax of their tour for when they returned downstream. She crept noiselessly out of the cabin, leaving her mother asleep, and stood on the deck of *The Sprite*, beneath the shade of its canopy, staring out over the great river, and knowing that they now approached the very heart of the desert.

The sight of her cousin Roddy in the main street of the ancient town's bazaar to which Mr. Bedales led his small party some hours later brought Henrietta to a heart-stopping halt in her tracks.

At first the tall figure, in dark blue uniform topped by a beige topee with a sensible linen square protecting the back of the neck, seemed to her to be just any uniformed young soldier. As her mother was never tired of reminding her, there were plenty of them in existence beside her nephew. And, though she had spent almost half an hour pretending to take a constitutional round and round the steamer's deck that morning, Henrietta, strain her good eyesight as she might, had seen no sign of the royal *Centaur*.

She had joined the landing party well-equipped with pocket money and followed by a bearer who attached himself the first yard they walked ashore—ready to carry her purchases. Her mother, pleading the desire to study her personal copy of *Lloyd's Guide to Egypt*, had remained behind to enjoy the quiet of a cane chair on the upper deck. The ship's doctor had joined her. Henrietta felt free to indulge her own whims.

And now she was forcibly reminded, as the tall uniformed figure turned towards her and looked into her eyes, of two things. Firstly, that the trio of fair-haired young subalterns had been absent from *The Sprite's* dining room at breakfast. Secondly, as she paced the decks of the steamer that morning she had noticed a large, sprawling island which seemed to be inhabited, in midstream. Its higher buildings, its few palm trees, had been quite sufficient to conceal on its far side any vessel requiring to remain unnoticed by other, passing river traffic. *The Centaur* was obviously at hand, and here was her cousin to prove it.

As her thoughts raced, her heart began also to beat rapidly, but Henrietta found that she herself was rooted to the spot. Her usual impulses, to run affectionately to her cousin when they met, or (as more recently) to flounce her displeasure, did not apply. Her gaze was serious. She knew, as Roddy took the initiative and walked towards her, that she loved him, and always would love him. But she wanted more than anything to warn him that he was about to be caught up in a royal drama that could send repercussions throughout the kingdom if it were not resolved.

Roddy came to within a yard of where she stood, and she saw that his face had changed. Although he could not have been more than a few days in Egypt, if her calculations were right, he had a bronzed, weathered look. His body also seemed harder, and the word she really sought, as she endeavored to analyze the change, was that he looked—older. It was a change that pleased her. But there was no time to let him know of such things. And yet what was she to say to him, now that they stood face to face? The one subject of the utmost importance, the question of the sacred scarab and the danger it might bring to both their prince and their country, was forbidden. Lance Morton had sworn her to secrecy, and she was a woman of her word.

She stood quite still, a lithe figure in pale lemon traveling coat and wide, matching hat drawn low over her high forehead by a gauze veil copied from Miss Summers' outfits and made only two days before at expert speed by a milliner recommended at Shepheard's Hotel.

She trembled a little as Roddy walked towards her. He frowned a little, perhaps not sure that the face beneath the veil was hers.

But with her cousin's first words to her, the trembling ceased, and a slow warmth of delight spread through her entire being. Gone were the dreaded "old girls," and the off-pat "how jolly to see you." There was no move to nudge her in the ribs; no nervous, boyish shifting about of the headgear or the feet.

Roddy stood close now. A rather elegant figure, she thought. He looked cool and poised in spite of the morning's tropical glare. Quiet but smiling eyes looked into hers

"Sabah el-full, Cousin," he said, in a low, controlled voice. But it was suffused with love, as he translated the singing Arabic words: "Morning of fragrance."

And Henrietta blessed the episode in the bazaar beneath the hill of the temple of Mahomet Ali in Cairo, where she had first heard the greeting, and learned the reply: *"Sabah en-nur,* Roddy," she answered. "It is indeed a morning of light."

Whether it was fortunate for the cousins or not, as they now stood face to face so far from home in a strange land, knowing in their hearts that they loved each other, they were within seconds of their discovery whirled away from each other and into the chattering depths of the bazaar. A camel had broken its hobble at the far end of the street, and its keeper yelled a warning only just in time for the crowds to scatter. Roddy and Henrietta had not understood the cry, but were thrown to safety, if to opposite sides of the narrow street, by the surge of the native crowd.

Henrietta found herself pinned to a fruit-stall while her young bearer made encouraging gestures to the shopping he still held safely in his arms, and Mr. Jonathan Fountain, standing manfully in front of his sister as the foul-smelling mountain of pale fur and angular bones that was the party's first glimpse of a camel at close range roared by, exhorted them all in a suddenly broad Yorkshire accent to "watch aht for theirselves."

Reflecting that what she had seen could hardly be described as the ship of the desert, though the runaway camel had a voice not unlike the boom from a steamer's funnel, Henrietta dusted herself down with the rest of the party, which had suddenly gathered into a protective circle around her, and tried to find Roddy again.

She did not have long to wait. Roddy himself rejoined the party with alacrity, and held out his hand—to Professor Clémence.

The small, sharp-faced Frenchman bowed. Roddy shook his hand with enthusiasm. Then he turned to Henrietta.

"Have you met my cousin, sir? Miss Henrietta de Vere Smith," he said proudly. Then:

"Henrietta. Professor Clémence is to join my party, y'know. As egyptologist. To—a very important person."

Beneath her gauze veil, Henrietta's face went white. Roddy could have no idea of the professor's hostile attitude to the British. And if she revealed what she knew, she would have to admit to the humiliating role of eavesdropper. More to the point, she wondered if Lance Morton knew of this appointment the Frenchman was about to take up. And how on earth would it affect the situation concerning the sacred scarab? It looked to Henrietta very much as if things were about to get out of hand. And unless she broke her promise of silence, she was powerless to prevent it.

For the moment, she decided, she had to play for time. But how long had she got? As the party re-formed in safely close ranks, hugging the side of the street, in case of a return of the ship of the desert, Henrietta found herself walking at Roddy's side.

She turned her face up to him, and asked in all innocence: "Is your steamer delayed for long, Cousin? *The Centaur*, I mean?"

He looked down at her sharply. "So you know that much, Cousin. You are well-informed. Surely you did not come here to seek out—you know the personage I mean—like some common tourist? If you knew how he needs solitude, and how he hates to be lionized...."

Henrietta's color returned. "How can you even suspect such a thing? If I came here at all by my own wish, it was to explore the great past, not to play foolish games with the present. And if you want for proof of how serious a traveler I am, there is only one thing left for you to know—"

Roddy took her elbow. "No need to take things so to heart, Henrietta. Look, I'll see you back to your boat, and you can explain there."

"I don't think you will want to linger when I tell you who has joined me on this voyage, Roddy."

He stopped. It was as if he already knew.

When she finally told him that Constance de Vere Smith awaited her on board *The Sprite* that very moment, and was probably at least half way through Mr. Lloyd's *Guide to Egypt*, he groaned aloud.

"And I was hoping to persuade His—our friend—to invite you to dinner on board *The Centaur* tonight! We've only one woman in the company, and she's proving the very devil. With you being a cousin and all that, I know he'd have welcomed you with open arms. You can always be sure of the discretion of us de Veres, he knows that. Except for one member of the tribe...."

"You mean Mama?" Henrietta's voice registered total dismay. She was at once wildly disappointed to miss the chance of dining with the prince, as her cousin's guest, and at the same time desperate to make good the situation so that she could be included, and thus play some role first-hand in helping Lance Morton in his vital undertaking.

But Roddy was now pushing irritably through the crowds, and the professor buzzed at his elbow, attempting to distract him from her company. She had to think quickly.

"Mama was most impressed when she learned that you were—your duties were—with—whom they are with," she panted, as grammatically as she could under the circumstances. She wished Roddy would not hurry so. Any moment now they would reach the edge of the town, and their figures would be easily discernible to any eagle-eyed watcher on the deck of *The Sprite*.

"It's me, I mean *I*—with whom she should be impressed, not the company I keep," he answered shortly. He was apparently not going to be as malleable in her hands as in the old days.

She tried again. "I mean that I think if we threw ourselves into her confidence, and made it a question of loyalty to—to the crown if you like, that she said nothing to our fellow passengers—then I think she would give her permission for me to go on board *The Centaur*."

It was then that she had her most brilliant moment of inspiration. "But why didn't I think of it before!?" she cried. "There's another way!"

The professor was hovering now, and it was the easiest thing in the world for her to encourage Roddy to give up the whole bad business of arguing it out, and certainly it did not suit her to have him come face to face with her mother now without the means to prepare her for the shock with some acceptable explanation.

A yard or so ahead of them, the last establishment in the street, was a café. At its tables sat only Egyptian males, and she knew she could not possibly join them. But she drew Roddy with her into the greater privacy and shadow of its wide awning. He had no choice but to follow.

"Roddy," she asked him, breathlessly, "do you trust me?"

He looked at his feet, and flicked somewhat uselessly at the layer of dust on the toe of his right boot with his swagger stick. "You know I do."

"Then will you tell—our host—that there will be a lady guest at dinner on *The Centaur* tonight who is known to you, if he will agree to her presence? That she is none other than your dear cousin, and that she will accompany the distinguished *English* archeologist who had come all the way from Brindisi to meet with him on a *very special matter?*"

Her voice dropped to a whisper. Professor Clémence had come dangerously close to where they stood.

"It means that I do not yet have to tell Mama of your presence in Egypt, Roddy, don't you see? If, that is, I have only to seek her permission to dine on *The Centaur* as the companion of Lancelot Morton!"

Roddy looked unconvinced. "Who is this fellow?" She could not be sure that it was jealousy that tinged his voice. He was after all a soldier on duty, and watchfulness must be his first reaction to any new presence in the camp.

"You will see, Roddy. I can promise you that his name will be on the guest list. I cannot explain now, but I *know*. As surely as I know that if we appeal to Mama's sense of patriotism and loyalty we can expect her to keep the secret of *The Centaur* to herself. Do you in truth believe that *anything* would prevent her from letting me dine at *his* table?"

"What I really fear, Henrietta, is that if Aunt Constance learns that I am aboard *The Centaur* she will not hesitate to make it an excuse to call on us herself. And I do not think I could bear the spectacle of your mama tête-à-tête with H.R.H. while my fellow subalterns looked on."

Henrietta plucked at his sleeve consolingly. "No one is asking you to bear with any such thing, Roddy. And I least of all. I have to be very careful indeed of letting Mama know too soon that you are here in Egypt. If she thinks I came all this way just to see you, she is quite liable to pack our bags and march me back home." As soon as she had spoken, Henrietta realized she had been indiscreet. Roddy was regarding her keenly, with what could be a hint of amusement in his gaze.

"And did you, Cousin? Come all this way to see me?"

She chose not to reply to his impertinent question, but her very silence gave him his answer, and beneath her veil she was blushing in a quite becoming fashion.

"Roddy," she returned to the subject in hand. "If Lancelot Morton dines with—with his patron tonight—then do I take it I would be welcome as his guest?"

He smiled, and gave a peremptory nod. His attention was distracted now by Professor Clémence, who was pacing up and down in the dusty street only yards from where they stood, gazing now and then at the fob-watch that hung ostentatiously from a thick gold chain across his checkered waistcoat. "Now that I know why you are really in Egypt, old girl," he told her, and as he spoke he gave her a playful tap on her graceful skirts with his officer's swagger stick, "I don't mind so much whose arm supports you—so long as I can clear it with—our host. But mind: one word to Aunt C., and you're lost!"

It was no use Henrietta stamping her foot into the sand at his words, because as soon as her cousin had finished speaking he turned on his heel in military fashion, having saluted her solemnly, and disappeared into the crowd, followed by the Frenchman.

Despairing of his complete return to his old ways, and knowing full well he had taken refuge in his boyish behavior only because she herself had accidentally revealed that she had followed him from London, Henrietta decided to call the shopping expedition to a halt. She looked round for her companions of the morning, and was soon on the return track to the jetty where *The Sprite* was moored. On one side walked her bearer, carrying her numerous purchases, and on the other Mr. Fountain, who had almost recovered from the incident of the runaway camel.

None of the party had noticed that a white-turbanned Egyptian, with rounded African features and very dark skin, who had sat motionless at one of the café tables while Roddy and Henrietta talked, rose from his place as soon as the professor followed Roddy into the crowded bazaar, keeping some yards from the two white men as he took the same path through the chattering throng.

And the mortification of Roddy's childish behavior to her was soon smoothed away when Henrietta set foot on the deck of the steamer again, and found Lance Morton waiting to take her parcels from the bearer and escort her to her cabin.

The first hurdle she had to clear since her encounter with Roddy was behind her within twenty minutes of their parting. The archeologist had, in her absence, made contact with the royal equerries—in the persons of the three young men Henrietta had rightly guessed to be on their way to join the prince's staff. He had stated his urgent business, without divulging it in detail, and had received word from the prince that if he undertook not to be too solemn about his mission at dinner, and to bring an attractive woman with him, then he should present himself on the far side of the nearby island at nine o'clock prompt that evening, from where he would be escorted on board *The Centaur*.

"I had no hesitation in promising to bring an attractive companion," Lance Morton said.

Henrietta did not think it was the time to be falsely coy. She wanted this invitation more than anything in the world, and she knew that with this man she did not have to pretend otherwise.

"If you would tell my mama that you wish me to dine on board a steamer not too far from this spot, that the host is a very distinguished person traveling incognito, and that you will return me safely before dawn, sir," she said in her direct fashion, "then I believe that can indeed be arranged."

He gave the sudden, generous laugh she had grown to like, and ran down the steps to the cabins in spite of the numerous parcels the bearer had off-loaded. Within minutes, the evening was arranged. Constance de Vere Smith knew enough about character and appearance to know that her daughter would be safe with Lancelot Morton. It only remained to select an outfit that would do them all credit.

It was not until after luncheon, as she rested on her berth to the music of her mother's light snores, that Henrietta realized with a start that she had left one important matter unresolved. Roddy had mentioned that the company on board the royal steamer included only one woman. But he had not named the creature. For creature of some kind she must be, if she valued her reputation so little as to travel unchaperoned, even—or especially—in such company. By process of elimination, she knew it could not be the Princess Alexandra, who seemed, poor lady, to have been kept in the dark about this impulsive return of her consort to the scene of his Egyptian triumphs. She calculated also that it could not be Maria Newcastle, who had learned of the clandestine journey through a friend at court, and would certainly not have suppressed the fact in the Bond Street chocolate house had she been invited herself. Of the other, shadowy female figures whom Henrietta knew, as well as any member of London Society, to flutter about the person of H.R.H., there was not one whom she could envisage escaping the marital nest, (for they were all of them safely married) for long enough to traverse Europe, the Nile, and back.

Suppressing her curiosity with a sigh, Henrietta lay back on her pillows and tried to sleep. She wanted to look her very best that evening, for the prince himself, for Roddy, and—for the solitary rival she was to meet. She would wear a dark amber gown, low cut, her hair would be swept high from the white nape of her neck, and she would persuade her mother to lend her the amber earrings. It amused her to feel them sway lightly above her young shoulders, and they were at their best in candlelight. For she was sure it would be a candlelit dinner ... and with the glowing picture of her own success in her mind's eye, she fell into a light, refreshing doze.

Some five hours later, wearing exactly the gown and jewels she had planned, and looking rather more stunning than she knew, Henrietta stood at the top of the gangway on *The Sprite*, a golden, glowing figure in the flares that had lit the steamer's decks since darkness swiftly fell.

With some agility, and in spite of her formal attire, she negotiated the gangway, and alighted in a small boat that waited at its foot. Next, Lance Morton took his place in the bows, facing her, and gave the word for the boatmen to slip the mooring. With a splash of oars, they moved away out of the circle of light from the starboard side of *The Sprite*, and onto the dark stretch of water between the steamer and the island beyond which the royal vessel waited.

Turning to wave dutifully to her mother before they were encompassed by the night, Henrietta saw that there was more than one passenger watching their departure from the rails of *The Sprite*. For a moment her gaze was held by the dark, admiring eyes of the American, Brian Dogharty, and she knew with a flash of intuition that it was he who had sent the gardenia to her cabin on their first night aboard.

The knowledge gave her elegant, burnished head an added tilt of pride as some thirty minutes later she crossed the deep-piled carpet of *The Centaur's* stateroom, to where the heir to the throne stood, her cousin at his side.

Then, with the merest nod to Roddy, she waited while Lance Morton was formally presented, before she in her turn moved forward. Her long amber earrings swayed in the light of a hundred candles as she found herself raised from her deep curtsey by a strong hand. She had never before been presented to Edward, Prince of Wales, and now she found that the legends did not exaggerate. She looked into gray eyes which smiled at her, and which she found nonetheless sad. Her hand was held fast, but there was no flirtatious tremor in the grasp. This was a man who loved women, but if he had been at the center of scandal, then it had not been by inclination.

The prince let go her hand at last, and turned to Roddy. "Some of us at least are fortunate in the cousins allotted to us by fate," he said.

Henrietta inclined her head in acknowledgement of the compliment. She hoped that Roddy appreciated it for the rare honor it was. But Roddy was staring straight ahead, as if on duty, and though her heart had danced at the prince's words, she was relieved when a slight pressure on her elbow signalled that she should move away, and turned to find Lance standing with a delicate tulip of champagne ready for her consumption.

The young uniformed subaltern, who held the silver tray from which Lance then took his own glass, seemed familiar, and when he left them with an almost imperceptible, disgracefully impudent wink in Henrietta's direction, she suddenly realized that this was one of the trio who had joined them in Paris.

The other two braves now stood, also in uniform, on either side of the state-room door, and as an Egyptian steward entered, carrying a silken shawl, a reticule and a fan, Henrietta realized with a shudder of anticipation that they formed some kind of guard of honor... for the "devil of a woman" Roddy told her was the only other feminine creature in the party.

The woman who entered, after a dramatic silence broken only by a subdued royal cough, wore a tightly swathed gown of palest cream silk. Her dark chestnut hair was drawn back from her face, and showed to perfection a straight nose, imperious cheekbones, and passionate dark eyes. The eyes were the only feature that contradicted what Henrietta's father had seen so clearly at the opera so many weeks ago. As if from a great distance, Henrietta heard her cousin present her formally to this woman who so closely resembled herself.

In a daze of shock and jealousy, remembering how Roddy had danced attention on this person in the intimate surroundings of the royal box, Henrietta registered the information that her name was Helena, that she was of a distinguished Greek merchant family, and that she would travel with the royal party for the rest of the prince's much-needed vacation.

But as she recovered her composure, Henrietta saw that there was one item in the Greek beauty's toilette more worthy of her apprehension, and no doubt the cause of the way in which Lance now stood as if rooted to the spot before her.

At her graceful throat, the woman Helena wore a heavy, golden chain, from which was suspended, set in delicate gold filigree, an ancient scarab, of white alabaster streaked with red. Against her glowing skin and the pale sheen of her dress, the scarab looked as if it had been lovingly fashioned for her alone.

It was the only jewel that she wore.

CHAPTER SEVEN

THE DINNER that followed in the adjoining stateroom was an informal affair, from which the Egyptian stewards were dismissed after the fourth course, and from then on the prince himself insisted upon serving his guests and keeping the decanters moving at a fast pace from one end of the eighteenth century table to the other.

At the opposite end of the table to Prince Edward, Henrietta was surprised to see the Frenchman, Professor Clémence. No doubt, she thought, as egyptologist to the royal party he would be expected to give good value and to supply information even at mealtimes. She noted also with approval that his dress was now somewhat modified, and that he wore a perfectly correct white tie.

The woman Helena sat on the prince's right hand,

and from where Henrietta was placed, on Lance Morton's right, and opposite her own cousin, she was able to observe with well concealed interest just how alike she and the Greek woman were—in appearance, though of course not in temperament. That had been evident from the moment of Helena's entry earlier that evening, and the more Henrietta studied her the more she found affinity in her sinuous, graceful movements and predatory gaze with some tawny member of the feline species. She was utterly thankful, for the first time in her life, that she herself had blue eyes. For now she saw what effect a really straight nose and high cheekbones, combined with too strong a spirit, could have.

But in other respects—the slim waist, the good height, the proud head—she would not have minded the comparison. She had to admit that in certain circumstances, such as darkness and at a distance, there was a distinct similitude.

The knowledge that in Helena she also had a rival, at least for the duration of the Nile journey, was also soon brought home to Henrietta. The prince, perhaps perfectly content to be in some part relieved of the woman's attentions, at least with an audience present, did not seem to notice the way in which his companion (for that she was his companion the jewel at her throat eloquently stated) flashed her eyes at Roddy, spoke most frequently to him, and as the night wore on offered him the choicest fruit from the silver platter before her. But Henrietta noticed, and took note.

Was her cousin deliberately encouraging this flirtation to pay her back for pursuing him to Egypt? she wondered. Or were his polite smiles and ready pleasantries the fabric of his duty as an aide-de-camp? The second possibility caused her more pain than the first. Was this the pointless social life to which Roddy had now succumbed?

But the undercurrents between Roddy and his cousin were not the only drama to be played out at the royal table that night.

As the hours sped by, and midnight came and went, Henrietta became aware that Lance Morton grew restless. There was no sign that the prince intended to retire. The usual custom of the gentlemen being left with the port while the ladies retired did not seem to apply when Helena was at table. There seemed every possibility that the night would pass without an opportunity for Lance to have private audience with Prince Edward. When he tried to turn the conversation to the subject of antiquities, it was Professor Clémence who monopolized the talk, and when Henrietta herself found the temerity to introduce the topic of the holy mosque of Mahomet Ali in Cairo, staring directly at the scarab which gleamed palely on Helena's bosom as she did so, there was a dramatic silence—broken with a complete change of subject by the prince himself.

If the prince had been already aware of the mission Lance had set himself, he could not have made it more clear that he was not prepared to hear him. And if that were so, Henrietta could only sympathize. Not even with the power and reputation of the whole country, of all his mother's dominion at stake, would the prince find it arguable that he should attempt to retrieve the sacred jewel from the throat of the tigress who sat at his right hand. Henrietta had looked into his eyes, and she knew.

But somehow it must be done.

Her chance to set things in motion came at last when the prince stood suddenly, and at once the other diners rose as a man.

"Music, I think." Edward beckoned a subaltern from where he stood sentry at the door. "My dear fellow, would you be so kind as to see if the Egyptian musicians are awake still?"

"Sir, I am too weary to sit here and listen to more of those drums and pipes." It was the Greek woman who spoke, in a low but forceful tone, which they could all hear. The prince leaned to whisper in her ear, then turned, as if remembering there were others present, and motioned to them with a flutter of his hand to resume their seats.

Henrietta, seeing that Helena now walked with the prince to the state-room door, remained standing. She was uncertain what the socially correct thing to do would be if either Helena left alone, and she remained the only woman in the dining room, or if the prince left with his companion. She tried to catch Roddy's eye.

Then, as she saw the prince bow over Helena's hand, his lips brushing the white glove quite tenderly, as if in taking his leave, she acted with that inborn instinct which so often saved her in difficult situations.

As Helena disappeared on to the deck, Henrietta left the table, and with a quick, lithe step approached the prince.

As she drew near, she stopped, and dropped a half curtsey. He smiled, absentmindedly. Had he noticed the likeness between her and the woman who had just left? she wondered.

"No need to stand on ceremony at this time of the morning, my dear," he said.

"Thank you, sir." Henrietta stood serenely before him, a figure in deep amber caught by the candlelight. He looked at her suddenly with rather more interest. She saw her chance. "It occurred to me, sir, that it would be perfectly splendid to take a turn on the deck, if it appeals to Your Highness to do so, and—and while the musicians play, to observe the night sky."

"Capital! Capital!" The prince turned to Roddy. "See to it, m'boy. But your cousin will need a cloak about those fine shoulders. These so-called tropical nights are damned cold!"

No sooner had one of the stewards produced a long woollen cloak for Henrietta than the party set off round the deck of *The Centaur*, the strange rhythmic cry of the flute and the muffled persistence of the drums accompanying them as they walked, rather quickly in the chill air, beneath the stars. To portside, the long line of the island was silhouetted against the sky. Ahead, the river ran straight for as far as they could see.

To her surprise, Edward walked quite fast for a man of his stalwart build, and as she kept up with him Henrietta's breath came in little clouds on the night air. On her other side strode Lance Morton, whom she had been careful to beckon to her as soon as the party left the dining room. It was the only way she could hope to help him further his cause, and speak with the prince alone.

But it was not so easily achieved. The prince's spirits had unaccountably risen with the departure of the Greek woman to her cabin, and he now seemed in the mood to talk.

"A wonderful land, this," he told Henrietta. "And tomorrow, we start for Thebes. Must see Thebes again. The tombs of the kings." He gave a strange, hard laugh.

"They say that in this country the king alone shall be sure of immortality," Henrietta said helpfully.

"The king, yes, and the queen no doubt as well," again this was followed by a curt smile.

The party marched on in silence, broken only by the thin cry of the music on the air.

"Good land to be a king, this." He spoke over his shoulder. "Eh, Roddy?"

"It's a good land to be a soldier, too, sir." Roddy's voice in the darkness behind her startled Henrietta for a moment.

"Do you think much of this soldier cousin of yours, madam? Does he treat you right?" Edward smiled down at her, and as the cloak about her shoulders suddenly slipped a little, he stopped and patted it into place.

She looked up once more into the sad eyes. But now they twinkled brightly at her. "I think you'd show him his place if he didn't!" he went on. "Tell me, what has he failed to do recently, that you both avoid each other's eyes for the whole of an excellent dinner?"

Henrietta leapt to the moment. "It is not my cousin's

fault, sir, that he is preoccupied. There is a matter of some gravity which he has to broach with you. My companion, Mr. Morton, has some information of the most serious kind to impart!"

To her horror, the prince reacted to her temerity by bursting into peals of laughter, and stopping in his tracks. Convinced that he would dismiss her out of hand, she gazed despairingly at Roddy, begging him silently to step forward and turn the moment to some advantage. But she was to be disappointed. Roddy was on duty, and knew his protocol. He made no move. It was Lance Morton who now took the bull by the horns and spoke up.

"Sir, it is remiss of me to allow my young companion to speak for me like this. And yet she has put my case well. As you know, I am an archeologist, and I specialize in the antiquities of Egypt, many of which I have already rescued from disintegration and abuse—before I had them shipped home to London."

The prince listened and nodded. Henrietta looked round, suddenly fearful that Professor Clémence would interfere. But there was no sign of the Frenchman, and she remembered that he had drunk an inordinate quantity of port within the space of the last hour.

"Go on, man," said the prince.

"But there have to be exceptions, sir. And such a case has been brought to my attention. At Your Highness's last state visit to these lands—if I am not mistaken—a private gift was made to Your Highness."

Edward grunted. "Several, actually." Henrietta held her breath.

Lance Morton went bravely on. "This was a jewel. A single stone, of great worth—because it is a holy relic of the alabaster from which the great Cairo mosque was built."

"Out with it! If you mean what I think you do, then you're a braver man than I took you for. It's the scarab worn by the splendid creature who was at my table this night, is it not?" The prince sounded only vaguely interested. He turned, and began to walk back in the direction of the state-rooms. Was it going to be an easier task than they had anticipated, Henrietta wondered, to retrieve the sacred stone? She was wrong.

The prince walked even faster now, and it was not until he stopped at the state-room doors that Lance Morton was able to give him his reply.

"Yes, Your Highness. It is that stone. But—there is more to it. The scarab is a sacred relic from the collection of antiquities belonging to a tribe of the eastern desert. The Dashawai. They are a proud people, and they live by proud tradition. The scarab was stolen from them by those who wish to make trouble—for our country, sir. To see to it that we are not welcomed here."

Edward looked more alert as he ushered the small group—now consisting only of Henrietta, her cousin, and Lance—into the warmth of the dining room. As the prince indicated to the steward who had waited up for him that brandies were to be served all round, he sat heavily in a deep chair, and gazed up at Lance Morton with serious eyes.

"You don't surprise me. But you don't impress me, either."

Lance Morton shrugged helplessly, and looked at Roddy. To Henrietta's delight, Roddy stepped towards the prince and said: "I think it's a bona fide situation, sir. There are dozens of these relics floating about, I know. But—it's not the first time I've heard this story. And the Dashawai are d- extremely clever fighters, to boot. I'd not like to find myself face to face with them on their own ground, sir."

The prince took his brandy and sipped it. "It won't come to that, boy. You're right—there are dozens of these things about. But you have to admit, the stone has a very rare quality. Tell me—Morton, isn't it? Tell me—what would these fellows want in the way of compensation?"

Lance Morton had not touched the cognac which the

steward had served him. Now he put the glass down, an expressively final gesture.

"Compensation would not put matters right, Your Highness. I cannot pretend to Your Highness that it would. In fact the implied insult, the implied deprecation of the object in question, would no doubt start off an incident on its own."

The prince was thoughtful now. "Where do these fellows hold out? The eastern desert you say?"

"They are nomadic, sir. But their headquarters at this time of year are beyond Assuan, to the east," Lance explained.

"We're not likely to bump into them much before the First Cataract, sir," Roddy chimed in. "I've studied this territory pretty soundly, and I think we'd be safe until then."

The prince stood. He looked Roddy fiercely in the eye. "Is a young puppy like you, much as I like you, trying to teach this dog tricks? Do you think I don't know this country?"

"I think, sir," Roddy said in respectful, but very clear tones, "that in the matter of the sacred pendant we are all of us reluctant to face one thing."

"And what might that be?"

Henrietta's heart went out to her cousin then, as he faltered only for a second, squared his shoulders, and replied to his prince: "That the lady who wears it now with such distinction has to be told that the Dashawai tribe—if I am to interpret my cousin and her companion correctly—want the alabaster scarab back. And that if they do not get it, then our party is in danger. And our country's good name in peril."

The effect of Roddy's speech on the prince was electrifying. His jaws worked as he fought with suppressed anger. Whether it was anger with her cousin or with his own helplessness in the teeth of such a situation involving his companion Henrietta was not sure. But in the end it was the royal blood that won. The royal blood, that is, that went in some fear of domineering women, perhaps from nursery days. Edward seemed to consider the matter for a brief moment. Then he bowed curtly in Henrietta's direction, and ignoring the two men marched to the doors that communicated with his private state-room beyond.

As the steward ran to open the door for him, the prince turned.

"It's out of the question, of course," he said, and left them.

In the silence that followed, the state-room's red and gold warmth seemed suddenly to turn to ice. The native steward, as if sensing trouble, slipped softly through the main doors and on to the deck, where he waited, a white-robed figure in the darkness outside, until he could be sure his duties were over for the night.

On the small dais across the room, the musicians had long since ceased to play. They sat gloomily, staring into space.

It was Roddy who made the first move to break the uncanny stillness. With a visible effort, he pulled himself together, and went to Henrietta's side. She looked up at him, remorse in her blue eyes.

"We had to try," she said. "There's so much at stake."

He nodded, his young face a mask of formality. His loyalties were still with the prince while he served as aide-de-camp, but his eyes told her that he felt for them all, and understood what she had tried to do.

"I'll see that your boat is ready." He turned to where Lance Morton stood looking thoughtfully out on to the deck. He held out his hand. The archeologist took it, and the clasp of their brief handshake was firm.

Both men made for the door, and Roddy opened it for Henrietta and her companion to pass through. Before she followed, Henrietta let the heavy cloak she still wore about her shoulders fall. It lay on the golden fabric of the chaise longue that skirted one wall of the state-room—a symbol of an evening that had somehow ended in disaster.

At the door, she paused again. "Is Professor Clémence not to accompany us back to *The Sprite?*"

Roddy looked slightly uncomfortable. "Er—I believe he left us before you took a turn on deck with H.R.H.," he said flatly. "I daresay he'd have managed to get another small boat to take him back round the island. Either that—" Henrietta had the distinct impression that her cousin was lying, and making a bad job of it, "—or he may have been offered a berth on *The Centaur* for the night. There's a lot the prince wants to learn about Thebes before we get there. And—" he finished lamely "—we've plenty of spare beds. We rattle around like beans in a bag, don't you know."

He still avoided Henrietta's eyes as their small boat pushed away from the steamer's side and she looked up to the rails, her gloved hand raised in farewell. But he seemed to be busy supervising the proper stowing of the ropes, and before they were in midstream he had disappeared along the deck towards the cabins not occupied by the prince.

Henrietta began then to shiver in the night air. She had been foolish not to realize that the temperature would drop so low in this climate before dawn. For it was almost day, and she half expected, as she stood once more on the deck of *The Sprite* with Lance Morton, to see the sudden light in the east that heralded the morning. But her companion would not allow her to linger. A protective arm about her shoulders, which she appreciated too much to find familiar at such an hour, he hurried down to the cabins.

As she had fully anticipated, there was a light in the window of the cabin she shared with her mother. Like all the mamas since time began, Constance de Vere Smith had waited up for her daughter.

Shuddering again, perhaps at the thought of the white lies she would now have to produce for her mother's benefit if she were not to betray the true identity of their host on *The Centaur*, Henrietta laid a warning hand on Lance Morton's arm a yard or so before they reached the cabin door.

"I would not disturb my mother unnecessarily," she explained. "I will thank you here, for a splendid evening. I am sorry it did not bring the result that you wished."

He took her hand. The gesture surprised her, but the contact was reassuring. "Your conduct this night has been superb," he said admiringly. "For one so young—"

She shook her head. "Perhaps my age and—my inexperience—lent me courage which I would not find at my disposal ten years from now."

"And I am certain it has not been wasted. Whatever the—the prince's reaction," he lowered his voice at the use of the name—"I believe that I should return to the attack as soon as is possible. I am not yet convinced that we have failed."

"But *The Centaur* proceeds to Thebes, now," she reminded him. "There can be no communication between the two parties. It is well known that the royal vessel will keep all the distance it can between itself and more common tourist traffic."

He led her to the rails. In the darkness across the river the graceful bird-like line of a lateen sail sped on an unknown journey. "You do not allow for the unlimited uses of a small boat on these waters. It can go like the wind, with the wind. And I shall not lose time to seek the ear of the royal party again. You shall see."

Henrietta suddenly felt very, very tired. She turned from the rail. "I believe my cousin also is to be admired for his part in what happened. It is not easy for an aide-de-camp to disagree with the man he serves. And I think he showed great diplomacy."

Lance Morton followed her. "I do not think, I *know*—that your cousin is a soldier. A true soldier. And that he has far to go. I observed him closely. And I believe that he has far to go."

It was an extremely surprised Englishman who

stood in the shadows of the steamer's awning that moment, expecting to be dismissed with a touch of a white glove and a murmured good night—only to find himself soundly kissed somewhere in the region of his left ear, and abandoned in a miniscule cloud of delicate English perfume that was to stay with him on his pillow until morning.

As Henrietta let herself into the cabin, she felt prepared to answer any question her mother might like to ask but the light that still glowed in the cabin showed that her mother had fallen asleep. And as dawn flared in the sky she curled herself beneath her cooling sheets, the mosquito net settled gently about her, and went to sleep with the image of her cousin's face in her heart.

CHAPTER EIGHT

THE EUPHORIC MOOD in which Henrietta went to sleep in the dawn after the tensions and irresolutions of the dinner party on the royal steamer proved however to be short-lived. Some hours later, she awoke to a sensation of nausea in her stomach, and the rhythmic hammering in her temples was echoed by the thud of the steamer's engines below where she lay.

There were no sounds from the promenade deck, or from the river shores, to tell her what time of day it was, or where they were. There was no sign of her mother in the small cabin. The other berth was neatly made up, and no kerchief or reticule lay about the confined space to show that Constance de Vere Smith was perhaps temporarily absent.

In an effort to seek more signs of her mother's whereabouts—maybe a note left beside her berth—Henrietta raised herself on one elbow. It was then that she knew just how unwell she was. She could not have moved had she wanted to. Her head swam, her neck was stiff, and the hands that clutched feebly at the mosquito net were burning. Helplessly, she sank back onto her pillows. As she did so, perspiration started on her forehead, and her whole body began to ache. She was paying the price of that walk under the stars with the prince. The swift changes of temperature had taken their toll. She had succumbed to a tropical fever.

She was unable to measure whether hours or minutes followed next, as she tossed fretfully from side to side, longing desperately for a glass of water, and yet unable to call out or reach the steward's bell. But time did pass, and *The Sprite* seemed to her to have been ploughing relentlessly on for an eternity when the cabin door opened.

The figures who stood regarding her solemnly swam before her eyes. She raised a hand to welcome them, only to let it fall helplessly to her side. She knew that the woman whose voluminous skirts almost filled the space between the berths and the door must be her mama, because no one else in their party had shown the temerity to wear black and white striped silk *and* a hat spilling with white roses on board. But the man at her side, a dark-faced Egyptian in a russet fez and European suit was unknown to her. That is, until Constance de Vere Smith announced him.

"I was unable to call the good doctor to you until some time after luncheon, Henrietta. The Muslims eat alone, you know, at a second sitting." She turned to her companion, who already showed signs of impatience. "Dr. Fayum—my daughter, Miss Henrietta de Vere Smith."

The doctor bowed curtly, but when he removed the mosquito net and held her wrist, Henrietta knew she need not be concerned about his bedside manner. His touch was expert, his gaze—as he gently pulled at her lower eyelids and looked into her blue eyes with his own black orbs—was totally professional and detached. She was in good hands.

"Madam," he said to Constance next, "you should not have hesitated to send word to me at luncheon. Your daughter has a very, very high fever. And a chill. It is a good thing that we journey on tonight, to Luxor. Tell me, are you prepared to spend the hours of darkness in nursing? We must get this fever down. Otherwise, I shall not be able to permit the patient to go ashore...."

Henrietta gave a smothered murmur of dismay at his words. Not to be able to go ashore at their next call, where they would stay in a hotel for the duration of their exploration of the great site of Thebes, would mean that the very climax of their tour was lost to them. For she knew that if she herself had to stay on board, then her mother would have to remain as chaperone.

But to her surprise, her mother's hand swiftly and gently covered hers. Her usually imperious tones were softened, as she told her: "Henrietta. Child. We have the whole afternoon, and then the night before us. We have the good doctor. We shall without fail be disembarking at Luxor, according to plan."

Weakly, Henrietta shook her head. It was not only the thought of ruining their tour that troubled her. It was the knowledge that she was now quite unable to watch out for her cousin's progress on the river ahead of *The Sprite*—and if Lance Morton found his opportunity to pursue his talks with the prince, she would not be at his side.

Mistaking the movement for sorrowing acquiescence, Constance de Vere Smith once more turned to the doctor, who bade her accompany him to the boat's medical headquarters—his own cabin—and bring a steward with her. There was medicine to be prepared, blankets were to be found, and a regime for the invalid was to be organized. With the excellent mother, he told her in his polite, sing-song tones, as nurse, he had no doubt that the charming daughter would make good recovery.

"But only," he told Henrietta, as he turned to the berth, and replaced her mosquito net with a firm hand, "only if she obeys orders!"

Henrietta tried to smile at Dr. Fayum, but the knowledge that she was a prisoner now, combined with her fever to send a slow tear spilling down her reddened cheek. As the cabin door closed and the voices of her mother and the doctor receded into the distance, she wept openly, helplessly. If only she could get word to her cousin! Or even to Lance Morton. She was apprehensive, also, that the latter gentleman would take her sudden absence from the general company as a slight. She could only hope that her mother would find it possible to rejoin the party at least for dinner, when her news would no doubt be circulated with all the speed and efficiency of the Belgravia set itself.

Resolving to tell her mama on her return to the cabin that she was on no account to miss dinner that night, Henrietta once more slid into an uneasy sleep. That, at least, was her impression of the befuddled state in which she now found herself. And when, moments later, a shadowy male figure in European dress stepped into the cabin, she had turned her face to the wall.

Vaguely, she was aware of movement. She stirred, anticipating her mother's command to sit up and take her medicine. But the voice that addressed her was not that of Constance de Vere Smith. It was the voice of Professor Clémence.

"Do not be alarmed, I beg of you, mademoiselle," he whispered. "I intend you no hurt. But—you must listen carefully to what I have to say. And—if you value the life of your cousin—then you must remember that I am in deadly earnest, and that I am to be obeyed."

Henrietta lay taut with fear at his words. At first she thought that the intruder was a figure in a feverish dream. She tried to wake herself. She struggled to turn.

When she did so, she saw that the professor was no hallucination. The face that now peered into hers was flesh and blood, and infused with an intensity that made her shudder.

"Sir," she managed to say at last, controlling her chattering teeth with a superhuman effort of the will, "you are doubtless aware that my mother has only just left this cabin, or I do not believe you would have had the audacity to enter in this way. But are you not also aware that she will return, within moments, and with a steward at her side?"

The Frenchman gestured impatiently. "I do not need long to convince you, mademoiselle, of that I am sure. I observed you last night, on board His Royal Highness' vessel. And I found that you are a woman of great intelligence and understanding."

"You will find, sir, if you do not leave this cabin at once, that I am also a—a person—of strong lungs," Henrietta threatened, but her weakness betrayed her then, and she sank wearily back onto her pillows.

The intruder leant forward, eyes gleaming almost fanatically.

"If, I repeat, you value the life of your brave young cousin—and I also observed at dinner that you do—then you must advise him, and your other English friends, to desist from this matter altogether."

Henrietta closed her eyes. She despaired of being able to get rid of the man, and now she could only hope that her mother would indeed return posthaste and surprise him. But then it occurred to her that if he were confronted in this way, and tried to extricate himself from the situation by any reference to the night before, then it would mean that Constance de Vere Smith would begin to ask questions. And in the innocent account she had given of the dinner party, Henrietta had skillfully avoided even the whitest of white lies—by a series of diplomatic omissions. She had really believed for a moment that it might be possible to continue the Nile excursion without her mother sailing on to *The Centaur* to confront both her nephew and the heir to the throne. But now she felt less secure.

"Be quick, if you must speak. And then—go." She spoke as fiercely as she could, and with the effort she felt perspiration run freely now from her temples and into the warm, damp space between her young neck and the pillows.

The Frenchman's voice came as if from a great distance.

"You will send word to your cousin that you wish to speak with him, most urgently. When we arrive in Luxor. It should not be too difficult."

She was aware that he had stepped closer to her berth, but she was too weak to remonstrate.

He continued: "When you meet, you will tell him that there are things here in this great country which are beyond his understanding. He must have no part in the events that are to come. He—and the other Englishman—have no place here, no role to play. And if they persist in the foolish interference which they tried to display last night, then—there are those who will have them removed!"

Between the full horror of his threat, and the audacity of his presumption that he could issue a command to a man like her cousin and expect to be obeyed, Henrietta could not decide which infuriated her most. She swallowed, tried to speak and struggled to sit up. By the time she had raised herself again so that she could see into his eyes before she told him exactly what she thought of him, the Frenchman had gone as quietly as he had appeared, leaving her with a fast beating pulse and a head that now screamed with pain.

The next thing of which she was conscious was a cool cloth on her brow, and the taste of some bitter liquid between her clenched teeth. When she looked back on this phase of their journey many months later, Henrietta was drawn repeatedly to the conclusion that her mama's skill and energies alone had saved them from disaster. The fever had her so in its grip that, left untended, it would doubtless have lingered for days. But in the determined teeth of Constance de Vere Smith's campaign, it reached its peak by midnight as *The Sprite* journeyed on, and as dawn gleamed through the cabin windows, Henrietta opened her eyes to find herself in clean, dry chemise, her hair combed, her bed neatly made about her exhausted limbs.

In the sudden delight and relief of feeling well again, she lay for a while without moving, her thoughts unclouded as her cool brow. But as her mother spoke, the memory of the Frenchman and the threats he had made flooded back.

"I have arranged for a litter to carry you to the hotel at Luxor." It was the old, imperious voice again, and briefly Henrietta wondered if the woman who had moved so quietly and deftly about the room for the long hours in which the fever had raged was indeed the same who now stood before her. "I told the good doctor we would succeed in our battle with this dastardly climate and these foreign ailments, and I was right!" Constance de Vere Smith announced to the world at large, as she retrieved a large leather valise from the floor and slung it triumphantly onto her own berth.

"How glad I shall be to stay even for a short while in an hotel again," she said. "As soon as I have selected a gown for your disembarkation, I shall repack and send for the steward. Now—something graceful, if you are to be carried." She began to talk to herself, as she rummaged through the open valise, and not until she held aloft an almost gossamer confection of palest pink did Henrietta find the strength and will to object.

"Mama!" She swung from under the mosquito net, long slim feet brushing the cabin floor and pale, golden limbs gleaming in the slits of light through the now shuttered windows.

Her mother turned. "You will find, if you attempt to stand, Henrietta, that you are quite disabled by this virulent fever we have fought together, and I would advise you not to try!"

Only too accustomed to her mother's thorough ways in any of her undertakings, Henrietta knew enough to believe her, but still she tried to get to her feet. Clutching at whatever support was nearest, she took two, maybe three steps. She swayed. The room tilted about her. With her mother at her side, she returned to her berth.

"Mama, I cannot, I simply cannot make my appearance at our hotel on a litter!" she gasped unhappily. "I *must* walk."

"If you are to be fit for the exploration of the tombs of the kings," her mother replied," then you will *not* walk off this vessel. Mr. Bedales is no stranger to these illnesses that beset his courageous patrons, and he has assured me that if you force your recovery unduly, you will relapse!"

It was this that resigned Henrietta to the knowledge that she would now be carried like some northern Cleopatra from *The Sprite*. If other travelers had suffered these fevers and relapsed, then she could not run such a risk. Whatever happened, she must be well again in order to find and warn her cousin.

For she had made up her mind that warn him she would. Not to take heed of Professor Clémence's threats, but to instil in him the need to act—in spite of them!

When at last she was established under the awning outside their cabin, a graceful if somewhat fragile figure in the gossamer pink, Henrietta was not as annoyed by her situation as she had anticipated. For the last stretch of their journey, to where they would disembark for Luxor, the Nile had begun to change character, and Henrietta's position, slightly raised on the litter, which itself was balanced on two sturdy benches, was one quite beneficial to the would-be sightseer.

At first she had hoped that she would be able to watch for some sign ahead of *The Sprite* of the progress of the royal steamer. But the long, straight line of the river which she had last seen before the fever overtook her had now given way to a series of giant twists and curves. And if *The Centaur* was ahead of them, however close, it would be a miracle if she would sight it now before they landed.

Giving in at last philosophically to the fact that she must be patient, Henrietta tried to turn her attention to the view that now lay on either side. In this, too, the river had assumed a new garment.

Beyond the great sandy stretches of its banks were long, natural paths across rough stone, and beyond them, high stone cliffs that made Henrietta feel, strangely, as if she floated on some inland sea.

It was beyond these cliffs, to the west, Lance Morton told her, that the ancient necropolis of kings awaited them.

"And to the east?" Henrietta, aware that they might be joined any moment by other members of the excursion seeking to enquire after her health, tried to infer in her tone that in calling his attention to the east, and the desert beyond, she wanted in fact to revive the subject so close to her heart at that moment. The menace of whatever lay awaiting the royal party in the eastern desert was now with her with every breath that she took. But if she were to take this opportunity to confide in Lance Morton the details of the strange visit to her cabin by the professor, she feared that the Frenchman himself might reappear and return to the attack. And for the moment, she felt too weak to endure a scene similar to that of their last encounter.

Lance Morton himself seemed in no hurry to reply to her question, and the moment of unspoken fear passed, as Constance de Vere Smith herself bore down on them.

"Sir," she cried, before she had even come to a halt, "I am sure that you, as a gentleman, will be prepared to give me your word in a matter that has caused me much anxiety."

Henrietta's heart sank. Was her mother about to

resuscitate the whole business of the dinner party at which she had clearly caught the fever? But Lance Morton bowed calmly, and, somewhat mollified, Constance de Vere Smith returned to her subject:

"Will you promise me that, as one of the most sober and mature of our little party, and one who seems to wield not the least influence on this gel, my daughter that is, you will see that she makes no foolish plans again in the course of this great journey we have undertaken—either to walk in the heat of the day, or to stroll unwisely in the cool of the evening? May I, in a word, as you, sir, to be at her side, as the elder half brother of her best friend's husband, at all times during our stay in Luxor, and if any foolishness should occur to her—to report the matter immediately to the one who is most concerned in bringing her back to health? In a word more—to myself?"

"Mama!" Henrietta's acute embarrassment at this appointment of Lance Morton as a kind of civilian bodyguard was only matched by her secret delight that the arrangement could be extremely useful in the whole matter of making contact with her cousin, and taking some action in the matter of the danger to the prince and his party. But, if she had intended to make any objection after her first bisyllabic protest, she was forestalled.

"If I understand you correctly, ma'am," Lance Morton spoke civilly, "you have excellent reasons for asking this of me—and for knowing that I would agree?"

Constance nodded, somewhat severely. She wore a dark lilac outfit for the journey to the hotel, and the matching parasol which she held clamped tightly down over her exposed features lent a vaguely dramatic aspect to her appearance.

"You do understand me, sir."

"For, as it was to all intents and purposes through my neglect, or at least in my company, that your daughter contracted this disabling fever, you can be certain that I of all people, as a gentleman, am obliged to see that it does not return?"

The formal bow with which the older man gravely embellished his speech to her mother, made Henrietta smile. Lance Morton was indeed her protector, and all the more valuable because he understood her mother to perfection. The pleased manner in which Constance now swept to the rails, as if the matter were closed, and gazed out on the small white-walled village they were now passing, denoted a triumph for both sides in the matter.

"It will be quite pleasant to find oneself in a proper town again," her mother addressed the waters of the Nile.

From the main path that ran through the heart of the village, Henrietta watched the figures of a group of women walk in Indian-file. On their heads they carried giant, earthen waterpots. They were darkly veiled, and their bodies entirely secret in long robes. She looked down at her own frivolous gown. In the glare of the day, it suddenly seemed without value and bereft of elegance.

She looked out again to where the women moved on, beneath a line of slim, tall trees. They seemed to be making for a well on the outskirts of their home. They were, she thought, no more than beasts of burden. And yet how graceful, and how feminine, they seemed.

She gave a small sigh, and at once Lance Morton moved to her side. He looked down at her, protectively.

Then he glanced over his shoulder to where Constance stood, as if making sure that she could not hear.

"You must be patient," he said in a low voice. "And you must trust me."

"I do," she whispered. "But—there is so much I must say to my cousin. And if my mother even suspects that I am in touch with him—"

"I can guess what would follow. I am not blind. But you have allowed yourself to become over-anxious. You must rest. Before you can carry this matter further, you must feel well again. And perhaps I can tell you something that will hasten that recovery?"

Henrietta nodded. It was true that if she saw Roddy now on the banks of the Nile, or the deck of *The Sprite* itself, she would be powerless even to walk to him—let alone do battle with the forces that lay in wait for him if he did not act soon. But the implied meaning of Lance Morton's words suddenly dawned on her. Hope sprang in her young breast, and for the first time since she had fallen ill her eyes sparkled a little.

To her relief, her mother moved away from them at this moment, attracted by a scurry of small boats that had joined them—if only to shoo them away as if they were a fleet of ducks on an English pond.

Lance Morton followed her antics with a slight smile on his usually serious face. "I have spoken to you before of the small craft and the way in which they can dart about these waters. And while you were fighting your fever in the confines of your cabin, I took it upon myself to seek out that soldier cousin of yours. I think, when you next meet him, that you will find him deeply embroiled in some plan of action to save his prince—and his country—from whatever fate awaited them in the eastern desert."

Henrietta's spirits soared with his words. She stifled an impulse to leap from where she lay, throw her parasol to the deck, and hug her companion.

But then she realized, with a slow sinking of her heart, that the news he gave her, the action he had taken, took no reckoning of what had passed between her and Professor Clémence.

She looked blankly out to where the landing place at Luxor now awaited them. The shallows of this sweep of the river gleamed dully between the steamer and the shore. The jetty was cluttered with baggage and beggars, with naked children and brown-limbed fishermen. Their shrill voices reached out to her, an alien sound in an alien world. Somewhere further along the jetty a donkey brayed.

"Look, look!" Miss Fountain and her brother had rounded the deck, and walked with some excitement towards them. "The donkeys are waiting. And we have been instructed, by Mr. Bedales, to bring our own saddles ashore! The ladies' saddles, that is. We have a long ride tomorrow, it seems."

Henrietta looked with envy upon the group that now assembled at the rails of *The Sprite*. The ladies chattered, and worried, and gave small, ecstatic cries. The lady who kept a journal made mental notes with vigor. The gentlemen prepared to proffer helpful arms and stalwart backs and sound advice. They approached the very height of the experience they all shared with the propriety and solemnity with which they would embark on a Sunday morning excursion to a village church. How brave, how fine they were! And she hoped with all her heart that her cousin was made of such good stuff. For if Lance Morton had indeed launched him on a plan to thwart the danger that lay over them now like a cloud, Roddy would have to deal with those forces which the Frenchman had warned her would stop at nothing to see that he failed.

CHAPTER NINE

THE SIGHT of the Englishwoman, Constance de Vere Smith, mounted firmly sidesaddle on a large gray donkey was one that the British consul in Luxor, a Mr. Mustapha Aga, believed he would never forget. He stood on the verandah of his long, low house by the river and watched her, as veiled and parasoled, a splendid figure in cream-colored riding habit, she moved off with her party on the two-mile ride across the sands to the great temple of Karnak—at the same time managing a graceful farewell to her daughter.

Henrietta, now wearing a becoming crinoline in white muslin spotted with pale green, reclined on a low cane bench in the shade of the consulate verandah. She wore no bonnet, since her outdoor clothes had been left in the care of Mustapha Aga's servants for that day. Her hand shielding her eyes from the glare of the light from the river, she watched the small party, led by Mr. Bedales and a local guide, until the light grew too much for her to bear. She was still pale from the weakness that was the aftermath of the fever. Her hand fell listlessly to her side.

The consul, turning just in time to catch the movement, at once hurried to where Henrietta lay, and clapping his hands, ordered sherbet and cold tea to be brought to the guest.

At that moment, Lance Morton joined the figures on the verandah, and an onlooker in the street between the consulate and the river landingplace would have seen a tall, formally dressed Englishman bending solicitously over the bronze-haired young girl, as if to straighten her cushion.

But Lance Morton was taking advantage of the consul's preoccupation with the trolley of drinks that had now been brought to whisper urgently into Henrietta's attentive ear.

"*The Centaur* has gone on ahead to Assuan. I shall not see your cousin now until we also reach the First Cataract—if then. But in a way, this is perhaps to our advantage. The travelers—your mother included—have two or three days here, when they will mingle with other tourists at every turn. Today, the antiquities at Karnak. Tomorrow, Thebes itself. It would have been more than likely that your mother came face to face with the royal party had they stayed in Luxor at this juncture."

The consul approached them at that moment, and Henrietta, accepting a tall glass of sherbet with a smile, told her companion: "I feel so guilty, sir, that you have not gone with the others to the great palace remains. They say the work was a triumph for the Rameses, both father and son."

Lance Morton bowed. "You forget, dear young lady, that this is not the first time I have explored this country. The rivalries of Rameses the First and Second are not new to me. And my promise to your mother was binding. At least we are able to pass the day pleasantly here, with our friend."

Mustapha Aga, who had (it now transpired) known Lance Morton for some years, joined them for the next hour, and entertained them with his many stories of the other intrepid explorers and archeologists who had come to Luxor in the years in which he had been consul. At one point, he clapped his hands, murmured in Arabic to the native boy who appeared and disappeared in seconds, and produced the large vellum-bound visitors' book which those who passed through his territory always signed.

"May I?" Her curiosity, as always, getting the better of her, Henrietta began to turn back the pages, to see if there were any names she recognized. For the previous year, she found a whole page taken up by a formidable list of visitors, headed by the signatures:

Albert Edward P.

Alexandria P.

With a long, slightly tanned finger, Henrietta silently indicated the passage to Lance Morton. Her eyes ran on down the same page. The names were those of the distinguished, official party that had visited Egypt with the prince on the occasion of the opening of the Suez Canal. Prince Louis of Battenberg; Lord Carrington; numerous other gentlemen of title—and the usual clutch of young equerries, from the celebrated regiments of Life Guards, the Horse Guards, and the Grenadiers.

It was the names of the young soldiers, all of whom must have known Roddy in London, that made Henrietta give a low sigh, and close the book.

She knew it was indiscreet of her, but her next words came almost involuntarily to her lips.

"It is sad that no members of the royal family have, it seems, called on you since the great days of 1869, sir," she said politely to Mustapha Aga.

The consul took the book from her as she spoke, and in giving his noncommittal answer he did not meet her gaze.

"It is a long way from your country, mademoiselle," he said. "And a state visit requires much preparation. Your prince was a great success—but—" he shrugged. "After all, you have a great empire, do you not? There are many other faraway places where he should also be seen."

It was then that Henrietta knew the royal progress was this time indeed incognito. And she felt a sudden wave of compassion for the princess, the mother of Edward's two children, whose name was so evident in the 1869 list of official visitors, but who now sat at home and presumably believed her husband was on some innocuous private holiday in Europe.

And yet, she had to admit to herself that she had found those sometimes serious, sometimes smiling gray eyes of the truant prince extremely appealing, whilst in the course of the promenade at his side on the deck of *The Centaur,* she had detected in his dry, almost curt remarks a quick brain, as well as a saddened heart. It was, she knew, presumptuous of her to compare her lot with that of a prince of the blood royal, but having languished for years herself in the shadow of the formidable presence and will of her own mama, she did not have to ask why Edward had to resort to subterfuge to be his true self.

The rest of the day, for which they were to be the consul's guests, passed in quiet leisure for Henrietta and her companion, and by the time afternoon tea was served she was delighted to find that she was able to walk without aid, and without a return of her previous annoying weakness, from the small drawing room where she had taken her siesta alone to the library where Lance Morton and Mustapha Aga once more awaited her.

When the bell had been rung for tea some quarter of an hour previously, Henrietta had been aroused from a light sleep on a chaise longue by a gentle touch on her shoulder. She had awakened to find a young Egyptian woman smiling down at her. She could not understand what was said to her, but the gentle, dark eyes, the soft voice, and the graceful robes worn by the woman all combined to give Henrietta a sense of wellbeing. As she followed her to an anteroom where she bathed her face and hands, Henrietta observed not for the first time that there was something very beautiful and mysterious about the way the Egyptian women walked, and about the garments that floated about their totally concealed bodies in the warm, scented air.

The contrast between the two images, of the women of the east and of her own civilization, was all the more forcibly brought home to her that evening, when, with Lance Morton at her side, she rejoined her mother in the lounge of their hotel.

Constance de Vere Smith was enthroned triumphantly on a carved sofa upholstered in red velvet, and her well-formed powdered shoulders rose from the restrictions of a lace-edged décolleté gown of apple-green silk as if in tribute to the monolithic remains she had inspected far out in the desert that afternoon.

The windows of the room in which she waited for her daughter's return faced the west, and afforded a prospect of the river at some distance. As Henrietta entered, the room was suddenly flooded with dull red light, and in the split second with which twilight came and went before darkness, her mother's figure was clothed in dramatic scarlet shadows.

The face that was raised to Henrietta for a daughterly kiss told her that the day's ride to Karnak had taken its toll on her mama. The skin was white under the skillfully applied powder. The eyes were slightly bloodshot, and the lids a little puffed with the heat. But of course, Constance de Vere Smith would rarely admit to fatigue, and it had to be said in her defense that she had only recently nursed her own daughter through a wearing night and day of fever.

Her first remark, in which she demanded why Henrietta was walking again so soon, proved beyond doubt that her spirits had not suffered from the ordeal she had clearly undergone in physical terms. She proceeded then to a detailed account of the excursion which lasted for the duration of the excellent table d'hôte supper, and concluded with the announcement that the whole party was to snatch twenty-four hours repose the following day, before the onslaught on Thebes itself.

Constance de Vere Smith made this announcement in full hearing of the rest of the group from *The Sprite*, who now took coffee at the adjoining tables. It was clear from the numerous raised heads and raised eyebrows that this was new to most of the party, and the way in which Mr. Bedales leapt to his feet and began, in a rush of words, to explain the reasons for his decision, left Henrietta in no doubt at all that the whole thing had been instigated by her mother—and was a clever ploy to gain a little time for rest and recuperation. The fact that, as Mr. Bedales explained, this meant a complete reshuffling of the timetable, was offset in the minds of the other travelers by the assurance that any extra expenses incurred would be met by his own company, and that the change of plan would mean that their charming companion, Miss Henrietta de Vere Smith, would be well enough to rejoin them for the greatest moment of their journey—the long pilgrimage to the valley of the kings.

In the flickering candlelight from the table at which they had dined, Henrietta's eyes glowed with sudden pleasure. It was clear to her now also that her mother had anticipated her probable need for a day's further respite before she attempted the ride to Thebes. Her motives had not been purely selfish in persuading Mr. Bedales that the party needed more time for this section of their journey. Once more she had shown that, though she would be the last to admit it, she had her daughter's welfare inexorably at heart. It was a pity that the process also involved trying to rule her daughter with her strong will. But for once Henrietta was grateful for the results.

The next day, while Constance de Vere Smith remained in the hotel and gathered her resources about her again, Henrietta was therefore at liberty to find her own legs in a series of undemanding walks into the small township of Luxor itself, with Lance Morton on one side and the American Brian Dogharty on the other.

Still wearing the green and white muslin, for its practical coolness more than for its undeniably becoming qualities, Henrietta carried a matching parasol of white trimmed with green, and wore a wide hat of white. As she walked through the Luxor bazaar after a late breakfast, her face glowing with new well-being, her eyes darting hungrily over the scene, the crowds of shoppers and itinerant merchants, donkey drivers and beggars, fell back a little to let her pass. There were very few women in the streets, and Henrietta and her two handsome escorts presented a pageant of intriguing novelty to the male crowd.

Not unaware of the impact she made, Henrietta pointedly shared her glances and her conversation equally with Lance Morton and the bearded American, but since the evening before she had decided that she would take the opportunity of an excursion without her mother's company to buy her some memento of the journey so far. Her mother's fatigue, and her indomitable scheming in their favor had somehow won her heart, and having had so few opportunities since Brindisi to spend her own allowance, Henrietta was in a position to express her feelings in style.

She told her companions, as they walked from stall

to stall, that what she sought was a jeweler, and one of the highest repute.

"I do not wish to impress my mama with my extravagance, or to express my appreciation of this adventure in any showy fashion," she explained. "In any case, I could not compete with the jewels which my mother already wears, as part of the de Vere de Vere heritage. But—"

It was Brian Dogharty who broke in: "But something truly Egyptian, of true craftsmanship, perhaps? No trash made to deceive the tourist, or empty his purse?"

Henrietta took his arm confidingly. "I can see that you understand. And Mr. Morton, also." She looked up into Lance Morton's face. (It must be explained that the Englishman already held her other arm lightly in his.)

"The requirements shall be met," he told her. "We shall seek out the best man to be found."

Then, to her delight, Lance Morton proceeded to buttonhole a swarthy, bare-limbed young Arab who had been offering his services as a guide for the last ten minutes, and address him in his own language.

As soon as he had understood the visitors' quest, the boy nodded eagerly, and beckoned to Henrietta to follow him at once.

His striped cotton tunic would soon have been lost in the crowd had they not then begun to walk faster in his wake, and after a few yards Henrietta, still a trifle debilitated by her fever, perhaps, was forced to ask for a reprieve.

Luckily, at that moment, their guide seemed to have found the shop that he had in mind. He stood at its entrance, in a low mud-built wall, and again he beckoned to Henrietta.

When she at last drew close to where he stood, Henrietta wondered for a puzzled moment if the boy had really understood their requirements. There was no display of merchandise, no window or stall in which a display could even have been mounted. The entrance to the plain, whitewashed building had no proper door, but was screened by a heavy tapestry... which the Arab boy now drew aside.

It was evident to them all that the boy was familiar with the place, and as if sensing a trick of some kind Henrietta did not enter at once, but gave a quick enquiring look at Lance Morton to see if he shared her hesitation. At once he called the boy back, and asked him several questions in fluent Arabic.

The boy, waving his arms excitedly, answered at once. And as he spoke, Lance Morton translated for the benefit of his companions.

"There is no mistake," he said. "The boy knows that we seek the best jeweler in the town. And this is where he lives." He listened further as the boy continued.

"The jeweler's name is Hamed. He is so famous for his skill as a goldsmith that only his first name is used. Hamed of Luxor. But—he is not *too* expensive! Especially, that is, if his customer is a beautiful English lady!"

To the accompaniment of Lance Morton and the American's quiet laughter, Henrietta then picked up the hem of her dress and stepped resolutely past the tapestry, her companions in her wake.

She found herself then in a small courtyard, and stood rooted to the spot by its unexpected beauty. Only yards from the dusty main streets and the hurly-burly of the markets Hamed the Goldsmith lived, it seemed, in an oasis. The courtyard was laid with white marble, and in its center a small fountain played. The fountain was surrounded by a wide circular seat of darker stone, polished so that it caught what sunlight was allowed in. Overhead, the branches and leaves of five young palm trees met to give shade and soft color to the air. On the waters of the small pond fed by the fountain, an English water lily gleamed.

As if bewitched, Henrietta moved forward and the

two men followed. The boy waited for them on the far side of the courtyard, and beyond him they could see into a dimly lit room, furnished with low, cushioned ottomans, and exquisite carpets on walls and floor. Somewhere, further in the recesses of the strange house, a woman sang in a low, monotonous chant. Then, as a man appeared on the far side of the room and beckoned to his visitors to enter, the music stopped.

As she stepped into the half light, Henrietta's impressions were legion; the soft silk of the rugs beneath her feet, the scented air, the black beads that were the eyes in the face of the man who waited for them.

Trembling slightly—but with pleasure rather than with fear—she took her place on the low ottoman which the goldsmith indicated with a slight motion of his head was where she was to sit. Lance and the American sat on two smaller, low seats, on the other side of a long table of black marble.

It was Lance who then dismissed the boy with a silver coin, and made the formal introductions, explaining Henrietta's purpose. Trying not to dwell on the sudden suspicion that their arrival had been anticipated well in advance, Henrietta looked about her. If the accouterments of the room were anything to go by, then Hamed was a very successful man.

As if he could read her thoughts with his darting black eyes, the goldsmith bowed—but without deference—watched her for a moment before he clapped his hands sharply. As if she had only paused to take breath, the woman then at once resumed her chanting. And at the same time the curtains through which the goldsmith himself had entered the room were parted by unseen hands, and a second woman approached the table, carrying a tray set with miniature cups of coffee and a plate of sweetmeats in pastel colors. The visitors looked at each other, quite convinced now that they had come to the house of a great craftsman, and that their business would not be accomplished in five minutes.

But it was the woman herself who caught Henrietta's attention. A slim but rounded figure, she moved silently on sandaled feet, and the almost translucent drapery of her garments swam about her as if in slow motion. Her head was veiled, and as she set the tray on the table before her, Henrietta noted that the veil was kept in place by a narrow fillet of pure, soft gold. Her face was half covered by a gauze of silver gray, and above it the woman's eyes glowed, dark velvet pools. With a catch of her breath, Henrietta saw also, before the woman turned away, that her eyes were outlined in skillfully-applied curves of artificial color; and that the lids themselves were painted gold. Then, as she moved across the room, Henrietta watched her go, and realized that the diaphanous garment she wore around her, which had seemed at first sight to be a silken skirt, was actually an exotically feminine version of pantaloons!

More covetous of the servant girl's garments than she had ever been of any Paris gown, Henrietta tried to turn her mind as she sipped her dark, sweet coffee to the business in hand. But, as was the custom of the place, no merchandise was brought to the black marble table until the refreshments had been consumed.

It was almost an hour later that Henrietta, therefore, was able to make her choice at last for her mother, between a delicate gold filigree bracelet which she knew would harmonize with the de Vere heirlooms if nothing else, and a thin gold circlet from which was suspended a semi-precious stone in a shade of green which would match several of Constance de Vere Smith's ensembles. The matter of choice finally settled—it was to be the filigree bracelet—the question of price was then broached. And at this point in the transaction Henrietta was heartily thankful that she was accompanied by Lance Morton.

Leaving it to his discretion, she allowed the archeologist to bargain, which was apparently the custom, in Hamed's own tongue; and as the two men launched into their discussion, she turned to engage in a quiet conversation with Brian Dogharty. But she was less than halfway through a first sentence when the sound of some activity in the courtyard attracted her attention.

With a slight snort of annoyance, Hamed also paused. He listened briefly, to a young voice speaking Arabic, and what Henrietta knew at once, unmistakably, to be an Englishman's voice speaking halting Arabic in reply.

Then, as if he disdained the idea of leaving his honored customers for a moment, Hamed snorted again, clapped his hands thrice, and called.

Outside in the courtyard, the voices were silenced. From within the house, the serving girl reappeared. She carried a sealed package ceremoniously before her, and as she wafted quickly and quietly past them there was no opportunity even to guess from its size what it might contain.

But not even the girl's sudden reappearance, or her mysterious veiled beauty, not even the mysterious package in her hands, held Henrietta's interest. As the graceful figure passed and repassed them and the strangers in the courtyard, having apparently received what they had come for from Hamed, moved away, Henrietta's head spun. For a moment, she thought that her fever had suddenly returned, and that she would be sure to faint. Desperately, she fought to retain consciousness. So controlled was her effort that her companions seemed not to notice that anything was wrong.

Gradually, she calmed herself. She smiled when Lance Morton informed her that the transaction was complete, and the price agreeable to all parties. She rose to go as if in a dream, and bowed to the goldsmith as if in some strange, formal dance.

It was not until the party was out in the street again that she allowed her control to go. Then, regardless of what Lance Morton and the American might think of her, she ran on ahead of them into the very thick of the bazaar, alone. For the young English voice she had heard in the courtyard was that of her cousin, who was, or so they all believed, on board the royal steamer, two days' journey away by now from where they stood.

CHAPTER TEN

TO REACH the Valley of the Kings, and the legendary tombs which were the highlight of their whole tour, the party of travelers led by Mr. Bedales was obliged to leave their Luxor hotel not long after five in the morning, and to make their way by donkey to the landing stage, where a variety of small local craft awaited them in the bright dawn.

From there, they crossed to the other side of the Nile, their native boatmen navigating as if born to the river—through crosscurrents, between small islands, and over difficult shallows.

Not quite certain whether this was the very spot where their revered founder, Mr. Thomas Cook, had almost drowned while bathing on a near-fateful March day a year or so previously, the members of the party sat in general as far into the center of the scudding vessels as was physically possible, and surveyed the rapid eddying of the dark waters around them with some apprehension. This was a very different journey from their steady, uneventful progress in their chartered steamer, and even for Constance de Vere Smith herself it held more latent fears than the swinging cable cars of the Swiss Alps so bravely endured at an earlier stage of the whole adventure.

For Henrietta, the crossing would, if things were normal, have been an event of unlimited delight. The slow awakening of the river, the creaking of the *shaduf* as the farmers moved on the horizon like tiny clockwork creatures, bringing water to their fields; the distant cries of men and birds in the strange glare of light that meant the day had come; to a young woman born and bred in London the scene was like a rich dream of ancient, ageless worlds. But as they sped on, the line of a wild bird in the wing of their lateen sail above her, Henrietta's heart was elsewhere, wildly winging on to where the river carried *The Centaur*. The steamer, as she now realized, which no longer carried her cousin....

Since the moment she had disappeared into the crowds of the bazaar the morning before, she had known no peace of mind. Roddy, whose voice she was certain had been that of the man in the courtyard at the home of the goldsmith Hamed, had already lost himself in the narrow streets. She did not even know, she realized as she ran on through the pushing huddles of merchants and shoppers, what he was wearing. If he traveled incognito, would he wear uniform? Would it be the best disguise of all? Or would he wear his civilian clothes, and pose as an ordinary tourist? And if so, why had he received such special attention when he called at the jeweler's house? And when had he learnt to speak Arabic? And why? The questions drummed at her brain throughout a sleepless night, and now pursued her across the Nile itself. And, if her cousin was, as she suspected, acting as a lone soldier now in the drama that had begun to unfold, she dared tell no one of his continued presence in Luxor.

As she lay in her bed at the hotel the night before, gazing wide-eyed into the darkness, she had even begun to ask herself whether she could now trust Lance Morton. The American who had accompanied them to the goldsmith's, who had also—if she considered the matter carefully—watched her rather too enthusiastically from the moment their eyes had met across the dining room in Paris: was he, too, not suspect now? She tried to remember to which of her escorts she owed the visit to the goldsmith, and in her confusion, which was somewhat aided and abetted by the remnants of fever in her system, she could not recall. All she knew for certain was that she must find her cousin, and that she must do so by her own efforts. So acutely suspicious of everyone had she become by the time she eventually found her way back to the hotel, a dusty, disheveled figure in green and white spotted gown, her parasol lost, her face drained of all color, that she asked her mother to inform the gentlemen who had been her escorts that a sudden attack of nausea, and the fear of actually being sick in their presence, had sent her scurrying back alone through the bazaar.

With the gift of the filigree bracelet in her reticule, greatly pleased with her daughter's choice, Constance de Vere Smith was perfectly prepared to stand between Henrietta and any gentlemen for the rest of that day, and mother and daughter had rested quietly for its duration, all the better to tackle the hazards which next morning faced the entire party.

Safely deposited by their native boatmen on the far shore, the ladies had not long to wait before the boat carrying their saddles pulled up on the rough beach. The dragomen scuttled forwards, sand flying beneath their feet, in competition to find the property of each of the riders in their charge. Unable to read English as they were, they did not attempt to unravel the mystery of whose saddle belonged to whom by studying the large luggage labels which Constance had insisted each of them tie to their shining English leather tackle. Rather, they watched the direction of the numerous multicolored parasols which pointed at the equipment in question, and, once in possession of a saddle, raced back up over the sand, their prizes high above their heads, until they were in their turn claimed by an imperious jab of a parasol and a cry of "Well done, my man!", or "Not that one, no *baksheesh* for that one!"

The caravan that eventually started off across the Libyan plain, which lay between the river and their destination, was as splendid and varied a spectacle as the progress some five hundred years before of the poet Chaucer's Canterbury pilgrims.

As the line of sturdy, gray-brown donkeys began to climb into the hills, the gentlemen of the party were in the lead, and a native dragoman rode to and fro, showing them the paths, and urging the donkeys on.

A second native rider shepherded the lady travelers some small distance behind, and as the heat of the day began to beat down upon them the parasols unfurled— so that from a distance, across the river, it seemed as if a string of brightly variegated balloons were bobbing in line into the haze above the plain.

Finally, the familiar figures of the stewards from *The Sprite* itself brought up the rear. They had chosen the strongest of mounts, and some of them even walked at the side of the heavily-laden beasts, the better to care for the great baskets of provisions which were strung on either side of their bellies. From these baskets, at precisely the civilized hour they would have chosen in the hotel, luncheon would be served, al fresco.

But in the meantime the great empty caves, the natural tombs of the hills, beckoned to the travelers, and the party advanced steadily.

The day had become so stifling, by the time the donkeys and their riders were all assembled at the mouth of the first cave deemed safe for exploration, that Mr. Bedales cried halt. The stewards tackled the baskets, white cloths were spread on the large flat stones that scattered the landscape. There was no wine, both in regard for the traditional temperance of Mr. Cook's more domestic excursions, and for the dangers of consuming alcohol in the great heat. Instead, refreshing lemon and orange concoctions were served, magically cooled by some secret of *The Sprite's* kitchens. Luscious melons were offered as a first course, and even Mr. Fountain was to be seen lapping the sweet juices from his chin with an eager tongue, though Henrietta wondered as she watched his simple pleasure how Professor Clémence, who had not joined them, would have fared at the temperance feast.

In spite of her fears and her growing exhaustion, Henrietta was hungry. She had fought her sense of helplessness every inch of the climb to the caves, telling herself that for this one day at least she could make no progress in finding Roddy. The excursion had been delayed for her sake, and was perhaps the most fascinating of a lifetime. As she sat at her mother's side, the great plain and the winding river now far beneath them, she made one final effort to fling herself into the spirit of the occasion. She began to eat her luncheon.

Less than an hour later, she stood with a group of her compatriots in the maw of a deep cavern cut in the hillside. The dragomen hovered at its entrance with the travelers, preparing to light the small magnesium flares which could be carried by one or two of the party into the depths of the cave.

Flares spluttering whitely in contrast to the redstone hills and the yellow earth about them, the group advanced. Mr. Bedales led the way, an Egyptian guide at his elbow. The torchlight illuminated his linen suit, and Henrietta noticed its creases and the intense gleam of his well-polished shoes on the cave's rough ground.

Behind Henrietta and Constance walked the other ladies of the party, and the gentlemen brought up the rear. They spoke in whispers, as if overawed by the ancient solemnity of their surroundings. Kings had lain here waiting for immortality. Their enemies, and the enemies of history, had despoiled their tombs. And yet, when one of the party stumbled somewhere in the dark, Henrietta distinctly heard a child-like giggle—perhaps of fear.

The cave that had been selected for exploration was now empty of all treasure, but the despoilers had been defeated by one aspect of the artistry with which the ancient dynasties had entombed their dead. The walls of the cave, as they came to its innermost depths, were carved in long panels, at eye-level, with pictorial scenes of triumph, of battle, of domestic bliss. And here and there were blocks of hieroglyphics, the ancient Egyptian writings, which their guide explained were hymns of praise to the exploits of the dead kings.

Enthralled by the thought of the history hewn into the rock, Henrietta begged one of the travelers who followed at her heels to allow her to hold a flare so that she might see the writing more clearly. She held it above her head, and narrowed her eyes in its glare, straining to decipher the ancient images. She wondered who the artists and scribes had been, and how many of them had finished their sacred work, and lain down their tools, only to be immured forever with their masters. But of them all, she reflected, it was after all the craftsmen who lived on ... in the work of their hands.

So engrossed was she in her examination of the panels, and of her own philosophy, that she did not notice when the rest of the party began to move away. Further into the cave, the floor sloped downwards, and the way led into a subterranean chamber where only the bravest travelers would venture. In the case of Mr. Bedales's party, this included everybody. They had come so far, they reasoned, that one more peril was but a drop in the ocean. They might stifle below ground, or meet the ghosts of the past, but they had learned in recent weeks that they always lived, to take the next train, the next boat, further into the heart of their adventure. And so, voices now silent, feet treading with added care on the sloping ground, the travelers, with Constance de Vere Smith caught up in their midst before she could miss her daughter, traveled on.

When at last Henrietta realized that her companions had gone further into the cave without her, she wasted no time in following them. The flare held high above her head, her shadow cast like a giant black and white silhouette picture on the cavernous ceilings, she began to descend the slope. But she had not gone far when the shape of the shadows seemed to distort, as if doubled in outline. And the outline that had been added to her own was the shape of a man.

The hairs at the nape of her neck rose under the ribbons that held her bonnet in place. She stopped in her tracks, listened, and took another step forward. The second shadow moved with her. She stumbled, and a stone rattled away into silence at her feet. She could not be sure, but for one terrifying moment she believed that she had heard a ghostly whisper:

"Henrietta!"

With a stifled scream on her lips, Henrietta turned then, and ran back up the slope towards the mouth of the cave.

As she did so, she dropped the flare, and it sizzled and died.

With the daylight now ahead of her, she could see her way, but her fear of falling made her keep her head down, watching for every stone and crevice that might trip her. In spite of this, she stumbled again, and almost unable to breathe as she pulled herself to her feet, she leaned for a moment against the rough stone wall.

It was then that she looked up again towards the entrance, and saw the outline of a man standing against the light. He wore a slim-legged European suit. He was hatless. She glimpsed short, curled hair touched with gold by the sunlight on the hillside. His face was still in darkness. But she knew at once that the man was her cousin Roddy.

Pausing only to glance behind her to make sure that

she was not followed, she ran towards the open air. Roddy waited for her, and as she reached his side he caught her arm in a firm grip, motioning to her not to speak. They stood in the mouth of the cave, staring into each other's eyes. Roddy's grasp on her arm tightened, and as if they both asked the same question they turned to see if the stewards and dragomen had noticed their presence.

Stretched in the shadows of a great rock, the stewards slept the sleep of the just. The remains of the excellent luncheon they had served lay around them. Further apart, where the donkeys were tethered beneath a small cluster of palm trees, the dragomen also sprawled in deep slumbers. Both stewards and dragomen were preparing themselves sensibly for the return trek.

In spite of the extreme danger of their situation, with Constance de Vere Smith only yards beneath them in the subterranean caves, Roddy and Henrietta found time to smile at the sleeping men, before Roddy whisked his cousin out of the cave, and into the shelter of a deep crevice between two great walls of red rock. It was not until they were several yards into their hiding-place that Roddy released Henrietta's arm. Panting, her emotions mingling alarm with delight, she scowled up at him. He stood before her, his elegant light gray suit unruffled, an infuriating smile on his bronzed face. She stifled an anxious moment when she wondered how he would exist on the return journey to the river without a hat.

"You frightened me!" she hissed at him. And then: "It *was* you at Hamed's yesterday, was it not?"

The smile disappeared. "You're all correct, old girl," he frowned. "But it's *I* who was scared. I don't mind admitting it. I heard voices, and thought the old rascal had arranged some kind of ambush for me. I don't know how long I waited in that demned courtyard, before the boy came. Luckily, it was he who had led me there in the first place, last week."

"Last week???" Henrietta could hardly believe her ears. She began to wonder precisely what her cousin was involved in. Was it the smuggling of gold, or of antiquities? Surely not.

"Roddy," she said, as firmly as she could in view of the effect his proximity had on the fluttering of her heart. "You're—you're not in any *trouble,* are you? I —I saw the package that Hamed sent out to you. Not that I meant to pry. But I have wondered for two whole days almost what was in it!"

"That's no secret between us, old girl," he replied airily. She tried not to flinch at his return to his youthful slang. "In fact it's the contents of that packet I have to see you about. And we must get down to brass tacks. There isn't much time."

"Well, tell me then. What was in the packet?" For an infuriating second Henrietta was tempted to make history repeat itself, and push her cousin into the soft sand that had gathered in the crevice, blown there by the wind from the desert, perhaps untouched for centuries until they stood there together. She waited.

"It's a copy. A perfect copy, in every detail, of the necklet and the alabaster scarab, and the filigree bands of gold that hold the stone in place. It was my idea. I'd heard of the goldsmith chappy's skill. And I went absent without leave from *The Centaur* to see the thing done."

Henrietta was speechless. For Roddy to have gone absent without leave was as extraordinary an event as, say, her mama descending into Mrs. Pillet's kitchen to wash the dishes in the scullery maid's place. It was unheard of, out of character, and—in its implications— akin to madness.

But when she considered what he had also done, commissioned a copy of the sacred necklace and stone, it occurred to her that to have a copy made one had to supply an original. Had her cousin then resorted to the ultimate madness, and stolen the jewel from the predatory Helena before he ran for it?

Her eyes must have expressed something of the genuine fear for his safety this last thought engendered, for Roddy anticipated her question.

"Never fear, old thing," he said earnestly. "I'm no thief. I'm too clever for that, if ye must know. I worked out that if this jewel thing is causing so much stir, then it must be well known. And with any luck, if I found a goldsmith who knew his trade, then he'd be sure to know enough about the sacred stone to make me a fair copy, unseen so to speak, don't ye know?"

For the first time for many hours, Henrietta found that she wanted to laugh. There was something so innocent about her cousin as he stood before her, confiding his tales of villainy and deceit. Innocent, and yet how brilliant in conception his idea had been.

"You mean that you are going to exchange the jewels, and if the Dashawai come out of the eastern desert to claim their property then they'll steal the false one, from the—Greek woman?"

Roddy shook his golden head in mock despair of her apparent naivety. At the same time he chose to ignore the deprecatory manner in which she described the beautiful Helena.

"That would be far too simple, and would mean that I first deceived the prince's friend—which is out of the question—and then would be left holding the infant. I—I mean the real, sacred stone. What would I do with that, I ask you?"

Henrietta had no reply to this. Instead, she waited for him to continue in his own stolid fashion with his account of what he intended to do. She had been used to it for almost twenty years, and it was too late now to expect him to change.

"You see, old girl, I have a *plan*."

She waited.

"And I've followed you up here because I knew the itinerary—don't ask me how—and I guessed that it was the one place in which I could speak with you alone. Even briefly."

"Do you mean you've been following us all the way here?"

"Wrong again, old thing. I got here first. I was here at dawn. My pony—splendid little Arab fellow—is in the leeward of these rocks. As soon as I've told you what I want you to do, I'll be off like the wind. No one will be any the wiser—and you can return to the party and go on to see the Colossi—they're very jolly, but a bit battered about—and generally have a good day of it."

Henrietta leaned against the rock. She closed her eyes. She did not feel at all faint. But she felt giddy, with a mixture of exhilaration and despair. She did not know whether she could take to the new Roddy, but she had to try. He had taken his first, faltering steps towards becoming a man of action, and had perhaps overdone things a little in the process. But having gone so far, if he needed her to complete the matter, she was prepared to do so.

"I'll try, Roddy," she said faintly.

"That's a good girl, don't want you to spoil your day out," he said brightly.

"I mean," she ventured bravely, "that I'll try to help. With your plan." The conception of the trek from Luxor across the Nile, into the hills to Thebes and back, as "a day out" was a novelty that had not occurred to her.

"Ah yes. The plan." Roddy beamed down at her. "It'll take a bit of doing. But there's a spot further on, at the First Cataract, where I think we can pull it off. I refuse to let H.R.H. to be put on the spot like this, you see, and I propose to return the *copy* of the sacred stone to the Dashawai, and let them ride off thinking they've scored on us. But H.R.H. will not have to go through the absolute hell of asking his—his friend—for the return of a gift. As he said the other night—it's quite out of the question."

Henrietta had closed her eyes during the rather long but quite clear account. She opened them, to make quite sure she was not dreaming, and asked:

"But that still does not explain why you need to see me about it, Roddy, does it?"

He looked down at her bewildered blue eyes, and reached out to touch a strand of dark hair that had tumbled from beneath her bonnet when they ran to their hiding place.

"I'd have thought that was obvious. The eyes are different, I'll admit that. Prefer blue eyes in a woman, personally. But the—the build is about the same. Same height, same demned proud lift to the jaw. Surely you've noticed?"

Gradually it dawned on Henrietta that Roddy was trying to tell her of the startling resemblance between herself and the Greek woman first noticed by her father at the opera.

"I do believe it has been noticed," she said in a small voice. "In fact I had wondered, at one time that is, if the likeness was the reason why you paid so much attention to—"

The way in which Roddy then threw back his head and burst into laughter made her fling up her gloved hand and touch his lips with her fingers. The gesture was one born out of fear, and was intended to silence him before they were discovered. But Roddy surprised her by making good use of it, and before she could withdraw her hand she found the fingers clasped in his, and his lips tenderly brushed the golden skin that showed through the tiny aperture where the glove was buttoned at the wrist.

When they at last found the courage to look into each other's eyes, both cousins were serious.

"I'd like to kiss you, Henrietta," Roddy said. "But there's no time." He let go her hand, and she lowered it to her side very slowly, as he went on.

"What I want you to do is this, old girl. There'll be plenty of dinners on board, after the First Cataract. There's a holy place out in the desert where they ride at night. It's a paradise out there, they've told me—the other aides, you know. Well, one night when we've managed to include you in the party, you're going to ride out there with me, old girl. There'll have to be a moon. You'll be disguised as that Greek woman, if that's what you call her—and at your throat I reckon the copy of the stone will shine like the devil. I'll have got word to the Dashawai that you'll be wearing the real thing that night. The spies on board *The Centaur* are ten a penny—they don't fool me—and it's the easiest thing in the world to feed them any information I choose."

With increasing admiration, Henrietta watched her cousin's face as he unfolded his plan. At last, it seemed that he had finished. She took a deep breath. It seemed a terrible thing, to put a stop to his plans, and to damp his enthusiasm—as she knew she had to do.

"Roddy," she said, keeping her voice as calm as she could in the circumstances. "You have to leave *now*. If you are seen by any other members of the party, I cannot guarantee your safety. It's not just that I don't want Mama to know that I came all this way because—" she stopped herself in the very nick of time from admitting to crossing Europe and half of the African continent in his pursuit—"I mean, it is of the utmost importance, Roddy, that you realize there are men, wicked men, who intend to prevent you from doing anything at all about the sacred stone. I sometimes think that they want to make trouble. That they don't want the stone to be returned to the rightful owners at all!"

Roddy looked very thoughtful. "And when I was ill—", she continued.

"When were you ill, Cousin? Are you recovered?" He took her hand again, concern for her plainly written in his blue eyes. But this time she tugged it away.

"A man came to my cabin, while Mama was out. It was the Frenchman. Professor Clémence. He told me that I must warn you, Roddy, not to interfere. I think if they knew you were trying to influence the prince they would not hesitate to kill you!"

Roddy patted her understandingly on the shoulder. The old, familiar gesture did not anger her at all. She drooped a little, from growing fatigue, and he placed an arm around her waist as he led her back towards the mountainside. She did not demur.

"You see, old girl," he murmured, "they're not going to know about this until it's too late. Nobody knows, except us. And when the Dashawai ride out of the desert under the stars and snatch the necklace from your throat, it'll all be over. You'll see!"

"Snatch the necklace from my throat?" she echoed. She was beyond asking questions of her own making now. And the touch of her cousin's hand at her waist made it hard to think clearly.

"You'll see, old thing," he repeated. "And now I think you'd better get back and make your excuses to the others, don't you?"

It was with a sense of unreality that Henrietta rejoined her traveling companions some ten minutes later as they emerged from the cave into the sunlight. She told them that she had felt a slight return of her faintness as they took to the lower slopes of the tombs, and had decided to stay behind and rest, in preparation for the afternoon excursion to the two Colossi. Her story was accepted without question. The party remounted slowly. The baskets were repacked. The small band of riders began the slow descent. And far below the line of colored parasols a fast Arab pony made its sure-footed way back to the river, where a great burnt orange sail flapped lazily above a fast sailing boat that waited for the rider.

CHAPTER ELEVEN

THE SECTION of the great Egyptian river on which *The Sprite* and its intrepid passengers now embarked was the setting for perhaps the least exhausting, and the most entertaining, part of their journey.

With the great monoliths and caves of Thebes still a glittering memory, the party spent the first day back on the steamer in well-earned repose. The spinster ladies were to be found in their shared cabins, unearthing the clothes that had not gone with them to their hotel in Luxor. The men who now remained strolled the deck and surveyed the last miles of Libyan and Arabian desert through which *The Sprite* chugged her way to the city of Assuan. Ahead of them, they told each other, was the furthest bound of their tour, before the return to Cairo. In the vast silence of the Nubian desert, to the east, was such unknown, unchartered territory that even their revered organizer, Mr. Thomas Cook, had as yet not ventured into its mysterious heart.

Not the least happy of the newly embarked human cargo was Constance de Vere Smith herself. For the realization that the three almost identical young Englishmen had apparently left the excursion for some mysterious destination of their own choosing, had at the same time brought to Constance the privilege, promised to her some time ago by Mr. Bedales, of a single cabin.

And while her mama luxuriated in the splendid isolation of a room—albeit to starboard—which would now be her home for the remainder of the steamer excursion, Henrietta herself rejoiced in the occasion the empty second berth in the cabin where she remained now gave her to spread her gowns in all directions, and think of her cousin and his plight undisturbed.

It had not been until she had sunk bereft of all strength after the day out at Thebes into the high, soft bed in the hotel room that the full significance of so much of what Roddy had told her in such haste that afternoon sank home.

Professor Clémence, if he intended his schemes and his threats to trigger off some discreditable action on the part of the royal party in general and her cousin in particular, had shown himself to be a master of the role of agent provocateur. Roddy was even now, she guessed, in close pursuit of *The Centaur*, and by the time they all reached the city of Assuan and the roaring boundary of the First Cataract, would be well on the way to starting a small war. And, if she had understood him correctly, as they stood eyes locked and hearts pounding between the great red stone walls of the rocks at Thebes, she herself was to play a major role in its outcome.

In the emotion of their encounter, and of their necessarily hasty farewell, she had not paused to question the part Roddy had mapped out for her. The thought of posing as the Greek woman who was her double was, she now realized, distasteful to her. But she had no say in the matter, at least not until she met with Roddy again. But by then it might be too late. He had in their recent encounters shown a talent for quick thinking quite new to her, and this might well be followed by speed of action to match.

But far worse than any play-acting he had in mind for her was the prospect of the actual, real-life disaster it might bring in its wake. As she lay on her narrow berth on the first afternoon of the renewed voyage, she found it quite impossible to sleep, for her mind throbbed every time she closed her eyes with the memory of the remark her cousin had made so lightly, about the replica alabaster scarab being snatched from her throat by the rightful owners of the true, sacred stone, by moonlight, and—it would seem—miles from anywhere.

As the full picture of what such a moment would be like etched itself graphically into her imagination, she actually clutched at her young throat where she lay. It was of no comfort to her at that moment to find her smooth, rounded flesh bare of any ornament whatsoever. But this did serve to swing her fevered thoughts from anticipating a (so far) entirely imaginary holocaust to the rather more immediate matter of what she should wear at supper that night on board *The Sprite*.

For, on the first night on the river again in some time, the captain and Mr. Bedales, aided and abetted by Brian Dogharty, Mr. Fountain, and Miss Fountain of Harrogate, had decreed that there should be a gala evening, and that the theme should be one of gentle nostalgia, in which they would be transported to the scene, now so far away, of the front parlor, or (in the case at least of Constance de Vere Smith) the great drawing room, for that most delightful and characteristic feature of their lives at home in England—a musical soirée.

At home in Belgravia, Henrietta had never been enamored of these occasions, and if at all possible had contrived to sit at the back of the rows of small gold chairs which the butler and parlor maid brought from the basement store on the morning of the day in question. At some suitably dramatic, and accordingly loud, turn of events—perhaps in the last verse of a heart-rending ballad, or the last allegro spurt of a rondo for piano and violin, she had been in the habit of putting a hand to her brow, feigning sudden emotion, and making for the door. If observed at all, and her mama was usually far too engrossed in her own triumphs to do so at these events, Henrietta then made her way to the green baize door and the warmth of the kitchen belowstairs.

But not only was there no green baize door, no Mrs. Pillet the cook, and no convenient back row of small gold chairs on board the steamer thousands of miles from Belgravia—there was also no inclination on Henrietta's part to try to escape.

The novelties and grandeurs of the voyage so far, quite apart from the extraordinary events which were unfolding clandestinely, hour by hour, for herself and her cousin, had resulted in a heightened sense of occasion for Henrietta in everything she did, and a strong interest in the character of everyone around her.

The growing ennui that had marred her days in London the previous Season had altogether vanished. Her frustration with the social round had evaporated, because the social round since they had taken the packet at Newhaven had assumed such gargantuan challenge. And now the fact that her companions at the proposed soirée were to be so similar in social standing, in outward appearance, in manners, (on the whole) to those she had left behind in no way constituted a threat to her enjoyment. She saw them instead as so many figures in a strange, new landscape of which she herself was part. Everything, from the valiant struggle of her mama to survive their marathon to the fashionable dots on the veil sported by their diarist-companion Miss Summers of Finchley, had become to Henrietta's fast-developing sensibility matters of intense interest and causes for admiration if not concern. She did not know it, but she was at last selecting for herself a role in life: the happy, willing conspirator in living life to the full. Like all the other intrepid conspirators who traveled with her into Egypt, she did so with zest and vigor.

In the knowledge that with a long, straight section of the river ahead of them *The Centaur* would be drawing away from them fast by now, and that as a consequence she would not see her cousin again for some time—if as he planned he caught up with the royal party—she threw herself now into the celebrations. It was an excellent way, she reflected, of making time pass while she awaited whatever fate Roddy had brought them to, and in any case, she thought that the idea of the musical soirée was an inspiration.

Some hours later, wearing a low-cut crinoline of palest blue silk, a pleated white underskirt swirling above silver slippers, a blue and silver fan in her hand, Henrietta stood at the rails of the steamer and waited for the dramatic moment when the light would turn into darkness, and the Egyptian sun slip in a single, swift movement into its own deep glow. She had soon learnt that here in the desert there was no such romantic nonsense as watching the sunset. There was light, and there was dark. And no two ways about it.

Having learned also, through her long night of fever, that with the darkness came the treacherous change of temperature, Henrietta drew a soft white cape around her bare shoulders as the moment approached. She knew that her mother would soon join her, from her cabin on the other side of the first deck, and she made no intention of starting the gala evening with a scolding. The silken ties of the cape firmly secured, she leaned again on the steamer's rails, and as the light failed she drew in a sharp breath of wonder at the deep velvet texture of the night.

Moments later, she knew that she was not alone.

And that her newly arrived companion on the otherwise deserted deck was not her mother, who would most certainly not have arrived unannounced.

Her long moonstone earrings glittering in the dark, Henrietta turned her head. She found herself looking into the ardent gaze of Brian Dogharty, the American. She did not know whether she found his proximity more disconcerting than his habit of admiring her silently from afar. She only knew that the interruption was unwelcome. With a most unpromising nod of her head, she returned to her scrutiny of the river at night. "You will soon become accustomed to the darkness," the pleasant Bostonian voice observed.

"You are too kind, sir," she replied. "I had thought the stewards had forgotten the flares."

"Ah!" She knew that he smiled. "There is much more than torchlight planned for tonight. I myself have been put in charge of a firework display. The Fountains of Harrogate and the ship's doctor are at this very moment lighting a thousand candles in the dining room. The stewards are preparing a flambeé dessert! There will be fire, and firelight, everywhere!"

In spite of her determination not to encourage him, Henrietta was intrigued by the information. There was nothing she adored more than a firework display ever since her childhood, and in the de Vere Smith household it was not the sort of event that had been encouraged. It was, to her father's way of thinking, too dangerous and noisy, and in her mother's view too frivolous by far.

Turning to the American, Henrietta asked if all was ready, did he know, in the saloon—for the concert? Since he knew so much.

The moonstones glimmmered. "How splendid your earrings will look in the candlelight, ma'am," Brian Dogharty murmured. "I have noted since that very first evening in our Paris hotel, that you have a gift for wearing the right jewel at the right time."

With a jolt of suspicion, Henrietta wondered if his

words were intended as some knowing hint that he was aware of Roddy's plan for her. They referred so aptly to the adventure that might lie ahead for her that the man must surely be informed? If he wanted to discuss what amounted to a national secret with her, however, he was going to be disappointed. She kept her mouth in a firm, closed line, and contented herself with the merest hint of a smile, as if at a compliment well-turned.

The moment passed. There was no answering smile in the man's eyes, and no sign of annoyance in the bearded face. He seemed, as he leaned on the rail at her side—but she was glad to note at a respectable distance—to resume his interest in the view.

He had been quite correct, she now saw, in his promise that she would become accustomed to the darkness. The view across the dark swirl of the waters where *The Sprite* passed was now filled with looming shadows. She made out a low huddled cluster of what she guessed to be mud-built houses. Above them a group of tall palm trees swayed in silhouette. Somewhere the bleat of a goat broke the silence, followed by the singing thwack of a stick brought down in a cruel blow.

On the bank of the river the goat then ran into view, and the figure of its master followed. A ragged outline topped by the usual fez. The long stick in the man's hand swooped again in the darkness. The goat fled. Further along the bank it sought refuge in a group of native workers who still plied the creaking machinery of the *shaduf*.

"I am inclined to agree with your brave countrywoman when I see how hard life is here for the natives. How endlessly they labor—and for such small reward." The American did not turn from the rail. The bleating goat vanished before Henrietta replied.

"My countrywoman, sir?" she asked politely.

"May I?" To her annoyance, he placed a hand at her elbow at that moment, and turned to where the usual row of cane chairs lined the deck. Through the softness of her cape she was aware of firm fingers. It was difficult to ignore their message.

She hesitated. "I am certain my mother will not now be long in joining me," she attempted to discourage him. He led her to the chairs. "But until then—" she said feebly....

"Until then you will suffer my conversation with all the politeness of your breeding!" His voice was all sardonic laughter, though he did not smile. For the second time since he had appeared at her side, she wondered what this man really wanted of her.

"That, sir, is not a word we use," she said stiffly, playing for time.

This time he smiled. He ushered her to a chair, and eased it away from its fellows so that there would be ample room for her silk skirts.

"Then, ma'am," he said suavely, "I give you *my* word that *the* word will not sully my lips again this evening!"

She settled helplessly in the chair, and looked round for some sign that her mother, or even some other member of the party, was about to join them. There was no one else in sight.

"But stimulating, general conversation—that is always welcome, Mr. Dogharty," she told him carefully. "If—if kept within reasonable bounds."

As if her words had some sensual, physical message wrapped in their formal rebuke, he moved his foot at that moment an inch or so away from the hem of her skirt. She looked down, and at once regretted the glance. It could so easily have been interpreted as proof of some interest in his proximity, which was not the case at all.

"I do not think that the countrywoman of whom I first spoke would have conceded to bounds of any kind in her conversation," Brian Dogharty resumed. He seemed not to have noticed her small lapse, and with some relief she attempted to engage in the polite discussion from which it seemed there was in any case to be no escape.

"Lady Lucie Duff Gordon. You have heard of her, no doubt?"

Henrietta was prepared to admit that she had indeed heard of the celebrated soldier's wife who had come so bravely to Egypt to die of consumption, but had succeeded in prolonging her life and in helping the poor and diseased of this land of Egypt. She had become a legend in her own time—and she was the sort of woman whom Henrietta admired with all her heart.

"Lady Lucie observed in one of her letters," Brian Dogharty continued, seeing that Henrietta's interest was aroused, "that Egypt is one vast plantation, where the master works his slave without even feeding him."

Henrietta wondered silently if by "the master" the writer had intended that the Nile itself was a tyrant to those who lived along its banks. But Brian Dogharty seemed to interpret the statement otherwise.

"As you may imagine, ma'am, this has some significance for us back at home. Not that our landowners are so powerful as the Khedive who rules these parts— did you know that even our steamer—*The Sprite* itself—is owned by that illustrious gentleman, and that gold, actual gold, had to change hands for its charter?"

Henrietta's eyes widened. Mr. Cook and his organization were full of surprises. Was there no end to their enterprise?

"Or as the petty princes who rule this region we approach now," the American went on, warming to his theme. "*We* have to watch our P's and Q's back home. We need our workers. Out here—life seems so cheap. The people have nothing."

"You talk of petty princes," Henrietta said thoughtfully. She did not want to launch into the controversial matter of slavery as such. "But I see no sign of their palaces! The most princely residence I have seen since we disembarked at Alexandria is, I think—apart from the great temples and tombs, of course—the house of a jeweler in the last town."

As soon as the words were spoken, Henrietta realized her error. She bit her lips in self-criticism. What was it about this man that made her so forget herself? Surely she was not so deprived of admiration that his glowing eyes upon her made her forget the loyalty she owed to Roddy, in both his life at the prince's side and as her beloved cousin?

To her relief, the moment went unnoticed, or so she hoped. For it was lost for all time in the excitement of two arrivals on deck: the flares that were brought by the stewards, and the brilliant, flame-clad figure of Constance de Vere Smith herself.

"Oh, the princes do not live in these shanty towns," Brian Dogharty told her casually, as he stood to his feet to greet her mama.

Constance was almost upon them, as Henrietta asked quickly of her companion where, then, did the local princes have their houses? She was once more strongly aware that the conversation had taken a turn that had some relevance to the matter she and Roddy had in hand.

"Do they live in Assuan?" she persisted. "Shall we see the palaces there?" She had to wait for her answer while the American eased her mother's form into a third cane chair, and bowed over a hand that flashed with rubies and diamonds. Constance de Vere Smith had not wasted the opportunity to dress for a gala occasion.

"I was about to tell your daughter, ma'am," Brian Dogharty said, "that in Assuan you will find the great merchants, the great entrepreneurs of this land. But the princes of the blood—those you will find far into the desert, that is if you have the temerity to make your way to their tents."

This last, third oblique reference by the American, if reference it was, to the adventures with which Henrietta had so far imagined herself to be quite secretly involved, still rang in her mind as she and her mother approached the dining room. The supper gong still rang out from the steamer, and across the Nile, as Constance de Vere Smith sailed in ahead of the other passengers, and proceeded to ensure that protocol had been strictly honored and the placement at table, mixed though it was due to the novel arrangements for the gala evening, had been organized with the proper social dexterity. Her lorgnette greatly in evidence above her shimmering décolleté, she moved imperiously from table to table, murmuring quiet satisfaction, until she reached her own corner table, which gave her the dominant view of the dining room she had acquired, in her usual fashion, from the first night aboard.

But tonight, she and Henrietta were obliged to share their table. The company was—apart from the de Vere Smiths—turned topsy-turvy for the gala, it was clear that Yorkshire miners were to rub shoulders with the party's equivalent of kings, when Mr. Fountain and his sister bowed and edged their way into their places opposite Constance and Henrietta respectively.

In the brief discussions she had conducted with her daughter on the social desirability—or otherwise—of the other members of their party, Constance de Vere Smith had found it difficult to take exception to the standing of their present companions. To have made a fortune from coal mines was not exactly, she calculated, the same as being In Trade. It was true that commerce was involved. But at a distance. And then, the gentleman in question was so polite, and his poor spinster sister so innocuous, that had exception been taken it would have been quite an effort to prolong. It was a narrow margin, a near thing—but they were in close quarters for some months, and it was characteristic of Henrietta's mother that she therefore assessed the whole thing, at least for the duration, as a cross she must bear.

Unfortunately, it became evident long before the main meat courses were consumed, that enjoying the new advantages of each sleeping in a single cabin had blinded both mother and daughter to the drawbacks.

In the matter of planning what they were to wear for each occasion, for instance, it seemed that disaster had struck from the start: it was as they sat down that Henrietta thankfully concealed the white pleating of her underskirt beneath the white tablecloth itself. It had suddenly dawned on her that her mama's choice of crimson for the occasion, and her own discreet blue, had almost landed them in the absurd situation of being dressed in a combination of the three colors of the national flag. She could only hope that no one present would notice, and could only thank her providential stars that the absent Roddy—for whom her heart ached even as the thought sprang to her mind—was not there to blurt out some jolly observation on how jolly fine both mother and daughter looked, to the eyes of any soldier or patriot in the room.

The second disastrous moment struck for Henrietta when she looked down, quite by chance, at her own fair décolleté, and became aware that a bright red pin-prick of unknown origin had suddenly appeared above the blue silk. A second later, she sensed a sudden stab rather higher, in the region of her left shoulder. Hastily, she plucked her fan from where it lay beside her plate, and making some semblance of snapping it open rather fast, as if overcome by the heat, she contrived to give a good strong tap at the place where she now realized she had either been stung by an insect—or to her mortification, bitten by a flea! The powder with which her mama had so far so successfully routed their natural foes had been removed, with mama herself, to the new single cabin—and Henrietta had at once fallen victim to the liberated pests.

The rest of the meal she spent in acute misery, of body and spirit, as the creature—or creatures—proceeded to feast upon her fair skin, and polite society forbade her to take action against them. Her mother was so absorbed in the excellent meal, and in giving their companions at table the benefit of her worldly wisdom, that she was for once unconcerned with Henrietta's appearance, much less with her plight. Mr. Fountain, fortunately for Henrietta, had made a great show from the hors d'ouevre onwards, of *not* letting his gaze fall on her bare shoulders, so she could hope perhaps that they would reach the end of the meal, with the only other member of the foursome doubtless too refined to remark on it, without any reference to the numerous red spots that now ruined her appearance.

It was with enormous relief that, after an announcement from Mr. Bedales to the effect that the musical soirée would now commence in the large saloon, Henrietta watched the other travelers leave the dining room, and keeping a strategic distance behind her mama managed to pull her white wrap about her shoulders, at the same time pretending to shiver slightly in the night air as they made their way on deck to the large saloon.

Quite against her inclinations of earlier in the day, Henrietta murmured as they entered the saloon that she would prefer to sit in the back row of the seats set out for the audience, near the main exit; she was afraid of a recurrence of her fever if she sat in the very center of the now crowded assembly.

While her mama forged her way, reluctantly agreeing to leave her to a place in the middle of the front row, Henrietta took the opportunity to give a final, quite efficacious scratch at one or two of the painful bites under cover of her shawl. Mr. Bedales then walked from the side of the room to a commanding place on the platform in front of the small orchestra— the same players who had appeared and reappeared throughout their voyage so far—and announced that before the charming company commenced its entertainment there would be an overture of infinite suitability: none other than that penned by the master, Signor Giuseppe Verdi, for his opera *Aïda*, which he had created for the grand opening of the Suez Canal not long ago, but unfortunately not quite in time.

As the spirited music struck across the stifling room

at her burning ears, Henrietta reflected miserably that if anyone in the company there that night knew what the spirit of Egypt was all about it was she: first fever, now fleabites, and tomorrow, for all she knew, assassination. She had in the first weeks of the year sampled the entire gamut of oriental experience. And as the ripple of applause that heralded the next item broke about her, she shifted once more on her chair. It was as bad as Belgravia. And no below-stairs to which to escape.

For the next hour, she endured a wavering ballad from Miss Fountain, a dubiously humorous monologue from the ship's doctor (why was it that medical men always displayed such exuberance when off duty?), and what seemed an endless duet for violin and piano from the orchestra's leader and the lady diarist.

Then, the pain of the fleabites somewhat abating, Henrietta sat up with renewed interest as Lance Morton made his way to the pianist's side and conducted a discussion with her over several sheets of music.

In the last few days, she had little opportunity of seeking him out, and had become resigned to the fact that their shared interest, in what was to become of the sacred scarab, had to be set aside until they found themselves closer to Assuan and to the royal party again.

Now, she looked at the distinguished, older man with some concern. His usually pale complexion and clear gray eyes were reddened and clouded. The eternal cigar was missing. He coughed more than once as he talked with Miss Summers, turning his head politely away from her—so that it was Henrietta who glimpsed the pain in his expression. There was no doubt in her mind as she watched him take his stand in front of the piano, in preparation for singing accompanied by the diarist from Finchley, that Lance Morton had contracted a fever. And if it were as debilitating as her own had been, what role could he now be expected to play in the action that Roddy had devised?

Her anxiety was momentarily allayed in the moments that followed, for Lance Morton, his fine head held high, white teeth gleaming in the fevered face, began to sing in a tenor voice of quite extraordinary sweetness. The song, a story of a man who returns to his home far in the English countryside after years in distant lands, was one she did not know.

As she listened, the voice and the words brought tears to her eyes. She sat very upright, staring ahead. She had a sudden heart-warming vision of her brother Charlie, trudging over the fields of his small Gloucestershire farm back home in England. At his side, his spaniel dog. A rifle under one arm. Low graystone walls on either side of his path. It was a scene she herself had always loved. And now, how far away it seemed!

The applause with which Lance Morton's song was received burst so loudly upon her ears that she realized she had been daydreaming for the last verse or two, and with an effort she brought herself back to the present, and stood with the others in the room to applaud again. But when a loud voice demanded an encore, she turned disapprovingly to see who it was. She could not believe that the rest of the audience had not noticed that Lance Morton was a sick man. Then, sure enough, he bowed, shook his head, and made a hasty retreat from the platform. To leave the room, he had however to pass close by to where Henrietta stood. As he did so, she reached out to him, and laid a hand on his sleeve.

"My friend," she whispered urgently, "I can see you are unwell. Why do you not inform the ship's doctor?"

"You are kindness itself," Lance Morton told her. Now that he was nearer she could see that he trembled. "It is something that must take its course. An old friend. The curse of my travels. Malaria. Promise me something, if you can?"

"Of course. Anything." Henrietta did not care now whether anyone else, or even her mother, noticed that she and Lance Morton spoke so urgently together.

"Promise me that if I am not well by the time *The*

Sprite moors at Assuan that you will see this thing through. You and your cousin."

Henrietta gripped his arm. "Get well, Lance. You know what stuff Roddy is made of. It is you who taught me. We will not let you down."

The last she saw of Lance Morton as he staggered through the door and out into the air was a picture of a man exercising almost superhuman control. His face now deathly in the light of the flares on deck, he paused for a second, and then with heavy tread made off in the direction of his quarters. As she watched him, she knew that for the duration of the voyage, she and her cousin stood alone. The American Brian Dogharty, in the conversation she had conducted with him that evening, had shown that either he knew too much about her secret activities, in which case she could not trust him with a single word more, or that his interest in her was entirely personal. She was inclined to settle for the latter explanation, and to take the three strangely relevant remarks he had made as mere accident and coincidence. Had he really been on the trail of the matter of the sacred scarab, would he have risked such blatant remarks?

As she turned to resume her seat, however, any worries that beset Henrietta were diminished instantly— in the face of a new dilemma. Above the feathered heads, between the jeweled ears, and beyond the shining baldness of the back views of the company, Henrietta was aware of a quiver of crimson, a swooping first note, and the gleam of diamonds and rubies on an eloquent hand. She sank, as if mesmerized, onto her chair. She drew her wrap about her as if, like some magic garment in a fairy tale of long ago, it would make her invisible.

Her mother had begun to sing.

And then, to her joy, the unexpected happened. Constance de Vere Smith—who rarely sang for her Belgravia set and never for her own family—had found her voice in the heart of the Nile. The intoxication of the journey, the grandeur of all they had seen, had done its work. The popular drawing room ballad she sang for the excursionists spoke of love unrequited, of feelings unspoken, of devotion lost in the grave. To its sentiment, Constance de Vere Smith brought solemnity and conviction. Her voice swooped and soared, and died to a whisper, and the very windows of *The Sprite* rattled in their panes as the applause began.

Looking back on the scene many months later, Henrietta considered it to have been the highlight of her mother's journey. It could have as well taken place in London, and yet it had not. It had needed the stimulus of their voyage to awaken the artist in her mother, and, strangely, the scene was never repeated.

But an hour after it had ended, a scene infinitely more dramatic took place on the steamer's deck.

The Sprite had been moored for the final celebrations. It would not have been practical to give a display of fireworks from a moving craft. As they came to rest, and the sandbanks close beneath them in the shallows took the steamer's weight, Henrietta found herself at her mother's side. Mother and daughter clutched at the rails as *The Sprite* lurched slightly into position. They were still gazing vaguely at the riverbank, waiting for the announcement that the firework display would begin, when a whisper ran through the line of passengers that waited with them. It began like a small spark in the prows, ran like a current through those nearest to the bow, and came to rest when it reached Constance de Vere Smith herself.

No sooner had the words of the rumor tingled in her ear than Constance took her daughter's arm, and marched her past the other passengers, to a place in the bow itself. As they came to a standstill, Henrietta still wondering what had prompted her mother to change their position so unexpectedly, the firework display made an impromptu start. From the bridge above where they stood, the captain of *The Sprite* could be seen gesticulating wildly in the light of a blazing candle. Then a rocket hissed into the darkness, and another followed. In seconds, the air above them was filled with sparks. Flying beams of fire burst into sprays of color, and died against the sky. The pungent, acrid smell that Henrietta remembered from bonfire nights spent at the homes of her friends in the country filled their nostrils. They were silent.

Then, as a giant rocket burst high in the air above them and showered the river with golden reflections, the cries began. Small gasps of surprise. Murmurs of respect. From Henrietta's mama, a furious bellow stifled almost too late, before she turned and marched her daughter back to her cabin for the night.

For some yards ahead, in the rocket's golden light, they had seen another steamer moored. The firework display must have been too much of a temptation for the distinguished travelers who now stood in the stern of *The Centaur*. Their necks were strained to catch the beauty of the fire in the sky above them. They wore dark capes against the night air. But they made no attempt to disguise themselves. And in one second flat Constance de Vere Smith had recognized the heir to the throne, and her sister's only son, standing side by side only yards from where she stood with her daughter. They had come two thousand miles or more, to find themselves confronted by a sight they could have seen any night of the Season, at the opera house itself. And no one would have dared attempt to persuade Constance de Vere Smith that coincidence alone had led the cousins, Roddy and Henrietta, to this moment far from home.

CHAPTER TWELVE

AT BREAKFAST next morning in the dining room of *The Sprite*, Henrietta was conscious not so much of the inquisitive eyes of the rest of the passengers and of the crew, but rather of the way in which no glances came her way. It was suddenly as if some rule had been laid down by the captain that passengers using the dining room before eleven a.m. should not on any account raise their eyes from their kedgeree, or let their gaze wander from their grilled mushrooms and bacon. The rigors of an English country house breakfast were transposed so successfully to the room that had been the scene of such gala festivities the night before that Henrietta found it almost impossible to believe that she was in the same place.

And yet the solid, moving form of the steamer was still beneath them and the determined chug of the engines as she made her way to her last halt on the great river before the turn for home told Henrietta unmistakably that whether her mother liked it or not, they were still in inexorable pursuit of *The Centaur*.

She had no doubt that their companions on the voyage would sooner or later expunge from their shared memories of its most dramatic moments the scene which had followed the discovery of the royal party in the blaze of lights from the rockets. No one had asked, and no one had been told, why she had been marched from the firework display by her mama. Nor did the stewards dare to question her mama's command to retrieve her luggage from her new cabin and return it, however late the hour, to where her daughter sat—in solitary confinement in their previous, shared cabin. It was clear to everyone, and especially to Henrietta, that Constance de Vere Smith intended to spend the remainder of the journey in maternal vigil in the portside berth, as before.

But Henrietta had some things left in her favor. By the time both mother and daughter awoke next morning, *The Centaur* had disappeared from view. There would be ample opportunity, she believed, to explain everything to her mother's satisfaction before they came within sight or sound again—if ever—of the royal party. She had not lied to her mother, as yet. She hoped that there would be no need to do so. Her mother had guessed at her duplicity in planning the Nile journey from the start, but she could still explain that Maria Newcastle had been at the hub of the whole business—and that she herself had been tempted and had fallen. It was to her advantage, she now recalled, that Maria Newcastle, a favorite at court in more senses than one, was an old rival and long-established enemy of her mother. She had observed them both at social functions in the course of the recent Seasons since her coming-out, and had judged their mutual dislike and disapproval by the extent of their cries of mutual admiration.

She would blame the whole escapade on Maria Newcastle. She would throw herself on her mother's mercy. She would even hope to rely on her mother's admiration for the prince. But she would not hope to persuade her that his presence in Egypt was purely a matter of revisiting ancient monuments. For at his side on the night before the woman Helena had stood. There was no other woman on deck, nor, as Henrietta well knew, on board. She had watched the Greek woman turn and push her way out of sight, past Professor Clémence and other members of the royal party who had been enticed to the stern to watch the display. But the move had been made too late. Mama had most certainly seen, and recognized, the cloaked figure so like her own daughter. And she had most certainly known what the role of such a beauty would be.

By discreet and whispered questioning of the steward as her mother at last rose from the breakfast table and led her back across the dining room, her head held high, Henrietta ascertained that they had a further twenty-four hours in which to reach Assуan, and that most of the journey would be spent full steam ahead. Knowing full well that her own journey would be spent in full confinement if she did not act fast, Henrietta determined to tackle her mama on their return to the cabin and throw herself on her mercy.

Constance de Vere Smith had distinguished herself by maintaining an almost total silence since the disaster of the night before. She had pretended to sleep as soon as the lights in the shared cabin were extinguished, and mother and daughter had spent long hours staring into the darkness waiting for the other to make first move. But they were both strongwilled, and both had much to lose. They had waited for the confrontation as long as possible. Now, as they entered the cabin and the door closed behind them, each knew that it could be delayed no longer.

But at this juncture, the fact that they had procrastinated to such an extent proved the saving of Henrietta's soul. For as they each sat gloomily on their narrow beds, each waiting still for the other to broach the subject uppermost in their minds, Constance de Vere Smith's eyes lighted on a long parchment envelope that lay amongst her objets de toilette on the miniature dressing table.

The envelope was addressed to Mrs. Constance de Vere Smith in an exquisite copperplate hand. Henrietta, watching her mother open it, could tell even at a distance that the missive was from a distinguished correspondent. It certainly showed none of the haphazard, ink-blotted image she would have expected had it contained a communication from Roddy. Whoever it was who had written to her mother, she could see in the moments that followed it was someone very important indeed.

As she read and reread the cream parchment, and then refolded it in its single fold before she returned it to the envelope, Constance de Vere Smith maintained a thoughtful silence. Once or twice, Henrietta thought she detected a slight frown between her mother's arched brows. But the brow above the eyes that were eventually turned on her across the short span of the cabin was smooth, untroubled. There was a short silence. Then Constance de Vere Smith spoke.

"There are times," she said formally, "my dear child," the tone still cold, "when one has to turn a blind eye to things which, in the normal course of events, would be of the utmost significance. Things which should not, I repeat, go uncurbed. Deception is not a peccadillo. Deception between mother and child is unforgivable." She sighed, and moved in a stately fashion to her bed. As she sat down, she retrieved her reticule from beneath her, and with a great show of ceremony placed the letter in its depths.

Henrietta waited hopefully. She knew better than to spoil what for her mama was turning into a dramatic moment to equal her performance on the steamer's small stage the night before.

"You see, Henrietta," she continued, "in this matter

151

of your unfortunate inability to break the ties of childhood... so weak are you in this matter, in fact, that we find ourselves half way across the world in its pursuit... in this matter I find that my role as a mother, who should in the normal way of things have the authority to stamp out such a comedy, has been drastically curtailed. In a word, I find that my hands have been tied. And by a friend in high places. I may say the highest in the land."

Henrietta sat dumbfounded, and wondered what her mother would have to say next. If it was the prince himself to whom her mother referred by the phrase "highest in the land," she must be suffering from some delusion triggered off by the shock of the scene on deck the night before. To Henrietta's certain knowledge, H.R.H. was not by any stretch of the imagination a friend of her mother's. Nor likely to become one.

The explanation was in fact never to be completed. Rather than question her mother and lead to the subject that seemed might otherwise stay unmentioned between them, Henrietta allowed her claim to friends in high places to go unchallenged. As she sat in continued silence on her own berth, she was soon to be rewarded for her decision.

Her mother stood again and took a single pace into the center of their cabin. She looked down at Henrietta.

"I have another close friend in the upper echelons of our Society, at home in England," she said icily. "You will not often have mingled in such company. And I hope that that small comfort will be left to me yet. For the—the person in question has developed ideas greatly above her birth, and has brought nothing but humiliation, and wealth, upon herself. Maria Newcastle—"

Henrietta suppressed a gasp of apprehension with some difficulty. Surely the whole story of Maria Newcastle and the gossip that had led them here to Egypt in the wake of the royal party had not reached her mother in some scurrilous anonymous letter? Had the whole way in which her mother had read and reread the copperplate writing only moments ago been nothing but a charade, given to teach her a lesson? She was not accustomed to such subterfuge in her mama—and she was soon to be relieved of her suspicions.

"Maria Newcastle—" her mother repeated, "is an example, I hasten to explain, that I hope will be a lesson to all young girls who find themselves faced with temptation. Temptation in the form of the favor of princes. The adventures of soldiery. The fleshpots. No—" she gestured to Henrietta not to interrupt her. "I use strong language, I know. And I use it advisedly. For, if you are to dine in the company which I saw revealed—exposed—with my own eyes under the glare of those wretched fireworks less than twelve hours since, then I owe it to my role as a mother to warn you. On board that vessel of shame that lies ahead of us, our dear prince—our dear Queen's own son—is beset by those who would beg his favors, by the ne'er-do-well young soldiery of our time, and—by the fleshpots in the form of That Woman."

"But Mama!" Henrietta jumped up from her bed, unable to believe her ears. The slight on Roddy's own profession, the slight on the prince himself, she could ignore. What she could not believe was that she had heard her mother say she was to dine with the unfortunate ne'er-do-well, and to be allowed at the table of the beloved but misled prince whom he served.

"Mama! Do you mean then that you have received an invitation on my behalf? That you agree I may go to dine on the royal boat? *The Centaur?* May I see? When is it to be? It was that in the letter, was it not?"

All the humiliation of the night before, and the anxiety of the sleepless hours that had followed, fell away from Henrietta in a moment, as she danced about the small cabin and paused only to hug her mother soundly.

"I am not at liberty to tell you what the letter disclosed—or did not disclose." Constance de Vere Smith resumed her normal portentous manner, clearly pleased by the embrace. "It is sufficient, in view of your recent display of deviousness...I'll not call it cunning... that you know you are to dine with His Royal Highness and company on the night after we arrive in Assuan. An equerry will call for you. They do not yet specify which of the numerous young men I do not doubt are cavorting aboard the ship that will be."

Not daring to mention Roddy's name, Henrietta hugged the knowledge to herself that if it was not Roddy who was sent by H.R.H. to fetch her to *The Centaur* it would not be long after that that her cousin would put in an appearance. As she reflected how worried she had been only hours before, with Lance Morton on his sickbed and her mother aware at last of Roddy's presence in Egypt, she wondered at her capacity for recovery. The announcement her mother had just made left her with only vague fears of what the night on *The Centaur* might bring. All that she knew was that she was soon to be with Roddy again, that there was no need for subterfuge anymore, and that she would wear her amber gown.

"You will, of course, have to wear something other than the amber gown...this time." Her mother seemed to have read her thoughts, and, caught out at last, Henrietta raised her eyes appealingly.

"Did you know where I was, then, Mama?" she asked weakly. "When I dined out with Lance Morton as escort?"

"I am mortified to have to confess," Constance said with the beginning of a wry smile, "that I was in fact deceived at the time. But now, of course, I can put two and two together. It is quite obvious that you were on board the royal steamer that night. And equally obvious that you cannot possibly wear the same gown."

With such momentous subjects as her own deceit and her assignations with her cousin dismissed and put in the shade by the issue of which dress she should wear for the next meeting, Henrietta was happily able to avoid the pending war with her mama, and for the whole of the next day, while *The Sprite* steamed on under the glare of day and the passengers lay in their cabins, or under the awnings on deck, mother and daughter busied themselves with needle and thread, whilst the stewards padded to and fro with flatirons and sponges and newly laundered linen. The result was that by the time *The Sprite* moored at the great city of Assuan, a gown of exquisite trimness and freshness, edged with white lace on its crisp black and white ground, hung in pride of place in the de Vere Smiths' cabin, and Henrietta herself prepared to disrobe and bathe in preparation for the evening before her.

It was not until then that she remembered the fleas. As she stepped out of her white cotton underslip, and began to unbutton her bodice, she heard a cry of horror from her mother's bed. Turning sharply, expecting to find either a scorpion nestled in the maternal bedclothes or a spider hovering in mid-air above them, Henrietta found that her mother was gaping at her own daughter. And more specifically, at the blotched shoulders that now rose revealed from the straps of the bodice.

"Henrietta! Where have you been? What have you been doing to come out like this? Your shoulders! The prince! What would your father say?"

With a despairing half sob, she almost threw herself from her bed and ran to where the dress they had prepared with such care hung in waiting. Having expected her mother to come to *her*, Henrietta watched with some amusement as she now wrenched the dress down, searched for scissors in her reticule, and began feverishly to unpick the narrow lace that edged the low neck of the black and white confection.

As she did so, she muttered to herself that this would never have happened had she not deserted her daughter in their dear little cabin. The Persian powder would have prevented this disaster, and in her selfishness she had carried it off to the privacy of her new berth. The lace trim removed, she then leapt to her feet again, rummaged once more in the reticule, and producing a small jar—began to shower the cabin liberally with its contents. "No daughter of mine goes before royalty with fleas in her corsage!" she cried. "I have a deep lace collar that will cover what damage has been done. And this, in the meantime, will ensure that those pests do not strike again!"

It was after nightfall that a tap at their cabin door and a whispered call from the steward announced that Henrietta's escort to the royal steamer had arrived. At her mother's insistence, Henrietta had remained resting, her shoulders dabbed every half hour with cooling lotions obtained from Dr. Fayum, until the very last moment at which she could safely begin to dress and still be in time for the dinner was upon her.

Unwilling to go to the dining room herself until she knew that her daughter was safely on her way to *The Centaur,* Constance de Vere Smith had sat with her, and was still issuing directives as to how to behave in the presence of royalty when the summons came.

With a gentle kiss on her mother's cheek, and a reassuring tap from her mother's fan, Henrietta opened the door of the cabin. She was, if she were honest, greatly relieved to find that the young equerry who waited for her some yards away at the top of *The Sprite's* gangway was not her cousin. She did not think she was quite capable, as yet, of conducting a meeting with Roddy and his aunt so far from home. The upstairs drawing room in the Belgravia house was bad enough, but at least there she had the long curtains in which to bury her face when things got out of hand.

But from now on, she knew in her heart, she did not want her meetings with her cousin and her mama to be the travesties of forced family heartiness they had always been of late. She hoped that when all this adventure she had so unwittingly brought down about their ears was over and done with—if ever that day came—a new era would dawn for them. An era in which Roddy could look his aunt in the eye, and speak his mind like a man. It was a scene she had long hoped for, and which had so far eluded them. But she instinctively knew that if all went well for Roddy now, in his plan to save his prince and his country from disaster, then his behavior in the presence of her mama would undergo a radical change.

So it was that she made her way to *The Centaur*, in the small boat sent for her, with a light heart. She wore her white wrap about her, and her mother's high white lace collar concealed the remains of her blemishes. To detract from the plainness of the collar, she wore her mother's diamonds. In her bronze hair, plaited in a daringly new way at the nape of her neck, there shone a cluster of diamond leaves. She knew that she presented an entirely different image from the first night on board *The Centaur* with Lance Morton at her side, and she took some comfort in the fact that it was also so different from anything the sultry Helena could hope to achieve.

From the expression in the eyes of the young equerry who sat facing her, as the small boat swept across the dark stretch of water that lay between *The Sprite* and the royal steamer, she also knew that the effect of her image was not unattractive. She recognized the fair young man as one of the three who had originally joined the Thomas Cook party in Paris, and he was, if she remembered correctly, the one who had also winked at her with the air of something of a conspirator on the night she had first been received by Prince Edward aboard *The Centaur*. Now the open admiration in his eyes, which she could see clearly in the proximity of their situation in spite of the darkness, gave her the courage she needed. She was still unsure what the evening would bring, or what would be asked of her as it took its course.

She smiled at her escort as their small craft drew near to the mooring chosen for *The Centaur*. A cry from its deck welcomed them in the darkness. A ropeladder swung lazily from the rails, and above it, as she looked up, Henrietta thought for a moment that she glimpsed her cousin's face. But the small boat moved on, to where a more negotiable boarding-ladder and platform awaited her. She gathered her white wrap about her in preparation. It was then that she looked at the sky, and from behind a low cloud, which she had thought earlier on was an unusual sight in the clear skies above the Nile, slipped a full, brilliant moon.

As the almost white light bathed the whole scene around her, Henrietta gasped at the transformation it made of everything she could see. She did not know it, but her own face gleamed silver, her eyes shone strangely, and the diamonds in her hair flashed like blue flames in the white glare from above. Opposite her, the young equerry's fair hair glowed silver, too, and the waters of the river on either side of their boat were like the mottled gray-green scales of a giant fish.

She had heard tales of moon-madness from her Nanny, and from the nursery-maid who had always served her tea in rooftop children's quarters in the London house on Nanny's day off. But she had never given much thought to whether or not she believed them.

Now, as she leaned to one side of the boat, and gazed into the strangely luminous waters, she wished that her hands were bare, as they had been when she fished for shrimps and crabs as a child on the beach each summer. Her gloved hands forbade her to dabble her fingers in the silver river. But they did not prevent her from gazing into its moonlit depths.

She did not know what happened next, exactly. She remembered a low cry of warning from the native boatmen who rowed them to *The Centaur*. At least she took it to be a warning. Nor did she quite understand why her escort leaned forward then, and pushed her even further to one side where she sat. Whatever he intended, however, the result was clear enough. The silver-green waters rose up towards her; she dipped, a black and white reflection, to meet them as they rose. She saw the waters part rather than felt them. And seconds later her heavy skirts dragged about her, her legs flailed helplessly, and the ice-cold river embraced her.

The flurry of cries on the deck of *The Centaur* told her that help was near. The equerry leaned from the righted boat, and gave her his hand. She grasped it, but her doeskin gloves had become slimy the instant they made contact with the water, and she slipped away from him, giving a low cry of terror as the boat also moved away on a sudden current from somewhere under where she now trod water.

The fact that she had never learned to swim was not her fault. She had often begged her father to allow her to join the laughing, screaming crowds of bathing belles that had frequented the beaches of the popular resorts on the south coast near London—even if they did have to go rather far out to sea, and behind a screen—to immerse themselves modestly. But he had adamantly refused; perhaps it was the only thing he ever had refused her. And now, as for the first time her chin went under the surface of the river, and she clenched her teeth in instinctive rejection of its stench and cold, it flashed across her mind that if she went under and were drowned, her father would never forgive himself.

With a last effort, she kicked at her skirts, and in the single, strong movement found herself brought closer to the drifting boat. She wondered why the oarsmen had made so little effort to return to her side. Could he not see that she was about to drown? Was he frozen into inertia by fear? She was about to forget every lesson she had ever learned on the subject of decorum, and scream at the boatman in terms she had once heard from the family coachman, when she was halted by a blow on the back of her neck. By now she was convinced that someone was actually trying to drown her, and certain that she had been saved from some lethal attack only by the thickness of the braided hair at the nape of her neck, she acted like lightning, and grasped at the missile with both gloved hands. This time, her grasp held on the rough rope of the ladder she had seen some moments earlier hanging from the royal steamer's side. As she took hold, the ladder seemed to draw her back to the boat. She glanced fearfully in the direction of the silent paddles. If *The Centaur* had been in motion, she would have been sucked to her death!

She had no hope now that the small boat would reach her, and she allowed herself to be raised inches from the water by someone who seemed to be straining to save her from the deck above. But her arms, stiff with the cold of the night, ached unbearably, and she felt herself slipping again. With a last renewal of her will, she regained her hold, but this time, as a voice she now recognized as her cousin's called encouragingly to her from the steamer's deck, she began to climb the ladder.

Any chance observer from the riverbank would have seen at that moment the extraordinary sight of a young woman in full crinoline climbing like some giant black and white creature of the depths against *The Centaur's* side. She slipped, and climbed on. Her white frilled underwear hung dankly from beneath her twisted skirts. Heedless of the impropriety of her situation, she grappled with the ladder, and triumphed.

With one last haul on the part of her rescuer above, and a cry of relief from her cousin further along the deck, Henrietta found herself at last astride the steamer's rails, and with a movement that was half leap, half fall, she landed on the deck—at Roddy's feet.

Had she been asked, and had she had time to reply, what emotion she would have expected to find on her cousin's face as he bent over her and helped her to her feet, a second after she had missed death by drowning, she would have found it modest enough to answer, "Terror mixed with joy." Or: "Anxious concern, laced lightly with love."

But she had time only, as she dragged herself upright in her heavy skirts, to glimpse what she could have sworn was a smile of triumph, laced with, if anything, an edge of cunning. And hoping that she had imagined the expression under the extreme pressure of the moment, she allowed herself to be supported the length of the deck until they came to the set of cabins she remembered had housed the Greek woman.

Waiting for her, in the first doorway to which Roddy led her, was a young Egyptian serving girl, dressed in the costume Henrietta so admired. Dark eyes looked at her sadly from above a veil. The girl's tunic, under her outer robe, gleamed dark orange in the shadows.

The steward who had now run to join them muttered briefly to the girl, who at once ran back into the cabin. Roddy let go Henrietta's arm, and told her: "The girl will take good care of you. Her mistress is already in the royal suite. You'll not be disturbed, old thing."

He looked her straight in the face then, for the first time that evening. His blues eyes were candid. "I say, old girl, I suppose you are all right, aren't you? I mean, it's no joke being pushed into the briny; and I can't recall, demme if I can, whether or not you're a swimmer?"

If Roddy was pretending his concern, Henrietta had to admit that he had become a convincing actor since the days when they were children together. But there was genuine affection in the way in which he now put an arm about her soaking shoulder, and half pushed her into the cabin after the serving girl. "We'll see you at dinner, Cousin? You're game, aren't you? I was pretty sure you'd rally, y'know. But I must admit for a moment back there you had me worried."

As he spoke, he seemed to realize that he had given himself away. But his natural concern for her compelled him to finish his sentence before the full impact of her rising fury was let loose.

She stood in the cabin doorway, her eyes blazing in the moonlight. Her gown dripped water still, and clung tightly to her slim body. He eyed her small waist, and the high breasts under her boned bodice. The lace collar her mother had sewn for her clung damply about her shoulders. Her plaited hair was perhaps the only thing about her whole person that was even remotely dry.

"I wouldn't have liked it if you'd gone under, Cousin," he finished.

The shout of anger with which Henrietta gave him her reply was heard in the city of Assuan, in the fisherboats almost a mile away, and in the engine rooms of *The Centaur* itself. Whether or not her own mama heard from the safety of the dining room of *The Sprite*, where she sat no doubt in serene belief that her daughter was at that moment at table with royalty itself, Henrietta could not find it in her heart to care.

All she knew was that she had detected her cousin in a conspiracy that had almost killed her. That he had arranged for her dipping, she had no doubt. That it would mean he had at last avenged the day in Frinton-on-Sea so long ago was no accident. Had she come all this way, for love of him, to find herself taught such a lesson at last?

As she advanced on Roddy, her wet fists flying, her teeth bared, Henrietta looked like some black and white kitten that had been teased too long. Her eyes shone with unshed tears. Her feet slipped treacherously beneath her. She ran, screamed again, thundered at her cousin's uniformed chest with small, furious hands, and found herself close in his arms.

As he gathered her close to him, Roddy quickly put his mouth to a shell-like ear, and in the split second before he once more released her, he whispered fiercely:

"How else could I have managed to get you into one of her gowns, old thing? Work it out for yourself. One day you'll forgive me, won't you?"

He stepped back from her then, and in the cabin behind her the serving girl began to lay a long, graceful evening gown of palest coral on the bed.

As if in a dream, Henrietta backed away from her cousin. Her fury at the trap he had set for her was unabated, but her comprehension of his ultimate purpose silenced her. She knew now that she loved a ser-

162

pent. A serpent of the old Nile. But she could not find it in her heart to deny her aid in the task that still lay ahead.

"I will join you in perhaps half an hour, Cousin," she said in a loud, clear voice. "Will you inform His Highness that I am none the worse for my escapade?"

Roddy bowed. There were two stewards now close by on the deck, and round the corner of the main cabin-block came Professor Clémence. Swiftly, more out of a sense of modesty than anything else, Henrietta drew back into the cabin. As she did so, Roddy seemed to try to convey some other information to her. He tapped at the pocket on the left breast of his uniform jacket. But she could not tell what he meant, and as the professor joined him he bowed again, noncommittally this time, and moved off towards the main royal suite.

It was true that Henrietta was none the worse for her experience. But she feared, as the girl began to help her to restore her appearance, that the night had more ordeals to offer yet.

As she donned the coral gown and surveyed herself in the Greek woman's gold-edged mirrors, she had to admit that she liked the effect. And the cold water of the river seemed to have eased the inflammation of the bites on her shoulders, which were now once more revealed by the gown's low-cut neckline.

She was thankful, too, that her diamonds had not been lost in the process of the "accident" that had befallen her. It was the one thing she would have found impossible to explain to her mama. The matter of the gown she would perhaps manage to explain, if given time. She hoped that her own clothes would be restored to her in mint condition before she had to face her mother again. But she doubted that would be possible.

She had finished refastening her diamond earrings, and noted how well they looked above the coral silk, when her diamond hairclip fell loose from her braids and onto the cabin floor. Bending to retrieve it, she saw a small velvet casket tucked beneath the skirts of the dressing table. It was clearly a jewel case, and this was perhaps its hiding-place. But it was carelessly closed, and carelessly hidden, and from one side of its half open upper section there spilled a golden chain, from which was suspended the sacred alabaster stone.

She gasped softly. And then, aware that the serving girl watched her with the same great vacant eyes with which she had been greeted, she straightened up, gave one last glance into the mirror, and hurriedly left the cabin.

Outside on deck, the young equerry who had escorted her from *The Sprite* awaited her once more. As she stepped into the moonlight, a striking figure in the slender gown, he gave an involuntary exclamation of admiration.

"Miss de Vere Smith," he said, "I hope you'll forgive me for what happened. It's your cousin's orders, you know—and I think he has good reason. But he's a rum customer. You never know what he's up to."

She took the proffered arm, and together they began to walk towards the royal suite under the stars. It was a warm, dry night, and Henrietta was reminded that they had in the last twenty-four hours traveled deep into the dry climate of the upper Nile.

Above them, the moon now seemed to throb in its own white glow in the great vault of a cloudless sky. If, as she now had every reason to suspect, the time had now come for the execution of Roddy's plan to return the sacred scarab in replica only to the Dashawai, then the weather at least for her ordeal was fine.

She groaned inwardly then at the prospect of what her cousin wanted her to do. She believed that she had the style to carry off the immediate challenge, of facing the Greek woman in one of her own gowns across the supper table. But she protested to herself that though Roddy was at last showing signs of becoming a man of action, it was she who seemed destined to do the hard work.

There was nothing for it, until they could talk in private, but to seem to concur.

She told the young equerry: "I do so agree with you, sir. My cousin *is* a rum customer." And with her back as straight as befits a soldier's wife, (which she had frequently to remind herself she was not) she marched to her fate.

CHAPTER THIRTEEN

IN THE HOURS that followed, Henrietta had to admit to herself that in the matter of organization her cousin had become quite skilled. There had been a time when she would not have trusted him to organize a fête in his own garden.

Now, she watched him manipulate a devious Frenchman—Professor Clémence—into conducting a tour by moonlight of the sacred pyramids of Philoe some seven miles into the heart of the desert; she heard him convince a brace of Egyptian stewards, who would no doubt convey the information forthwith by fast messenger to the Dashawai, that the lady Helena would be the guest of honor on the excursion; and she was at his side when, at last, he took his prince into the privacy of the royal drawing room after supper and persuaded him to see that the lady in question was confined by some happy pursuit or other to her cabins for the duration of the night.

Prince Edward seemed also to have acquired some respect for her cousin's abilities, for he made no objection when Roddy asked for the private interview to discuss a matter of utmost urgency requiring immediate action, and it was he who asked if Roddy's cousin could not at the same time join them for champagne, to make up for the accident she had suffered at the hands of the royal boatmen.

In the course of the conversation with Prince Edward, Roddy began to show his other new gift for diplomacy. He told the prince that it was for the sake of the safety of the lady Helena herself that they must at all costs keep her from joining the excursion that night.

"You see, sir," he explained, "the matter of the sacred scarab, however much I risk Your Highness's displeasure in bringing it up again, must now be faced. There are spies about you—I think we accept that there always are, to some degree. And they work for the Dashawai. To these men it is anathema to see their sacred relic of the temple worn by a infidel woman."

The prince flicked the cigar he was smoking, and looked thoughtful. "I find that a bit strong, Roddy. She's not as bad as all that, is she?"

Roddy paused, choosing his words. "By 'infidel' I mean not of the faith, sir. Of course no insult is implied."

Edward smiled at Henrietta. He had already registered his total approval of her appearance during the course of supper, but now she detected something of the conspirator in his gray eyes. She would not have been at all surprised, had she not known that it was strictly forbidden to royalty, had H.R.H. ventured to wink at her.

But Roddy pressed on. "Whether or not the—er—the young lady in question persists in flaunting the jewel so openly, in the very land where it belongs, she would

167

be in danger if she ventures abroad on a night like this. The holy pyramid is of special significance to pilgrims at full moon, sir. Professor Clémence will tell you himself. It is, I would like to suggest, madness even for Your Highness to go—in view of the hostility the whole business has started."

Edward nodded. Again he smiled at Henrietta. "I have no doubt, my boy, that you have some plan up your sleeve. But if you have, I don't want to know. Is that understood?" Roddy's earnest face visibly brightened at the words. He turned to Henrietta, as if to convey that he had told her he could do something about the situation, and he had.

But since the mention of Professor Clémence, Henrietta's thoughts had been elsewhere. The Frenchman's presence on *The Centaur* disturbed her greatly. Throughout supper she had been conscious of his barbed smile, and under the current of his smooth discussion of Egyptian antiquities, which had practically dominated the table, she detected a cynical mind and a hostile spirit. She did not think he had forgotten the threats he had made to her concerning Roddy. And he must know that Roddy was behaving rather strangely. But she hoped that the professor thought that she herself had forgotten the interview in her cabin when she was almost delirious with fever. So that he could not be sure that she had alerted Roddy, or not.

While Roddy assured the prince that if he did decide to take action it would only be against some real danger, and that whatever happened, he knew that the incognito and clandestine nature of their little holiday discounted all possiblity of the prince's own participation.

"I give you my word, sir," he ended, "that I shall act with discretion, if I act at all. And that your name will not come into it. But—in return, I need some guarantee from you yourself, sir."

Horrified, Henrietta looked at her cousin to see if he had lost the use of his senses. To ask such a thing of royalty was just not done. Her gaze went next to Edward himself, to see what effect the demand had had. The gray eyes glinted rather dangerously, she thought.

"You know my situation as well as I do, sir." The title, used by an heir to the throne, was ominously formal. "You know my limits. You can only drive me to their furthest extent!" He flicked his cigar again. It was a gesture Henrietta was learning fast to dread. "But—" the dry, curt tone she also feared had crept into the royal voice. "It had better be worth it!"

With that, Edward burst into laughter, and gestured to Roddy to refill their champagne glasses. Gratefully, Henrietta let the sharp bubbles tickle her nose. It was a delicious, and cooling experience, and she savored it to the full. It might be the last time she had such luxury, if the way in which her evening had started was anything to go by.

Relaxing a little himself, her cousin deposited the champagne bottle in its basket. He did not retrieve his own glass. The moment was still too serious to see it through with a drink in his hand.

"I promise you that it is, sir. Otherwise, would I have the temerity to ask such a thing of you?"

Edward sipped his champagne. "Ask away, Roddy. Ask away."

For a moment, Henrietta feared that the prince had grown bored with the whole business. And she could not have found it in her heart to blame him if he had. He could not possibly know, as she did, of the extent to which his prestige, and that of the crown of England was at stake.

Roddy cleared his throat. "I would prefer it, sir, if you yourself were to make your excuses, and not join the party tonight. It is a delicate matter, and I do not choose to explain myself further. But it suffices to say that there is only one way to ensure that the lady Helena stays safely in her cabin for the night. And it is only because her life depends on it. I'm sure of that, old girl—" he turned to Henrietta, as if in need of her support at such a moment, which well he might be, "—if I dare to refer to the solution."

There was a long silence. Henrietta, guessing at once at her cousin's meaning, was glad that there were no servants in the room. She knew now why Roddy had requested an entirely private audience with the prince. She did not know where to look, while Roddy himself stared at the ground awaiting his reply.

It came at last. The prince's voice, to Henrietta's relief, was pleasantly calm.

"We're both men of the world, Roddy. And I take your meaning. The safety of our honored guest on board *The Centaur*, the lady Helena, depends on myself. What could be more apt? Rest assured that I shall see to it in person that she does not leave her cabin again tonight. And, of course, that means also that no one on board is to know of any strategy used to make certain of my success. If you will ascertain on my behalf, sir, that the coast is clear, I'll make my way along the deck as soon as I've finished this excellent cigar!"

On his return to the royal suite, where she had waited for him, Roddy came straight to Henrietta and stood, a hand on each of her bare shoulders, while he gazed seriously into her eyes.

She hoped that he would not notice any of the remaining signs of her sufferings at the hands of the pests on which her mama so advisedly waged war. But his eyes did not roam.

"He took it all much better than I could have hoped for, Cousin," Roddy said. "And he's produced a masterstroke which even I had not thought of!"

Not at first understanding what he meant, Henrietta gave him a puzzled look.

"What I mean is, old girl," he went on, "that at this very moment the entire crew thinks that the prince is cosily installed for the night here, in his own suite—I've told them all that he's had a sudden attack of fatigue and won't be riding out to Philoe with us. And therefore, as there's no trace of activity from the lady Helena's cabin—it's all in darkness—no one will question it if she—or someone very like her at a distance—emerges from that direction all ready for the night's excursion. Off duty, you might say!"

"Roddy!" At the indignity of her cousin's implications, Henrietta found herself blushing. She had, of course, heard rumors of the Prince's indiscretions, but who had not? His popularity was in some ways based on the legend. And in her own surmise, she found that he concealed a warm heart beneath the royal armor of dry humor, and needed all the affection he could get. But it was a different matter, to hear from her own cousin's lips such phrases, and to find herself a conspirator in such things.

"Don't let it worry you, old thing," Roddy said, somewhat too cheerfully she thought. "All that matters is that H.R.H. has at last found fit to listen to my warnings. It's true he has not yet agreed to hand over the real stone. And I doubt he ever will."

Henrietta was reminded then forcibly of the casket of jewels she had stumbled upon in Helena's rooms.

"But, as you know, I've allowed for that," Roddy continued.

Again, he tapped at his breast pocket, and this time she noticed that it bulged rather heavily, and detracted from the usually impeccable line of his uniform.

"Is it the replica?" she whispered, gazing fearfully at the door to make sure that they were still alone.

Her cousin nodded. "You'll soon be wearing it, old thing. And even Clémence won't know that both the girl and the necklace are copies, if we keep you both well apart!"

The casual way in which he referred to her as a copy, as if the Greek woman was in the original mould and she herself had been thrown together in some bazaar, as the replica scarab had been, was all Henrietta needed to vent her wrath once more on her cousin. As

171

they were in the prince's apartment, she could hardly fly at him physically as she had done some hours before. But fly at him with her tongue she did.

In no uncertain terms, she pointed out to him that no shadow of a replica of a woman would do what she was about to do for him that night at Philoe. It took real flesh and blood, and the de Vere spirit to achieve such things. Though he winced visibly at the mention of their mothers' family name, she went on ruthlessly. She reminded him that it was he who purported to be the coming young man of action, but she who seemed fated to do all the acting when the moment came. And she ended by objecting strongly to the way in which he had so blatantly contrived, with the aid of his fellow officers and men, to have her tipped into the Nile on her way to a royal occasion.

At the sight of her comically protesting face, as she recalled the way in which she had so nearly drowned, Roddy could resist her no longer. He stepped towards her, his arms open to receive her. In another moment, she would have flown into them. But a discreet cough somewhere in the region of the cabin door reminded them that they had other things to do. Roddy turned, to find a young subaltern waiting to speak.

"The horses are ready," the subaltern announced.

Roddy asked: "And the cloak?"

The newcomer nodded. From behind his back he produced a long cape of white silk. It had a foreign look, and Henrietta guessed that it had come either from Greece, which she now knew was Helena's homeland, or from Egypt itself. As she placed it round her shoulders, and Roddy himself smoothed it into place, she had to admit that it was a garment of great beauty. It was warm and light and graceful. She would not have minded had it belonged to her. She would wear it for that night with some pleasure.

As she stood in the center of the room swathed in the white silk, Roddy could not take his eyes from her. He pulled himself together with an almost visible effort, and told her: "I'm afraid you'll have to trust me with your diamonds for a while, old thing." His hand went to his pocket. "You'll be wearing only one jewel tonight. And if you would readjust the string or whatever it is at your throat—open it up a bit, I mean," he went on in what Henrietta felt was an unnecessarily unromantic vein, "then I'll fix the thingamabob around your neck."

As her cousin came close to her again, and reached out to place the scarab's golden chain about her throat, Henrietta found herself trembling. She could not tell whether it was from fear of what the night might bring, or from the effect of Roddy's proximity upon her whole being. As his hands brushed her skin her heart beat faster, and she was afraid that he would hear it. But he himself seemed unduly preoccupied with the fastening of the catch at the nape of her neck, and the moment passed.

"I do wish that this whole thing could be over, Roddy," she said, as soon as she could be certain that her voice did not betray her feelings for the young man who stood so close.

He stepped back, and surveyed the effect of the necklace with some satisfaction.

"No more than I do, Cousin," he replied. "But it will come to an end, and a successful end. I'm sure of it. And when it is all over, why then, we have tomorrow night to look forward to."

"Tomorrow night?" she said weakly. "Am I still to be here tomorrow night?"

"Well, shall we say here and there?" Roddy cheerfully answered. "Back on *The Sprite*, to comfort your mama with tales of the royal table, and to get ready for the fancy dress reception."

"The fancy dress reception?" she echoed him again. She had already surely endured enough dressing up to last a lifetime, and she had always abhorred what seemed to her the whole foolish business of masquerades.

"H.R.H. doesn't like the idea either," her cousin told her. "But—a certain person insisted. Said she's bored with all this. And when she was told that our—our host—is too well known a face to set foot in a city as big as Assuan, and that no one could leave the boat by daylight, she blew up rather. Said if there wasn't a party or something jolly soon, she'd be going back fairly smartly—and by train."

The cousins left unsaid the obvious fact that both of them heartily wished that the Greek woman had gone home by train long ago, and left them free to enjoy their Egyptian encounter to its full. But they were not free yet to do so. As Roddy so aptly put it as they left the royal cabin, and Henrietta made her way along the deserted promenade under *The Centaur*'s awnings— only to return at once, the hood of her white cloak draped low over her forehead, the scarab gleaming from its folds at her throat:

"There is work to be done."

The party that stepped ashore some ten minutes later from the royal steamer consisted of Roddy, the white-robed figure of Henrietta herself walking with a rather more sensuous sway than was her custom, a clutch of subalterns, two dragomen who were to take care of the horses, and Professor Clémence himself.

From the moment the professor appeared, Henrietta was careful to keep as much distance between him and herself as was possible. She had noticed thankfully at several stages earlier in the evening that there was little love lost between the Frenchman and Helena, so that it was not likely to excite comment now if she ignored him completely. He was after all egyptologist to the prince, and not to any hangers-on in the party. But she was careful all the same to make sure that he did not look into her face. For she knew that her blue eyes would be the first thing to give away her true identity.

It was not until they had mounted, and had ridden

some three or four miles out into the desert, that Henrietta felt free to allow the hood of her cloak to fall back from her hair. She was relieved to see that the professor, a poor enough horseman, flagged some way behind the main party. Roddy and his fellow soldiers, and she herself, were excellent riders. It was safe enough. The Frenchman would have only a back view of her, and her hair would look much like that of the Greek woman, silhouetted against the sand dunes under the now brilliant moon.

In fact Henrietta was never to know whether, as they approached the holy pyramids in the light of the moon, the professor—who should after all have been acting as their guide—had fallen behind on purpose. She and Roddy now led the small party of horsemen into the desert, and in spite of her apprehension that they would be attacked, or worse, she began to enjoy the ride.

They were about seven miles from the river when the pyramids suddenly appeared on the horizon, a cluster of low cone-like shapes squatting in the dunes like some eery alien visitors from the sky. But it was an optical illusion, like so many of the vistas in the desert. And as the party rode close to them, between them, shafts of white light struck like arrows as the horses crossed and recrossed in the path of the moon.

No one spoke as they rode. There was no need for explanations, or for lectures. The professor was in any case now some distance behind. The pyramids breathed their own message in every great stone. In the night air, which was so pure out in the desert that Henrietta found it almost intoxicating, it was as if the stones sang.

The only sound, as they rode to and fro, was the soft thud of the horses' hooves in the sand.

And then Roddy reined in his horse. The soft thudding seemed to have increased in volume. The others halted at a sign from him. The sound of flying hooves now filled the air. Henrietta's last picture of her cousin was as he dismounted, and led his gray Arab horse into the shelter of a pyramid. His fellow officers followed. The dragomen, eyeing each other with some uncertainty, seemed to wait for some sign before they would move. Suddenly, there was a hoarse cry from the direction in which the Frenchman now rode towards them. As it reached them, the dragomen also took shelter. In a single moment, Henrietta found herself alone.

Too late, she spurred her great white Arab horse. It was a spirited creature, and for a second it resisted her command. She dug with her heels, hampered by the white cloak. She was almost blinded now by the strange intensity of the moon, and the alabaster scarab glinted in its gold filigree like a flame at her throat.

When the attack came, it was swift and sure. Henrietta knew from what Roddy had told her that the Dashawai were the greatest horsemen of the eastern desert, and that if they rose to the bait, and came for their sacred stone, they would ride like the wind to snatch it from the infidel.

But it was not only the scarab they now snatched from the night. Henrietta had a glimpse of fierce black eyes in a hawk-like face. The man who rode towards her, or rather to one side of her own white steed, was hooded in the traditional white headdress of the nomad tribes. He came so close that she felt his breath upon her cheek. She steeled herself for what she knew must come. The necklace would be torn from her throat, and she must not fall from her horse as the rider passed.

But she need not have feared a fall. The air filled with the sound of hooves, and the cries of the half dozen riders who followed the man who now rode down upon her. Again she braced herself. And then she was astonished to find that she rose in mid-air, her white cape flying about her with the speed of the movement. And still she did not fall.

Instead she felt a strong, lithe arm about her waist. The rider's breath was hot now on her face. She gave a single cry, and heard it as if from a great distance.

She was aware, vaguely, that she had called her cousin's name.

But by the time the riders from *The Centaur* had rounded the corner of the pyramid from which they had hoped to observe the occasion of the return of the duplicate scarab to the rightful owners, the Dashawai had disappeared as swiftly as they had come, riding into the silent desert at furious speed under the moon. With Henrietta born on the saddle of the leading horse, like some human trophy in an ancient war....

CHAPTER FOURTEEN

"MY NAME is Hassan."

The hawk-faced, dark-eyed leader of the Dashawai sat cross-legged in his silken tent, and stared almost insolently at his captive.

"And I am the leader of my people. The guardian of their birthrights: the rightful keeper of the holy scarab."

With all the self-control she could muster, Henrietta prevented a nervous hand from flying to her throat. She had, since the moment of her abduction at Philoe, been in a very nervous condition. It was not surprising. She had set out from *The Centaur* as a decoy, surrounded—or so she thought—by heroes and friends. By the next morning, she had ridden into a distant Arab encampment in the arms of an Arab princeling. A prisoner. And she had no way of telling whether her cousin and his fellow soldiers were on her tracks.

At first, she had refused the food and drink which Hassan had offered her. She found it more dignified to maintain silence, and to fast. But as the hours passed by and the sun rose to its midday zenith, her good sense made her change her tactics. If she were to be rescued now, it would not be until darkness fell. No one, however brave, could hope to attack the Dashawai in broad daylight on their home ground and succeed. Roddy himself had told her what fierce fighters they were. And now that she sat staring as proudly as she could manage into the eyes of her abductor, their leader, she could well believe that he was right.

"You have what you wanted, then, if you are the guardian of the sacred stone," she said. But her voice lacked conviction. The one aspect of the plot to avoid trouble over the scarab that she had never liked was that it depended on passing a duplicate for the original.

"You are an intelligent woman, as well as beautiful," Hassan replied. "Surely you do not expect me to accept that bauble at your throat as the holy relic belonging to my people?"

His words came as a great relief at that moment to Henrietta. She had wondered at first why the scarab was not immediately wrenched from her neck on her arrival in the encampment, by some furious member of the tribe. Then she had decided that this would be a ritual to be performed only by the hand of the sheikh himself... and that in all probability it would be followed by an equally ritual slaughter of its wearer—herself.

Now, if the sheikh had indeed realized that the jewel she wore was fake, she was at an advantage. She had not committed the mortal sin of wearing the true stone round her infidel neck. And her life might therefore not be forfeit. She could only hope that she was right.

As he continued to gaze at her, the expression on the sheikh's hawk-like features then visibly softened.

"Nor do I believe," he continued, "that you are the infidel woman who has sinned against my people. And against her own. You are too proud by nature, I think, to demean yourself by trailing in the wake of this English prince."

Stung to the quick by this insult to Prince Edward, whom she now felt she knew almost as a friend, she jumped to her feet. But Hassan waved her slowly back to where he had commanded her to sit, and clapped his hands. Almost immediately, a serving girl crept into the tent, and waited for the sheikh to give her some command. He spoke quietly to her, his eyes still on Henrietta, in Arabic. She could not understand what he said. But when he had finished, the girl came to her, and in sign language showed her that she was to accompany her, and that she would be bathed, and given new clothing.

Henrietta was only too glad to agree to follow the girl. She rose again, and gave a small, imperious nod of the head in the direction of Hassan. The sheikh smiled, and returned the compliment. She turned on her heel, aware of the softest of carpets beneath her now bare feet. (Her shoes had been removed the moment they rode into camp, to prevent her escape across the sand and rock that surrounded the area, she assumed).

But in the entrance to the tent, she paused. "I cannot help wonder," she told Hassan, "at the excellence of your English. It is by far the best I have encountered since my arrival in Egypt. May I ask you how you came to acquire such a skill?"

Hassan rose to his feet. He walked over to where she stood. She noticed that his bearing was graceful, for a man, and that his shoulders were wide and strong beneath his native robes. He looked down into her eyes, and she found that, in spite of her situation, she liked the proud expression, mingled with gentleness, that she saw in them.

"It is quite simple," he said. "I was at school in England. My father wanted it for me, and I had to obey.

They turned out to be—as you say in your country—the best years in my life."

"May I ask which of our schools you attended?"

The reply almost sent Henrietta reeling with shock and surprise out into the open air beyond the tent.

"Why, Eton, of course," Hassan replied. "Where else should I go to school?"

Concealing her surprise as best as she could, Henrietta played for time, and began to examine the fine lines she now could see in the dark face close to hers. It was just possible that this man could be the same age as her brother. It was worth a try.

"My name is Henrietta de Vere Smith," she announced in a loud, clear voice. She did not have to wait long to know that she had judged the sheikh's age correctly.

His whole demeanor changed. He threw back his head, and laughed aloud, then drew her back into the tent.

"Charlie's sister! You are the little sister of one of my oldest friends, and I have snatched you out of the desert like a beast. Can you forgive me? What can I do to make it up to you? And tell me, before you are dragged away by that foolish girl to bathe and change—how is Charles de Vere Smith, after all these years?"

If she had expected that the long friendship with her brother, and the long talk he now had with her about the old days, would make any difference to her situation, she would have been mistaken. But Henrietta did not. She was a sound judge of character, and she saw nothing in Hassan to denote a possible change of mind. He wanted the scarab, the true stone, for his people, and he would probably still kill for it—if he had to. But now that she knew more of him, she was willing to gamble that this might not be necessary. Honor, it was true, had to be satisfied. But bloodshed was not necessarily its obvious accompaniment.

She had not, however, studied the Arab mind to its

full extent, and she was still to endure even greater surprises at its hands.

She had been returned to Hassan's tent after a delicious, aromatic bath in a large tent reserved for the women of the encampment, and was, in spite of the serious nature of her position, delighted to be dressed in the Arab garments she had so admired on the women she had encountered in her travels so far.

Managing much more gracefully to sit on the silken carpets now that she wore the voluminous, diaphanous trousers under a cotton tunic and short over-cloak of silk, she prepared for her long vigil before Roddy came to her rescue by asking her captor to tell her more of the old days in England, with her brother.

As she listened, her heart ached for Charlie's good humor, and the comfort of the touch of his tweed jackets. She knew he had not been ideally placed at Eton, but he had done his best—surrounded by brilliant minds and as brilliant athletes. And the more she studied Hassan, the more she realized that he too must have shone at the ancient school.

"But enough of the past!" It was Hassan himself who at last brought their conversation, which had turned into a kind of Arabian Nights in reverse, to an end. With a start, Henrietta sensed that her moment of truth was upon her. If only Roddy would come!

"Whatever educational background I may once have shared in common with your countrymen, Miss de Vere Smith," Hassan elaborated, "their ways will never be mine. In our long talk here today, however, I have become strangely drawn to you. In spite of your pale skin, and your forward manner."

Henrietta would, if it had been an Englishman speaking, have hesitated no longer and marched out of the tent at these words. But it was her abductor who addressed her, in soft, enticing manner. A manner that turned the insult to a white woman, and an Englishwoman to boot, into a caress. In any case, had she left the tent, she knew that she would have got no distance at all.

As Hassan now rose to his feet and came towards her with his panther-like walk, she looked around for some other means of escape. All she could see was a wide silk curtain, slung from the apex of the tent to the floor, and forming a partition between Hassan's quarters and the rest. If she did manage to cross to it before he reached her—and the expression in his dark eyes told her that he intended to follow his last words with action to match them, she might only find that she had delayed whatever fate he had in mind for her. It seemed more than likely that beyond the silken curtain there lay the sheikh's own bed.

He had reached the spot where she now half reclined in fear, and stood looking down at her with an amused smile, when there was a movement, and a laugh, from behind the partition itself, and as the silk curtain lifted at one end, a small figure darted across the tent to her side.

By the veiled head, the embroidered tunic, and delicate velvet slippers the newcomer wore, Henrietta knew that they had been joined by a girl child. By the jewels at her ears and brow, she calculated the child was probably a princess, or at least high-born. But for all her decorative appearance, she seemed to care only for the ragged wooden doll which she now held out for Henrietta's inspection.

It was Hassan who spoke first, addressing the child in Arabic. At his words, she hugged the doll close again in slim brown arms, and bowed slightly to Henrietta.

"You are welcome to my father's home," she said in perfect English. "It is not often that we receive so beautiful a guest, and from so far. We beg to inform you that we hope you will stay with us for many moons."

In spite of the fact that this was precisely what she intended to avoid, Henrietta was touched by the child's manner, and relieved by the miraculous timing of her arrival. She knew that this must be Hassan's daughter, from the way in which she spoke English. And there was a strong family likeness in their melting brown eyes. But she also knew enough about the ways of the Muslim world to refrain from asking Hassan any question concerning a female relative, and more especially concerning a wife. Whoever it was who had mothered this small creature, it was unlikely that Henrietta would be told.

"Thank you." Henrietta returned the bow with a smile, and held out a hand for the doll. Solemnly, the child asked her:

"Do you not wish to know her name?"

Henrietta examined the plain cotton gown that had been sewn in rough, child-like stitches for the doll.

"I would like to know," she said, "who has made this dress so well. And then I would like to know the name of the doll."

The dark eyes beamed at her. "It is I, Sara, who made the gown. And the doll's name is Victoria."

At the proud announcement, Hassan visibly strove to conceal a wince. And Henrietta guessed that he had but little control over this particular member of his tribe if she managed to name a doll after the Queen of England.

"I named her Victoria," Sara continued, "because my father brought her home to the Dashawai from far away, when he was at school in a country ruled by a woman of that name. It is a thing unheard of, you know, amongst his people."

"You mean for a woman to rule?" Henrietta asked.

"No. For a man—and such a man as my father—to be attached to a doll!"

Henrietta knew that if she laughed at that moment, her life would be forfeit. Hassan strode angrily back to his own ottoman, and clapped his hands.

A young serving girl appeared at once from behind the curtain. Henrietta, to conceal her amusement, had begun to examine the doll in greater detail.

"Remove this daughter of our tents at once to her

own quarters," Hassan told the newcomer. "She has provided quite sufficient entertainment to our guest for one day!" To Henrietta's amazement, the girl seemed to understand. Any moment, it would transpire that this was some English Nanny transported from Kensington Gardens in London, her darkened skin acquired in years spent in the desert. But as Sara ran to her nurse's side, Henrietta called: "You have forgotten Victoria!" And the child turned.

"I brought her to you because she is an English doll, and she is broken. It is her arm. I have bound her with silk, but I think she needs proper attention."

"I am honored to be asked to help," Henrietta replied. "And I give you my word that it will be soon that your doll is returned to you, in the best of health!"

"Thank you. And now, I must hurry. I have to learn to groom my new pony. Father tells me that in England if one owns a horse, then one must know how to care for it. And it is the same thing with our people, you know."

While Henrietta was spending the first hours of her captivity in this fashion, her cousin—convinced that she was injured, beaten, perhaps dead—spent the time organizing a search party, and hiring the fast, desert horses he would need.

The fact that he and the royal party had stood helplessly by as Henrietta was whirled away under the stars the night before might have caused his shame, but it also had taught him a lesson. The Dashawai knew this region: he did not. They had the fastest Arab horses, probably the fastest in the world. He would find the same caliber steeds for himself and his companions.

He chose two of the young subalterns to go with him, and informed the prince and the rest of the company on board *The Centaur* that he was going on reconnaissance, just in case things got unpleasant. They were to be moored below the First Cataract for several days—an all too brief idyll for the Prince of Wales before they had to turn for home. It was an idyll, however temperamental his companion, which his aides-de-camp knew they should be careful to preserve. For the moment, Edward was not to be told of the disaster that had befallen his party at Philoe.

"With any luck," Roddy told his chosen helpers, "we'll have her back in time for the fancy dress affair. I hope so, at least."

But the other task, before him before he rode out into the eastern desert, was more difficult than anything else he had ever had to do.

He had either to tell his aunt, who no doubt still waited the return of her daughter from the supper party she had so recently allowed her to attend, that the daughter in question had somehow disappeared into the unknown—or he had to tell her a lie. And he knew enough of both his Aunt Constance and his own nature to feel that a lie would lead to worse recriminations than the truth. He had always been a bad liar, and he did not intend to improve.

He was hard-pressed for time, and impatient to don the disguise of nomad riders he had planned for the search party, but first Constance de Vere Smith had to be faced.

Having sent word to her via a steward on board *The Sprite*, he stood waiting for her summons, his knuckles white as he gripped the steamer's rail. Some yards upstream *The Centaur* slept at her moorings. Beyond the mud roofs and white minarets of the town of Assuan the desert merged into the sky. He was not afraid of his aunt at that moment. He could think of nothing but his cousin.

"Tell me, nephew," Constance de Vere Smith boomed, "it was you, was it not, who composed the forgery—the letter purported to be from H.R.H. himself?"

Roddy sat at her side on a chaise longue in the main stateroom, the only place on *The Sprite* where one could have a conversation in any comfort. His blue eyes looked straight into hers.

"It was not exactly a forgery, Aunt," he said. "It was penned by an aide, (though dictated by myself) and written in the third person, if you recall. H.R.H. was not asked to sign it. But every word of it was true! It is common knowledge that he demands the utmost secrecy when he is abroad in his private capacity. He gets little enough peace as it is. And when he invites a young lady to dine, then it is expected of her guardians that they do not divulge the matter."

"It is a thousand pities that in this case the 'guardian,' as you deign to describe your cousin's mama, was not also invited to dine with our dear Queen's son."

"That was impossible, I'm afraid, Aunt," Roddy said firmly. He did not intend to give in to her on every account. "And at the next spree, a fancy dress affair—Henrietta will once more be with us for the occasion if I have anything to say. And once more she will not be expected to arrive with a chaperone. It's the numbers, you see, Aunt. We're rather unevenly divided over on *The Centaur*."

She was not to be so easily diverted. In the teeth of the news of her daughter's disappearance, which Roddy had successfully assured her was due to a temporary whim—he did not say on whose part—to rush off into the desert and explore, she was rather more disturbed by the way in which she had in the first place been flattered into allowing Henrietta to go on board the royal steamer.

"To be promised an invitation to the palace at a later date is not so important to me, Roddy. Though I do look forward to meeting our dear Queen again. But to hint that if I keep this whole thing secret I am helping some national crisis is, I think, going a little too far." She gathered her reticule from where it lay at her side, as if to indicate that the interview was at an end, and Roddy could not believe that he had got through it so easily.

As he escorted her to the deck, he knew that he had not managed to pull the wool over Constance de Vere

Smith's eyes with his half-truths. She held out her hand in farewell, and as he took it, she said:

"I shall expect my daughter to report back to me here within five hours. That is, before dark. Will you inform her of this when you go to this—rendezvous you claim to have with her in the desert? And will you also inform her that, if she is not here by nightfall, then I shall have no alternative but to report the matter to His Royal Highness, in person!"

Her words still rang in his ears as less than half an hour later he joined the two fair-haired young subalterns who were to ride with him. It was perhaps fortunate for Henrietta that her disappearance had assumed greater importance than the fact that she was in Egypt at all. The account he had given her mama of an escapade which he insisted was to be short-lived had at least forestalled any questions about what he and his cousin were doing only yards apart from each other in two Nile steamers, when Constance de Vere Smith had gone to such trouble and expense for the precise purpose of removing her daughter as far from Roddy and the unhappiness he had caused her as was physically possible.

He was sincerely glad that he was not going to be in Henrietta's shoes when that moment of reckoning came. And come to think of it, he told himself, as he marched down the gangway and away from her mother, his infuriating cousin had not yet given him his answer to the very same questions. What was she doing following him up the Nile? And exactly whose idea had it been?

But as he rode out, half an hour later, from the suburbs of Assuan, his mood darkened. However light he had made of Henrietta's absence to her mother, he knew that it was a matter of life and death. And he had to face, as the three Arab horses, their heavily-robed riders looking neither to the right nor the left, broke into a gallop in the direction of Philoe, that the abduction of his cousin by the Dashawai was entirely his own doing.

He had selected the two young royal aides who rode with him now because he knew, from the rigorous training they had once undergone together at the Royal Military Academy, that they were skilled riders, born survivors, and could keep their mouths shut if needs be. They had been together in several escapades over the years—not all of them recently involving their employer. Sankey, the one who rode on his left, had always got them out of trouble, while Smithie, the one on his right, had nerves of iron and a good record as a boxer. Not that their best friends would have recognized any one of the three as they now were: their faces darkened, their hair boot-blacked, and their uniforms supplanted by all-concealing robes similar to those worn by the desert nomad tribes. As for the horses they rode, they were the fastest that their pooled resources had been able to hire. For Roddy was convinced that had he been so well-equipped the night before, instead of trapped in the shadows of Philoe by awkward, second-rate mounts while the Dashawai sped into the darkness, he would never have let them get away.

Looking back on events, he also remembered how the Frenchman, typically hesitant to join an affray, had mysteriously disappeared on the return ride to *The Centaur*, and had reappeared at breakfast that day with a conspiratorial smile in Roddy's direction. He must have known that the prince could not be told of the disastrous attempt to decoy the Dashawai with the fake necklace and the fake woman who wore it. It seemed to suit his purposes, whatever they might be, only too well.

But when they came to Philoe again, things were very different. It was daylight. They were three determined men. They knew roughly the direction the kidnappers had taken the night before. They stood stockstill for perhaps three minutes, their trained soldiers' eyes and minds alert. Then, with a brief, murmured consultation together, they wheeled in the sand. Moments later, they were off... three specks on the horizon... and then lost in the glare of the desert at noon.

Captive as she was in Hassan's princely tent, Henrietta had been quite unable to reconnoiter the Dashawai encampment which she had first entered under cover of night. Had she done so, she would have found that the sheikh's quarters lay at the far end of a stockade, and consisted of not one but three tents, linked by narrow corridors. The silken curtain from which Sara had so fortunately interrupted her audience with the sheikh in fact concealed just such a linking passage—beyond which lay not, as she had feared, the royal sleeping quarters, but a more general, family room. It was through this room, and beyond, that Hassan's most secret hiding-place awaited. A perfumed, darkened sanctuary against the murderous heat that now beat down on the stockade as the desert air pulsed in the afternoon sun.

The conversation which ensued when Henrietta found herself reclining on a low couch in the retreat was not at all what she had expected. For one thing, her captor did not seem in a hurry to press his attentions on her. For another, he himself reclined at a distance, on a second couch. And what was more, they were not alone. A young male Arab stood guard at the entrance that led, she imagined, to the outside world. Another at the entrance through which they had come. Beyond that, the middle section of the tents was shrouded in silence. The sheikh's household slept.

"How good it is to rest in the heat of the day!" Hassan yawned as he spoke. "And with so beautiful a companion." He reached for a platter of fruit on a low marble table before him.

Henrietta stifled an impulse to snort scornfully at the remark. When she spoke her voice betrayed none of the fear she still felt. But her original fear of Hassan was now tempered by the scene she had witnessed between him and his daughter. She had to admit to herself that she found him intriguing, and attractive. But this only made her situation all the more dangerous. If she wanted to escape, she had to stay on her guard every minute.

"I do not know how it is possible for a man to rest when he has been insulted, as you claim you yourself have been, Hassan."

For a moment anger lurked in the soft brown eyes.

"I have not forgotten the cause of insult to my people as well as to myself. The original theft by the infidels who then gave the alabaster scarab to your prince has only been matched in audacity by the way in which a fake has been sent to the Dashawai tents in its place." He paused, to bite into a pale green fruit which Henrietta did not recognize. "I am merely taking my time in deciding exactly what forfeit I shall command. That is, in addition to the return of the true stone."

"But in this I agree with you," Henrietta cried. She sat upright, and her eyes shone in the soft light that the great vault of the canopy above shed on the scene.

It was at this point that the sheikh raised his head sharply. He listened for a moment, as if he heard something move and waited for its presence to reveal itself.

"Did you hear something, outside?" he asked Henrietta.

Henrietta rose. If she had calculated aright, their long walk through the three tents must have brought them to the perimeter of the Dashawai encampment. She knew that Hassan's quarters stood apart. And if they were close to the wooden stockade, then it was not unlikely that they would hear the stealthy movements of an intruder bent on invading the place. Supposing Roddy had found the way across the desert to her? If he had, then she would know for once and for all that he was made of stern stuff.

"I think not," she replied casually. "It was nothing." Her heart had begun to beat loudly, and she had to fight to keep her breast from rising and falling too fast under her silken tunic.

"Ah, yes, as we were saying," Hassan continued. "Then you do agree with me that such insults deserve revenge? In my country, forfeits would be due. A life. A lifetime's imprisonment, perhaps. But—first I must have the true stone, back here with my people."

Outside, in the glare of the afternoon heat, Roddy lay full length in the sand. He held his nomad hood over his mouth and nose, but still he felt as if his whole body had been invaded by the gray-yellow grit which surrounded him as far as the eye could see. A fly buzzed at his ear. He dare not move to brush it away. His eyes burned. The roof of his mouth felt like leather.

But none of these hardships could hurt him in the way the words he could hear scalded into his heart. He had crept up as far as the stockade, leaving his horse with Sankey and Smithie in the shelter of a great rock that stood some yards from the encampment. They were within shouting distance, but had agreed that not one word would be uttered unless death threatened Henrietta herself. If Roddy could find her, he intended to lead her swiftly and silently to safety.

And now he had found her. Only to hear her agree with the man who had abducted her that the true stone should be returned to the Dashawai. And to do so in honeyed tones that matched the man's own cunning tongue.

Worse was to come. "Of course," Hassan continued, "there is one life that could be forfeit, and yet not lost. Do you know whose life?"

Roddy could have sworn that Henrietta purred in reply to this. He could not distinguish her words, but he knew that she was hardly discouraging whatever was going on in the sheikh's tent at that moment.

The man's silken voice continued. Roddy wondered how on earth the fellow had learned to speak English so well. If only he had talked to her in Arabic, Henrietta would not have been able to agree with his nonsense.

"It is your life of which I speak, Miss de Vere Smith. You could spend it here, with me and my people, in perfect bliss. In splendor. If you wished, we could travel. I am a great traveler. You could have your heart's desire—"

At this, Roddy's hand went to the knife he had concealed in his robes. There was nothing but the fear that he would put his cousin's life at risk to stop him from leaping the stockade and bursting into the tent to cut down the man who spoke to her thus. But, his soldier's training stronger than his anger, he stayed where he was. There was no sense in risking all their lives until the moment when a really good chance of escape had come.

"My heart's desire at this moment, Hassan," Henrietta said, "is to be returned to the Nile. My dear mama must be extremely anxious. Did you not meet my mother when Charlie and you were at Eton?"

For a second, Roddy could not believe his ears. When the implication of his cousin's words had sunk in, he wanted to laugh aloud. So this prince of the faith, who abducted innocent girls and lived in outlandish style, had been to Eton? The information at once gave him more hope. To his certain knowledge, no man had yet left that particular establishment who could challenge a pupil of the Royal Military Academy in any field of the martial arts he cared to name.

Equally encouraged by Henrietta's remarks, Roddy decided that he must soon return to where his colleagues waited, inform them of the true lay of the land, and settle on a plan of action.

"So far as I can tell, chaps," he whispered to Smithie and Sankey some twenty minutes later, having wriggled his way back to the rock on his stomach, "there is only one way in, if we are on horseback—and that's in at the beggar's own front door. Everything seems very quiet. I have reason to believe my cousin is well-treated. They probably think that there's no one in the

British party who would have the nerve to follow them out here in this no man's land."

"And they're wrong!" Smithie's blue eyes gleamed above his golden moustache. Sankey echoed their sentiments with a grunt. Both men fingered the knives they carried, as Roddy did, beneath their robes. The horses, sensing their unrest, pawed at the sand.

Roddy put a warning finger to his lips. "If those horses start making a noise, we're lost. There's nothing for it but to wait. We are not going to bump into any guards at this time of day, it seems. But after dark— it'll be a very different kettle of fish. This desert will be teeming with them, you'll see. And that's when we'll move. It'll be the very last thing they'll expect. We'll ride straight in at the only gate, and snatch Henrietta—the way they took her from us. Until then—we have one sip of water every half hour, and we wait...."

The fact that Henrietta had quite sincerely agreed with Hassan on much of what he said about the scarab—and had not actively disagreed with his declaration that it was she he would take as the price his honor required from the British—seemed to lull the sheikh into a less watchful mood, and as the afternoon drifted on Henrietta was relieved to find that his eyes ceased to be fixed intently on her face, and she was able to concentrate more on working out how she could escape. She was aware that almost twenty-four hours had passed since her abduction, and if a search party had been sent out for her it would by now have combed all of the desert for miles around. As she had not yet been rescued, she could only surmise that some other plan for her safety was afoot. It had been some hours since Hassan thought that he heard a movement outside, and nothing had come of that brief moment of hope that Roddy himself had come for her.

She did not know what she would do with her freedom if she did manage to get out of the encampment. She had no knowledge of the stars to guide her, and the journey from Philoe the night before had been so swift and strange that she could not summon the strength to notice the route. If she left on foot, she would be at the mercy of any wild creature that stalked the night. She shivered at the prospect of coming face to face with a yellow-eyed dog in the dark, and at the thought of her bare feet in contact with the treacherous sand and the snakes it harbored, she almost fainted.

But escape she must. And in the anguish of her need to get back to the river, to her own people, and to find her cousin again, she clutched the wooden doll which she had with her still to her breast. It was then that she remembered that Sara had spoken of a pony. And she knew what she must do.

Her chance to ask Hassan's daughter where her pony was stabled came after nightfall, when the women who comprised his household assembled in the center tent of the three. Hassan announced to her as their siesta came to an end that he had to meet with his elder tribesmen, and that she should await him in the safety of his women's quarters—where she would be given her evening meal.

The occasion was formal, and the women sat in silence as serving girls moved amongst them with plates of sweetmeats and rice. There was no sign of a hierarchy, by which it might have been possible to tell whether the women were wives of the sheikh, or which might be Sara's mother. And she knew it was hopeless to ask questions in such company. Even if they had been able to understand her, it would have been the height of rudeness on her part, and would have made them suspicious and hostile.

But in Sara's case, silence was clearly an impossibility, and the small girl, sitting on the far side of the low table where Henrietta had been placed, began to chatter in English—to the frowning disapproval of her nurse—from the moment the food was served.

It was the simplest matter for Henrietta, then, to

bring the conversation round to the subject of Sara's pony.

"I'd love to see him," she said. "Do you not go to say good night to him? What color is he?"

"I am not allowed to go out to the stables at night," Sara told her. "But I'm glad to see that you still have Victoria with you—for I always say good night to *her*. Tell me, when do you think you will find a toymaker who can mend her for me?"

At the mention of the wooden doll, Henrietta went very still. If the child was forbidden the stables at night, it would take more than polite interest in the color of her pony to get her to break the rule. The discipline amongst the women seemed to Henrietta to be very marked. She knew from her few hours in the encampment that it was a life she could not endure.

"I think," she said confidingly, "that only an English toymaker will do. But I do know of such a man. He is not so far from here. It would mean taking a journey. But I would soon be back."

As she spoke, Henrietta looked straight into the child's eyes. Would she take the hint? she wondered. And if she did, would she have the spirit to do something about it?

She did not have long before she received her answers. Sara's eyes sparkled back at her. The nurse did not seem to notice.

"Surely you would not ride by night?" Sara asked. "Even for Victoria's sake."

"Of course I would not dream of it," Henrietta replied. "For one thing, I do not know which way the great river lies from here."

At once, Sara jumped up from her place at table and ran to the partition which gave on to her father's tent—beyond which was the way out into the open encampment.

"Come, it is a fine night—I'll show you which way the river lies!" Before her nurse could protest, Sara had lifted the silk curtain, and disappeared. With an apologetic glance at the nurse, Henrietta followed.

Moments later, she stood with the child patting the mane of a small, sturdy pony. "His name is Rameses, after the king of olden times. Do you like him? I think he likes you." Sara looked up at Henrietta with eyes seemingly incapable of any deceit.

"Sara, if I asked you to let me ride your pony, now, would you agree? Would you trust me to bring him back to you—and Victoria, if I get her well again?"

The child thought for a moment, a frown between the fine dark brows.

"There are guards everywhere at night. I don't think you would get away. And if you were caught, then I think my father would be very, very angry with you. Are you not his prisoner?"

Henrietta marveled at the strange ways of a people that could make so young a girl accept such tyranny in her own father. It was true that at home, in most families, the patriarch ruled the household. But often with a gentle hand. In her own case, it was her mother's hand, but the effect had been much the same: she was not afraid of her parents, nor had she ever had true cause to be.

She searched desperately for some way in which to persuade Sara to allow her to ride the pony, but could think of nothing, until the child put out a hand to caress the doll which she still carried with her.

"If I promised to bring back Victoria, would it not please your father? You say that he loves her." It was a last, perhaps hopeless attempt. But as she spoke the child's frown died.

The brown eyes looked up at her. "Do you promise to return? Shall I tell him so?" Henrietta gripped the hand that still caressed the doll. She nodded. "You can give him my word."

Then, with Sara watching for the guards, Henrietta unleashed the pony, and whispered reassuringly into its ear as she patted its neck. Together, the woman and the child crept under cover of darkness out of the stables. Only yards away, the taut canvas of a large tent gleamed with the lights that burned within it, and the sound of men's voices raised in discussion made them pause.

They stood very still. Sara touched the pony's muzzle, a signal to keep silent. Henrietta held her breath. The voices receded. As she mounted the pony, riding astride with perfect ease now that she wore her native dress, Henrietta sensed that the night was filled with movement other than her own. There was no sign of a guard, and yet she knew she was watched.

"If I do not go now," she whispered to Sara, "it will be too late."

The child nodded in agreement, and gave a light pat to the pony's haunch. It was apparently a familiar signal, for the pony then moved forward, making for the blur of an opening in the stockade. Beyond the gap in the high fencing, Henrietta knew that she would come face to face with the guards. Only speed would save her. She dug her heels into Rameses' hide, and in response he broke immediately into a fast trot.

It was then that things began to happen so quickly that Henrietta faltered. Beyond the stockade, there was a rush of horses' hooves and a cry. From the tent where Hassan and his elders were in conference rushed a guard with a lighted torch in his hand. Its orange flare lit the whole of the open space in the center of the camp, and the gap in the stockade towards which Henrietta now rode at speed. The guard shouted, and two more hooded men appeared in the pony's path as he approached the only way out. Then, framed in the entrance to the tent, Hassan began to hurl orders at the men.

If they had not turned for a split second to see what now came out of the desert and the darkness in a roar of hooves, they would have stopped Henrietta in her tracks, and her escape attempt would have failed.

But as she herself reached the open, three horsemen

rode towards the entrance to the camp. They were dark-skinned, hooded riders on Arab steeds. They wore white Arab robes and for a moment as the pale figures whirled towards her out of the dark, Henrietta believed that the Dashawai guards had heard the alarm and left their posts outside the stockade. But as the leader drew close, she saw that in the dark, dust-streaked face the eyes that shone at her were fiercely blue. The rider was her cousin. With a leap of her heart she knew that Roddy had come to her rescue—and proved himself, as she had always hoped he would.

But she was not free yet. Danger lurked beyond the camp in the shape of the night guards. The single figure at the door of the main tent had been joined by many more. Already, while two of the riders held back, the Dashawai began to run at the leader, knives glinting in their hands.

Henrietta stopped the pony as she reached Roddy's two companions. One of them hissed at her to dismount, as the pony would not have the speed to flee with them when they left. She did so, and turned back to call to Roddy, preparing to ride behind him. The pony trotted back in the direction of the stables, and she had no choice now but to wait for Roddy's help. But he seemed in no hurry to join her. To her horror, as lights appeared from all directions, she watched him dismount, and stride towards the regal figure of Hassan.

Hassan did not move. On each side of him, an Arab waited for his command to fall on the intruder. But it did not come. As the men came face to face, the noise and confusion that had filled the air suddenly died away. Henrietta thought that her heart would stop, as Roddy began to speak.

His voice was loud and clear, and his challenge rang through the night.

"I know you speak English, Hassan. Yes, I even know your name. And in the name of our own Queen, and of my cousin, whom you have held here against her will, I tell you that your so-called honor is worthless! A man who would snatch a woman and bear her back to his prison is no man. The scarab was all you asked for. I offered it to you. It should have been enough."

The guards stepped forward menacingly, waiting for Hassan's command. But the Dashawai leader merely smiled. "But my friend, the real jewel would have been enough. You should not have added to your gift this jewel of a woman who has spent this last day with me. For now, not only will I wage war with your country until I retrieve my people's sacred right, but by the end of the fight, your cousin—if it is she you talk of—will be at my side. And willingly!"

The final insult was too much for Roddy. Before anyone could move, he had hurled himself at the sheikh. Smithie at once started to dismount; a hand-to-hand fight was just his style, and they could see that Roddy had not a chance against the Arabs who now flew to Hassan's side. But Sankey put out a restraining hand.

"Wait!" he said. "Henrietta, you must face it—Roddy is beyond our help if he does not get out of this in one minute from now." Tears of fear for Roddy's safety sprang in Henrietta's eyes, but she knew there was nothing she could do. She called his name, but he did not seem to hear her. She took the hand that Sankey offered her, and leaped up to ride before him. The horses whirled about, and faced the open desert.

She turned, straining to see if Roddy followed. But the last glimpse she had of him was as he flew at Hassan, fists flailing. And Hassan replied, with an expert, lethal punch that sent her cousin reeling into the sand at his feet before the guards closed in on him.

CHAPTER FIFTEEN

"FIRST IT IS you who rides off into the desert on some impromptu whim, and then your cousin disappears in the same way!" Constance de Vere Smith rebuked her daughter, in severe tones, as she watched her changing hastily into a simple day gown, and smooth her wild hair into the heavy braids she had worn when she last left *The Sprite*, little knowing what fate lay in store for her.

"It is not his fault. You must believe that, Mama," she said. "And without his show of courage, his splendid effort, I would have been lost in the desert, perhaps for good. I am sorry to have caused you so much pain, but I did not mean to. And now I am to see His Royal Highness after breakfast—I really cannot linger to discuss it further." She knew that if she was submitted much longer to her mother's questioning she would have to fabricate a whole series of lies to avoid admitting that she had spent the last hours in the seclusion of a silken tent with a handsome sheikh.

Little guessing at the memories of those hours that were racing still through her daughter's mind, Constance de Vere Smith looked at her fondly for a moment, when she thought she was unobserved. For all the trouble it had caused, she was heartily glad to know that Henrietta was safe, and she had to admit that that nephew of hers had shown rather more style and spirit than she had thought he had in him. It was going to be very embarrassing if they returned to England with the news that he had been lost in the desert while saving his cousin from some wild prank.

"I trust that His Royal Highness will agree to send out a search party forthwith?" she remarked. Henrietta, hastily fastening a last button at the neck of the dark blue cotton crinoline she had chosen for the occasion—for she anticipated that a sensible outfit would be required for whatever she had to face next—told her mother that she was sure the prince would do whatever had to be done. Then, not waiting to choose a pair of gloves or a bonnet, she seized her Arab costume from where she had flung it on her bed, pushed it unceremoniously into a small valise, and gave her mother a warm embrace on the cheek before she ran from the cabin.

"There is nothing for it, sir," she told Prince Edward less than an hour later, as she sat closeted with him in the royal stateroom, only Smithie and Sankey with them, "but to return the *real* scarab! Oh, I know this man, Hassan. He is a true tyrant, and means what he says!"

The kind gray eyes looked thoughtful. Edward had dressed and breakfasted early to receive her, and obviously took the business of Roddy's capture very seriously indeed.

"There are too many problems attached to its return," he played for time. Everyone in the room knew that he referred to the woman Helena, who was most unlikely to let a rare jewel be taken from her possession. If, in the first place, the prince even dared to try.

"But we must get my cousin back! Alive...." At the voicing of the knowledge that Roddy did indeed look as if he was asking for death as he attacked Hassan, her voice trailed sadly away. Edward noticed her emotion, and leaned forward to pat her hand. She was glad then that she wore no gloves. There was such comfort in his touch, and she felt that she was pleading with a human being, and not with the heir to the throne.

"He succeeded in finding where I was, he risked everything." The others murmured their agreement. "Sir—if I promised to return the real stone and at the same time to preserve the goodwill of all those concerned, to do it surreptitiously in fact, would you then have any objection?"

Edward did not reply at first. She held her breath, hoping he was not a mind reader. She had never forgotten the half concealed jewel casket in the Greek woman's cabin, and with the replica stone still concealed in the valise she had brought with her, amongst the veils of her Arab dress, and side by side with the wooden doll she had clutched in her flight, she could easily switch the two alabaster pendants. No one would know even, except herself and Hassan. She could see only one drawback that mattered: she would, if she did this thing, be guilty of theft—and from a friend of the prince.

She was contemplating whether or not to confide in Prince Edward that she knew where the real pendant was kept, when an urgent knock at the stateroom door brought her back to the present sharply. A royal aide came in, and stood before Edward, stiffly at attention.

"What is it, man?" Edward's tone revealed that he was not pleased at the interruption.

"A matter of the utmost importance, sir. A message from the Dashawai!"

In the fearful hush that settled on the room at his words, Henrietta could hear the painful beat of her own heart. She knew what came next. There was only one message a man like Hassan would send now.

"If the property of his people is not returned by sunset, then the fate of the brave Englishman is sealed. He will die."

"Did the word 'brave' come in the message, or is it an addition by yourself, boy?" Edward asked.

"It was the actual words, sir. Sent by word of mouth, but nonetheless not a word altered."

Henrietta looked at the Prince with a wan smile. If the sheikh himself thought so highly of Roddy, then Prince Edward must surely now know that her cousin was a man of action, wasted on the foolishness of life in high society. But how terrible to think that the discovery had been made too late.

She got to her feet, royal protocol thrown to the winds. She ran to Edward's side and knelt, taking his hand in hers. Tactfully, the three men in the room averted their eyes.

"Sir," she pleaded, "can we leave a man like this to die?"

He frowned. It was against all they both believed in, he knew that, but the thought of attempting to retrieve the scarab from the present owner was more than he could face. Sensing his hesitation, Henrietta plunged recklessly on: "Sir, if I undertake to do this thing alone—if no one knows but the people who now stand here in this room that I am to do so—and if even they do not know the means by which I shall do it—will you not at least give me your royal approval?"

Edward patted her hand again. Her frank blue eyes, her obvious sincerity, coupled with the great beauty of her face as she pleaded for her cousin so bravely, moved him more than he could admit even to himself. He sighed heavily.

"Am I to understand that you love this brave cousin of yours?"

Henrietta did not have to think before she replied. "Of course I do, sir! And he loves me, I know it. But whether anything was to come of our love was another thing—and now, if we don't bring him back, I'll never, never know...."

Edward coughed, perhaps with embarrassment, perhaps with concealed emotion. He looked at the soldiers who stood about the room waiting for his word. He looked again at the girl who now rose to her feet before him—a stunningly beautiful creature in her fear for the man she loved, he thought.

"Let this young lady have anything she needs to make her task easy," he commanded at the room at large. And as he finished, Henrietta came to his side again, and curtseyed deeply. Then, as the soldiers began to assemble at the door to escort her from the royal presence, she leaned towards the heir to the throne of England and bestowed a chaste kiss of gratitude on the high forehead... before she ran from the room.

The first thing she did when she sat in conference with her three aides in the main saloon was to open her valise and take out Victoria, the wooden doll. "Smithie, you look as if you're good with your hands! Tell me, can you mend this poor creature for me—quickly? It is very important that I take her back with me to the camp, fully restored to health."

Smithie looked down at the toy, now deposited firmly in his great, boxer's fists. He did not know how to refuse Henrietta, nor did he know how to mend the doll. But he nodded, and said gruffly: "Anything for old Roddy, you know that."

"And you, Sankey," she turned to the other hero who had come for her in the desert. "There is so much I have to thank you for already, but there is one thing more. Tell me, are you willing to help?"

As the means to help Roddy slowly became a reality, Henrietta's beauty glowed from her face. She was, it seemed, doubly alive, now that she was able to act at last. She was irresistible. Sankey could find no words, but he nodded.

Moments later, he had cause to regret his impulsiveness.

"The Greek woman, Helena!" Henrietta almost hissed the name. "Do you know what hours she keeps? Does she breakfast alone?"

Sankey told her that he was not sure, but he thought that she did, on most mornings. He did not reveal who her companion might be when she breakfasted *à deux*, but it was unspoken between them that they knew for sure that morning that she would be alone. The prince had already started his day, as they knew very well.

"Then, Sankey, I want you to go to her, and to suggest a turn on the deck. It will do her complexion good, but you are not say that! Could you perhaps infer that you have missed her company, something flattering of that nature, as you have been absent these last hours, and want a jolly partner at your side for a constitutional. It's a beautiful day!"

She seemed then to see the color slowly drain from Sankey's young face, as he swallowed nervously, his blue eyes wide with incredulity. She had surprised herself with her own powers of invention, she had to admit. But it required nerve to carry out her plans, on the part of them all.

While Sankey recovered his poise, and muttered that he would do his best, Henrietta rummaged once more in her valise. This time, she did not allow her companions to see what it was that she extracted from its depths, and being gentlemen of good birth they naturally averted their eyes while she did so. By the time she had concealed the scarab in the smaller reticule she carried, Smithie had gone to seek help in mending the doll, and Sankey had stepped bravely on deck and made for Helena's quarters.

Ten minutes later, as the Greek woman's laughter rang out across the river at some remark made by her escort, Henrietta watched them disappear round the corner of the main cabins in a brisk walk. Knowing that she had less than two minutes in which to achieve her task, she wasted no time. With a rapid glance about her to make sure she was not observed, she slipped into Helena's cabin, and closed the door softly behind her. To her relief, the room was deserted. The dressing table was scattered with half closed jars, and its glass surface was smeared with powder. The bed was in disarray. Clothes were flung everywhere, as if the wearer had not been able to choose an outfit for the day. It was a room inhabited by a self-willed, lazy creature, Henrietta observed to herself as she crossed the deep purple carpet, swiftly, making straight for her quarry.

Sure enough, the casket was in the place where she had seen it. From it, as before, the jewels spilled haphazardly onto the floor beneath the dressing table. Among them was entangled a golden chain, and as she unwound the other necklaces from it with shaking hands, Henrietta saw with a sigh of relief that it bore the alabaster pendant in its filigree setting.

Exchanging the two pendants took only a second more. But she was running out of time. She flung the duplicate back onto the other jewels, tucked the real stone into her reticule, and fled back to the door. As she reached it, the sound of a woman laughing—rather foolishly, she thought—approached. She held her breath. Had Sankey not managed to hold the Greek woman's attention longer than this? If she returned to her cabin now, she would bring Henrietta disgrace for life—a thief caught red-handed on royal territory—and Roddy's death would be inevitable.

Her heart drumming in her ears, she waited. The laughter stopped. Through the lace curtains at the cabin door, she saw two shadows pass... and continue along the deck. She was safe!

Henrietta knew that if she were to return the true pendant to the Dashawai then Roddy would indeed be saved. Hassan was a man of his word. They had until sunset to do his bidding. But in the risk she was taking for Roddy's sake, Henrietta knew that she risked even more for herself. If she returned as she was to the encampment, Hassan would know her at once. She knew that he had sworn to make her his, as forfeit for the insult offered to him by the theft of his tribe's relic and the duplicate which Roddy had hoped to fob off in its place. Her only hope of surviving to return with her cousin to the Nile was to go to the encampment alone, in her native dress. She would find Sara, and give her the mended doll. Around its neck would be the true pendant. She knew that Sara would at once take Victoria to her father, who had almost betrayed his love of the doll before a woman, so deep did it go. And she knew that he would need no prompting to be told the true nature of the jewel with which she would adorn it.

It was an incongruous trio that rode out from Assuan an hour later, into the eastern desert. Henrietta had insisted that she go alone, and they, Sankey and Smithie, compromised by saying that they would escort her as far as the spot at which the encampment could be seen by the naked eye. Then, so that the scouts who watched for the Dashawai would be sure to know that the British did not intend to make further trouble, they would leave her, and ride back towards the Nile.

It was high afternoon when Henrietta, dressed in her native veils, riding astride a white Arab horse, rode towards the Dashawai camp, alone. She knew from the hours she had passed there that Hassan would at this time be resting in his own private quarters. His household would be asleep. She would find Sara, and together they would ascertain Roddy's whereabouts. For they must leave the encampment together, or not at all. She was not to be disappointed. As she rode to the gap in the stockade, she waited for the inevitable challenge. But the guards stood at ease, and just within the encampment she saw the reason why. The child Sara stood, waiting—and when she saw Henrietta, who now held the wooden doll before her on the saddle, she ran to her, shouting her pleasure. It was a scene of such innocence that the guards were not to suspect that the visitor had any other errand in mind.

As Henrietta dismounted, Sara came to her side, and took Victoria lovingly into her arms. Smithie had done a good job, and the repair was undetectable. The child hugged the doll, and then hugged Henrietta.

"I knew you would come back! I knew you would keep your promise! Come, we must find Father. We must show him Victoria. And the beautiful scarab she wears—is that the one you wore when you first came to the Dashawai?"

Henrietta felt a pang of remorse then, as she told the child that it was another, a sacred stone, and that it would give more delight to her father, when he saw it, than the return of Victoria herself.

"But I cannot be seen by your father. Do not ask it of me, Sara," she told her as she knelt in the sand, to look the child in the face as she broke the news to her that they would not meet again. "I have to go back to my own people. And with me I must take a friend who is held captive here. Sara, can you help me? Do you know where they keep the Englishman?"

There were tears in the child's eyes. But she held them back, stoically. Life amongst the Dashawai bred strong character, Henrietta thought, as she waited for the reply that meant so much to her.

"I think it would be good to take your friend from here," Sara said after a long pause. "He is in the bad place. The place where it is forbidden for me to go."

In the glare of the sun, Henrietta had to narrow her eyes to follow the direction in which Sara pointed. It was to a large tent set apart, on the furthest perimeter of the stockade. She noticed that round it stood a small string of camels. And beyond the animals she now saw that there was a second gate, though fast closed, in the stockade. In moments, a possible plan for her escape with her cousin had formed itself in her mind.

"Sara, I have to say good bye now. Do you understand? Can you forgive me?"

The child's lips quivered, but again no tears fell. She nodded, and hugged the doll in her slender arms.

"It is just possible," she added in a low voice, "that my father may decide to send me to school in England. He has often mentioned it."

Henrietta almost laughed aloud. "Well, then, who knows but that we might not meet again? And the ponies in England will not disappoint you, I promise!"

There was no time to watch the small, sad figure that crossed the encampment towards the three great tents where Henrietta knew that Sara would find her father, and the pendant would at last have been returned to its true home. As soon as that happened, she knew that Hassan would guess who had brought it, and the cry would go up. If he found her in the confines of the stockade, she would never leave it again—it was something she had never questioned.

Without the sheikh's daughter at her side, however, Henrietta knew that she was more likely to be challenged, and she sped to the edge of the stockade as fast and as silently as she could, and then skirted it until she came to the "bad place" where Roddy was captive.

Trying to move silently, her breath coming now in great panting sighs from exhaustion and fear, she drew close to the tent, and then lay flat in the sand, out of sight, while she tried to listen.

The things that she heard in the moments that followed were engraved forever on her heart. She heard her cousin give a low cry. Then silence. There was a grunting sound, followed by what could have been the swish of a rope or cane—or the low hum of a knife thrown very fast. Again Roddy made some sound. Again there was silence. And then he spoke.

"You might as well give up, chaps. Or kill me now and be done with it. For I'll not tell you anything that will harm my country—or the prince. We've done nothing to hurt your people that was not the dirty work of some other power. And who they are you may well guess—do your own work, damn you."

His words were cut short by another sharp cry. She had never heard Roddy make such sounds, and her blood ran cold. She knew that she had to get him away, as fast as she could. And she was all the more determined, now that she had heard him at his very best— her brave, stoic cousin, whose spirit was so much stronger than she had ever dreamed.

But there was more to come. A voice, speaking in English, began to give Roddy orders. "You will return to your prince, alive, if you so wish. Before we torture you further. On one condition."

"It's no use. I'll not listen to you," Roddy said. His voice was calmer now.

"I think you will. After all, there is much to live for."

Henrietta did not recognize the voice as Hassan's. It had a different accent—and there was something familiar about it. If she had to guess the nationality of the speaker, she would have said that it was French. And with that realization, she realized also who the speaker was. It was Professor Clémence, the egyptologist who had been so elusive in the recent days on *The Centaur!*

"It seems a very little thing, to start a skirmish or two against these natives," the professor continued. "After all, you are a soldier—are you not? It is your trade." Roddy replied calmly again. "To be a soldier is no trade, Clémence. It is a profession. And one that lives by honor. If you think that I am going to stake my country's reputation in Egypt by starting a war with the Dashawai just to save my own skin, then you have underestimated me. It is out of the question!"

Reflecting that they had indeed all underestimated her cousin, Henrietta closed her eyes as she heard once more the swish of whatever instrument of torture was being used on his poor body. If she ever saw him again, she wondered, would he be scarred in any way? If he were, she would not care. They would be brave mementoes of the time when she had learned the true steel of his nature.

But for the moment, all she must think of was how she could free him. She opened her eyes again, and found herself gazing into the great liquid eyes of one of the camels she had seen from across the encampment. The horrific pungent smell that emanated from its creamy white skin, the strange hanging folds of the mouth, the menace of the sharp hooves, none of this could discourage her from the plan that now took shape in her mind.

The sight of a trailing rope from the camel's long neck showed that it had broken its tether. Sooner or later it would be missed. But as yet there was no cry of a camel driver calling for the stray. She had to act fast.

"I know you and your kind only want to see the British out of Egypt," she could hear Roddy saying now. "And you might as well accept the fact that we're here to stay—for some time yet." His voice was tinged with exhaustion, much lower than before. She thought she even heard a yawn. How typical it would be of her cousin that he would yawn in the face of his captors, with death only moments away!

"I will leave you to your slumbers for a while, sir," the Frenchman said. "But when you are refreshed, I shall return to the argument. This knife makes a splendid ally in debate, does it not?"

"Good of you to let a chap snatch a snooze!" Roddy replied, and Henrietta loved him at that moment more than she had ever done, and she waited, her hopes high now, for some sign that the torture had ended for the time being. As she crouched close to the tent, an observer would have seen that she also held a long rope in her hands—and that at its far end a large camel stood patiently waiting for her command.

It was some five minutes later that she heard the sounds of departure. If she was not mistaken, the

Frenchman had left the tent. But there would be guards to see that Roddy did not try to escape. With any luck, however, she thought that the guards would be posted outside the tent, watching for intruders as well as preventing Roddy's flight. Still holding the camel's tether, she took a deep breath, and wriggled under the edge of the tent where she had lain in the sand. If there were guards inside, then she was lost. But she had to risk it. It was a gamble she was willing to take, now that she loved Roddy more than ever, and knew for sure that he was the man she wanted to spend the rest of her life with. If that was to be only one minute, or twenty years, then providence would decide. In the half darkness of the tent, she called Roddy's name.

A whispered reply not far from where she lay on her stomach on rough ground—there were no such niceties as carpets in this place of terror—led her to Roddy. She half crawled, half scrambled to his side, hoping against hope that the tether would reach so far.

When she looked down into her cousin's face, she saw that he had indeed been brave. It was caked with sweat, and a light weal from some blow cut across one cheek. His lips were parched and swollen. But his eyes glowed with unbroken spirit.

"Is it you, old girl?" he croaked. "How on earth did you get here? Did those bounders Sankey and Smithie let you come back alone?"

"Sssh... they are not far off. And there's no time to argue. Roddy, can you stand?"

She looked about them, making doubly sure that they were indeed alone. Outside the tent, the shadows of the guard told her that as she had hoped they watched the open space of the stockade.

"Roddy," she whispered again, as her cousin staggered to his feet, and swayed a little, gripping her arm as he did so. "Have you ever ridden a camel?"

"As a matter of fact old girl," he replied, as he walked

with her to the place at which she had found her way into the tent, "I have."

Together, they crouched low again, and wriggled their way back into the stockade. The camel still waited, and Roddy, scrambling to his feet, gave a grin of pleasure.

The cousins looked at each other for a long moment, in the glare of the desert. Disheveled, dusty, in clothes that would have done justice to a pair of beggars in the streets of Alexandria, they had no eyes but for each other.

"And to tell you the truth, old thing," Roddy said, "it's a rather jolly experience!"

In the long, strange journey across the sand that followed, on the great ship of the desert they had commandeered, Henrietta did not always agree with her cousin's verdict on camel-riding. At first the motion made her slightly nauseous, but she breathed hard through her nose and tried to think of other things. As they gathered speed, making a straight course at last for the Nile, she began to think of the man and child she had left behind. Hassan and his daughter belonged to their people, the Dashawai. She accepted that, and was relieved not to have to fight for her honor or her freedom with the handsome Arab anymore. She had had a narrow escape—and yet the experience had not been wasted. She had learnt much of her own character and desires under the ardent gaze of the sheikh. Whether or not she would ever see him again, she was not sure. But if the child came to school in England, who was to tell?

By the time the cousins had come into sight of Assuan, the darkness fell—swift and sure as ever—about them. Ahead of them, the light of torches and lamps sprang up in the town. "We'll skirt the place, old thing," Roddy called to her over his shoulder. "I don't want to attract too much attention, and we must look very odd like this."

"Like some fancy dress wallahs, old thing," he shouted again, a hundred yards further on. And suddenly, with extraordinary skill, brought the camel to a slithering halt in its tracks. Still clinging to his waist, Henrietta looked fearfully about her. Had they been followed?

"What is it, Cousin?" she asked. For the first time since she had found him again, her voice trembled. The need to lean on someone had caught up with her, after all the trials of the last two days. And now that there was someone she could rely on, she faltered.

"The fancy dress supper! Unless I'm mistaken—and after all that's happened I hardly know where I am— unless I'm mistaken, old thing, it's tonight!"

The disheveled young native couple that boarded *The Centaur* an hour later looked as if they had lived all their lives in the eastern desert—he as a camel driver, with the smell of the beasts about him, and she as a dancing girl. At first the watch mistook them as from the cabaret, which had been ordered to entertain the prince and his household at the height of the evening's festivities. But one look into Roddy's blue eyes and one word from his companion, in her customary, flawless Belgravia English, told them they were wrong.

"It's a fancy dress do, demmit, isn't it?" Roddy asked them, and strode on, with Henrietta's hand tightly in his, to where the native music throbbed in the night.

As they stood at the entrance to the royal stateroom, Henrietta told Roddy firmly, "I really must not be too late tonight, Cousin. Mama has been very patient, you know—and I hardly thought it fair, the way in which you asked her to look after the camel."

"Look here, old thing," Roddy answered. "All that mattered was to convince your Mater that we'd been on some kind of a lark. It's what she'd expect of me, and it's what she got. After all, she's also got her invitation to the palace for the next Season. And that's as far as I'm prepared to go."

"Is that how it's seemed to you, Cousin?" Henrietta asked, her voice suddenly rather sharp. "A lark?"

"Well, you must admit, old girl, it was a lark—and you came out of it with flying colors."

"But Roddy, you were nearly killed! How can you make so light of it?"

"It's all in a day's work for a soldier. And thanks to you, the day has ended rather neatly. I say, do you know what I'd like more than anything, this very minute?"

Henrietta looked up into his face. The scars, the dust, and the weariness in his eyes made her heart cry out. If he had made the first move, she would have flown into his arms, and stayed there. She wanted more than anything to kiss him, and be kissed.

"What is it that you would like, Roddy?" she whispered.

He grinned. "A nicely chilled, sparkling, bumper-great glass of champagne!" he replied, and before he could say another word his cousin had flounced into the royal presence ahead of him, so far as it was possible to flounce in the diaphanous trousers she still wore.

By the end of the evening, the truth of the French attempt to discredit the English in Egypt was out. They could be sure that Professor Clémence would not dare show his face again, now that Roddy was free to inform the prince of his true role: agent provocateur. Lance Morton, who had reappeared, in much better health, confirmed Roddy's story, and embellished it with the fact that the whole thing went back much further—to when the scarab had been stolen by Clémence himself—a year ago or more, and given to the prince to put the whole incident in motion.

But Clémence was not the only one to be routed by the turn of events. The Greek woman had glowered at Henrietta from the moment she re-entered the room. She wore the duplicate scarab at her throat, as a fit jewel, (Henrietta had to admit) to go with her choice of costume. It was clear that she had no idea that it was a forgery. So much, Henrietta thought, for her good taste!

It was Edward himself who instigated Helena's departure. Perhaps in all innocence, perhaps not.

With Henrietta on his arm, he crossed the room to where she stood. For a moment, dark eyes flashed in the proud face, and an answering glitter sparked coldly in Henrietta's own blue eyes. As the two women, so alike in every physical way and yet so unlike, stood face to face in silent hostility, the prince cleared his throat. "My dear," he asked, "do you not admire the authenticity of the costume our new friend is wearing? Quite the real thing."

Helena, who had clearly examined every flowing line of her rival's native costume as they advanced upon her, now turned a remote gaze into the distance, in fact to where Roddy, his face now glowing proudly in the aftermath of his ordeal and escape, had made some inroads on a magnum of champagne with his fellow soldiers. The fact that he wore the robes of an Islamic tribe did not seem to have endowed him with their teetotal habits.

Henrietta's heart beat painfully as she waited for Roddy to sense that the Greek woman's eye was upon him. Would he look up? Would he leave his cronies and come to them? She did not think she could bear it if she saw once more in his face the admiration she knew he had once harbored for this foreign beauty. But her anxiety was wasted. Roddy heedlessly continued to enjoy himself, and Helena dropped her gaze. With an insulting curl of her lip, she told the prince:

"It is perhaps a fit costume for a consort—of a camel driver!"

Henrietta was hardly able to suppress a gasp of indignation. Not only was the remark a direct insult to Roddy, but, with Henrietta on the arm of the Prince of Wales himself, it could be construed all too easily as a gibe at her own escort. But a slight, warning pressure from the prince's hand made her decide on discretion. She waited to see how he would respond.

When Edward at last spoke to the Greek woman, there was a tone in his voice that Henrietta had not heard before. It was not a sound she would ask to hear again. The icy politeness was tinged with iron. It was no longer a man in the toils of a beautiful woman who spoke. It was the heir to the throne of England.

"My dear," he said, "there is something I have to tell you—if you will forgive an apparent change of topic of conversation. I cannot bear to deceive you, though it is on a small matter. It would not be honorable if I did."

"You are free to speak, sir," Helena replied. "As always." Her own voice was void of emotion.

"It concerns the scarab you wear at your throat. Your beautiful throat. A gift from me, but alas a gift made falsely. Or shall I admit to not knowing—that the scarab is false? I am sorry to confess that it is not in fact a true relic. It is valueless. I have been misled, and I would not do the same to you."

The change that came over the Greek woman startled even Henrietta, who had long since been aware of her volatile nature. The dark eyes darkened. The proud nostrils flared. The splendid shoulders quivered. And with a single move, Helena had wrenched the offending chain from her throat, and hurled it to the ground, where it lay at Henrietta's feet.

"This journey, this wretched, filthy river," she snarled, "has been the worst experience of my life! And you, sir, are welcome to the stone—for stone is all it is. I have long thought so, but did not wish to bring discredit on your own knowledge of such things. Keep it! It is a fitting souvenir of our relationship!"

While the rest of the company averted its eyes, Helena then stalked from the stateroom. As she marched, she called to a steward in a loud voice. Her bags were to be packed, and the times of the first available transport back to civilization were to be ascertained.

As soon as she had disappeared, the uneasy silence

that had fallen during her last speech was broken by polite murmurs as the assembly made some pretence of reassuming the evening's celebrations. But no one was sure of how to behave, until the prince himself set the pace.

For a moment, he stood watching the Greek woman's departure in stony-faced silence. Then he gestured to a steward to retrieve the scarab from where it gleamed on the dark red carpet at Henrietta's feet.

But Henrietta laid a restraining hand on his arm, and with a swift, graceful gesture, bent to retrieve it herself.

"If Your Highness has no objection," she said, her most disarming smile lighting the eyes above her veil as she looked up into his, "I would very much like to keep this—this souvenir. For my own memories of this voyage have been both pleasant—and remarkable."

Edward smiled down at her. "You are worthy of some more valuable token of my regard. For there is very much more for which I have to thank you than saving the best of my young aides from certain death, and the country—my mother's country should I say—from a most unpleasant war."

For a moment, as the gray eyes held hers, Henrietta did not mind that Roddy had still not come to her side. It was true that there had been no time at all since their escape for them to talk. But their adventure had brought them so close, she now felt for certain that it would not be long before the unspoken love that they felt for each other would, on his side, soon be declared.

In the meantime, she would savor the joy of an evening spent at the prince's side, and the look in his eyes as he held a glass of champagne to her was more than compensation for her cousin's absence.

"I think you are well aware, my dear, just how much you have achieved in Egypt? But—one thing still puzzles me."

Henrietta waited. The prince reached out with his free hand and touched the gauze veil gently.

"I cannot for the life of me fathom," Edward said, "how you are going to drink this champagne if you do not remove this delightful article of apparel and allow us to see your face!"

Let COVENTRY Give You
A Little Old-Fashioned Romance

THE PLIGHT OF PAMELA POLLWORTH by Margaret SeBastian	50119	$1.75
DANGEROUS LADY by Barbara Hazard	50120	$1.75
THE CONSTANT COMPANION by Marion Chesney	50114	$1.75
KISSING COUSINS by Anna James	50122	$1.75
SERAPHINA by Jean Merrill	50124	$1.75
PETRONELLA'S WATERLOO by Sally James	50125	$1.75

Buy them at your local bookstore or use this handy coupon for ordering.

COLUMBIA BOOK SERVICE (a CBS Publications Co.)
32275 Mally Road, P.O. Box FB, Madison Heights, MI 48071

Please send me the books I have checked above. Orders for less than 5 books must include 75¢ for the first book and 25¢ for each additional book to cover postage and handling. Orders for 5 books or more postage is FREE. Send check or money order only.

Cost $_____   Name _____

Sales tax*_____   Address _____

Postage_____   City _____

Total $_____   State _____ Zip _____

*The government requires us to collect sales tax in all states except AK, DE, MT, NH and OR.

This offer expires 1 September 81   8095

NEW FROM FAWCETT CREST

DOMINO by Phyllis A. Whitney	24350	$2.75
CLOSE TO HOME by Ellen Goodman	24351	$2.50
THE DROWNING SEASON by Alice Hoffman	24352	$2.50
OUT OF ORDER by Barbara Raskin	24353	$2.25
A FRIEND OF KAFKA by Isaac Bashevis Singer	24354	$2.50
ALICE by Sandra Wilson	24355	$1.95
MASK OF TREASON by Anne Stevenson	24356	$1.95
POSTMARKED THE STARS by Andre Norton	24357	$2.25

Buy them at your local bookstore or use this handy coupon for ordering.

COLUMBIA BOOK SERVICE (a CBS Publications Co.)
32275 Mally Road, P.O. Box FB, Madison Heights, MI 48071

Please send me the books I have checked above. Orders for less than 5 books must include 75¢ for the first book and 25¢ for each additional book to cover postage and handling. Orders for 5 books or more postage is FREE. Send check or money order only.

Cost $_____   Name _____

Sales tax*_____   Address _____

Postage_____   City _____

Total $_____   State _____ Zip _____

*The government requires us to collect sales tax in all states except AK, DE, MT, NH and OR.

This offer expires 1 September 81

8096